Tiger One–The Dragon of War
by Christopher Corson

For Uncle Lawrence, the poet who never got to write his story.
For my father, the pilot who flew into hell so others might live.
And for every quiet man who carried more than he could ever say- alone.
And for the women who bore the weight of those silences.

Contents

PREFACE

War stories are often told through the lens of history's victors—grand strategies, triumphant battles, and the leaders whose names echo through time. But wars are not fought by maps and generals alone. They are fought by men—some barely more than boys—whose survival is measured in seconds, and where every choice carries the weight of life and death.

This book is inspired by the life of Kurt Knispel, the most successful tank gunner/commander of the Second World War. It follows his actual path through four years of combat, with the battles and his role in them drawn from the historical record. The other characters, conversations, and much of the surrounding detail have been fictionalized for the purpose of storytelling. The aim is not strict biography, but to bring to life the human spirit, moral choices, and atmosphere of the time. Any resemblance to persons other than Kurt Knispel should be understood as purely literary.

Tiger One is different.
It's not your typical war story. This is historical fiction grounded in truth—an emotionally charged, dramatized account of Kurt Knispel, the highest scoring tank ace of World War II.

He began at just 18 years old, riding a bicycle through his Sudetenland village—he didn't even have a driver's permit. By the age of 24, he was commanding a Tiger II tank—the most expensive and feared hunting machine on the planet—and had become a legend in armor warfare.

In four relentless years of combat almost all on the Eastern Front, he crossed staggering types of terrain: from the frozen forests near Leningrad to the boiling oil fields of the Caucasus, the ruins of Krakow, the hedgerows of Normandy, and the final collapse in Hungary. Each battle—Leningrad, Tikhvin, Krakow, Maykop, Kursk, Korsun-Cherkassy, Caen, and Hungary—was chosen for its emotional gravity and dramatic intensity. He fought in burning heat and subzero cold, across mountains, forests, and farmlands—thrust into the front line between the clenched jaws of two of the most brutal empires of the 20th century: Nazi Germany and Stalin's Russia. Dodging death in both offensive thrusts and desperate retreats, he bore witness to history's most merciless and brutal battlefields.

He wasn't chasing a cause or a medal. He was just a kid—barely out of adolescence—caught inside the gears of two of history's most violent war machines. At least 96% of his combat time was spent on the Eastern Front—but one popular account (*Panzer Aces*) places him briefly at Caen in July–August 1944. Whether fact or legend, it underscores the scale of a young man swept into the conquest and collapse of continental empires. While others wore the badge of ideology, Kurt quietly resisted the Nazi regime that tried to claim him. And somehow, through it all—as everyone else looked away—he stood up for his humanity. Alone.

During the war Commander Alfred Rubbel (author of *The Tiger Project*, 2004) and Gunner Knispel had actually worked together for over two years during the early campaigns on the Eastern Front. After the war, Rubbel later spoke of his direct experience with Knispel with deep respect: *"As a person, Kurt Knispel was willing to help selflessly. He shared his food and drink with his comrades and, if necessary, even the shirt off his back. All of us who knew him felt safe in attack or defense, regardless of whether Knispel was in front or behind us. He never left anyone out, no matter what the situation."*

Rubbel also wrote, *"Kurt wasn't a man for parades or politics. He belonged to us the frontline soldiers."* One of the most defining scenes in this novel—the Krakow Incident—draws directly from a real incident committed during the German advance into Poland. I, personally, first came across accounts of this particular event in 2017, and it stayed with me. That haunting image—soldiers witnessing unspeakable acts, forced to choose between looking away or standing apart—was the spark that led me down this path. Though dramatized, the emotional core of that scene reflects real wartime accounts and the moral fractures that war carves into those who endure it.

This book does not condone Nazi ideology or totalitarianism. Instead, it explores the complexities of individual morality, honor, and duty—offering a rare and unflinching view from the German side, a perspective too often left unexplored.

Im myself, am a Vietnam-era veteran from a family with four generations of U.S. military service—including my father, who flew 75 missions in a P-51 during WWII, and my daughter, who attained the rank of USAF Colonel—I've witnessed the moral and emotional struggles soldiers endure. My mother also lost a brother in WWII (very likely in the The Battle of the Hurtgen Forest, 1944) , a reminder of how conflict touches every corner of a family. Lost a great uncle in WW1 (Meuse-1918 Argonne Offensive). These kinship ties shaped my understanding of the psychological and physical toll of war—and they permeate the narrative of *Tiger One-The Dragon of War*.

This isn't a story of black-and-white heroism. It's about the gray— about men trapped between duty and conscience. Like *All Quiet on the Western Front*, it is a tale of transformation, not triumph. It's about what happens when a young man, raised to admire warriors, finds himself in the chaos of war—and discovers that solace comes not from glory, but from the brotherhood of those beside him.

The Eastern Front was unforgiving.
Cold: -49°F (Belarus)   *Heat:* 104°F (Stalingrad)

These were not just battlefields—they were elemental forces of suffering. It was in this brutal landscape that *Tiger One* unfolds, blending fact with emotional truth. This story traces Kurt Knispel's actual combat path over four years of war, aligning key scenes with the battles he fought—real locations, real units, and real historical stakes. While grounded in history, some events are dramatized to explore deeper themes of loyalty, resistance, and loss.

Tigerphobia: There Was a Reason for the Term
The Tiger tank wasn't just powerful—it was terrifying. To German crews, it symbolized invincibility. To Allied and Soviet forces, it embodied fear itself. After early encounters, commanders on both sides warned their tankers to avoid direct engagement. Their guns couldn't penetrate the Tiger's armor, and the Tiger's 88mm cannon—arguably the most powerful of the war—could destroy a Sherman or T-34 from

beyond return range. The Tiger didn't just dominate the battlefield—it haunted the minds of those who faced it.

Why This Story Matters

But war, like the Tiger, is not just about firepower. It's about survival, humanity, and the decisions men make under impossible pressure. History is not neatly divided into villains and heroes. Some of the worst crimes were committed by men convinced they were doing right. And some of the bravest acts came from those who despised the flags they fought under. *Tiger One* is about that contradiction. Kurt Knispel—dismissive of politics, defiant in manner—he let his hair grow long, sported a goatee, and refused to conform. Despite his unmatched combat record, he was denied the highest honors by the very regime he served. He was a warrior—but not the kind they wanted. This is the story of a man who was both a soldier and an independent thinker. A man who proved that the greatest battles are not always external—they are fought within.

Step into this world—the frozen wastelands, the treacherous mud, the scorched grasslands of the Eastern Front. Feel the thunder of the Tiger tank. And witness the mind of a man who dared to think for himself.

This is not just a war story.
This is his story finally brought to light.
This is *Tiger One – The Dragon of War*.
— *Christopher Corson*
Austin, Texas

The German invasion of the Soviet Union—Operation Barbarossa—ignited the largest and most brutal conflict in human history. Over ten million soldiers would clash along the Eastern Front, making it was the single deadliest theater of World War II. This is one man's story.

Chapter 1—Before the War, 1938

Czechoslovakia, October 1938. The radio crackled in the corner of the Škoda auto factory, nearly drowned by the rhythmic thrum of presses and welding torches. A German announcer's voice echoed across the workshop—measured, deliberate, full of promises: peace, prosperity, unity. Just days earlier, under the Munich Agreement, Britain and France had agreed to let Hitler annex the Sudetenland—on the condition that it would be his last demand. He had promised peace in return. Now, the message was clear—change was no longer coming. It had arrived.

Hearing the radio crackle with the latest announcement, Kurt Knispel wiped his hands on a stained rag, not bothering to look up. The words were clear enough—Germany had taken the Sudetenland without a single shot fired.

The machinery clanked around him, but something had shifted. His older brother, Conrad, was out in the hills hauling stone on a construction crew. Stefan—Kurt's closest friend—manned the line beside him, quick with a joke, fluent in Russian, always slipping a phrase or two into conversation like a secret code only they shared. Things were changing faster than anyone had expected. For now, Kurt kept his head down and listened, the oil on his fingers suddenly feeling heavier than usual.

At home, the tension was thick, pressing on them like a storm about to break. Their father, a veteran of the Great War, said little about the looming conflict, insisting it was just another political flare-up that would pass. But their mother saw through the silence. She had already buried loved ones once, and she feared the signs too well to be fooled again.

And then there was Kurt's brother, Conrad. The golden son. The strong one. He had always led the way—first to walk, first to fight, first to win their father's pride. But that hunger to be first had its cost.

After annexing the Sudetenland in 1938, Germany, breaking all promises in March 1939, invaded and occupied all the rest of Czechoslovakia.

At home, Kurt sat with Conrad and family discussing what came next now that they were officially part of Germany. Kurt's dad welcomed the change. His mom was far more concerned. The self-assured older brother, Conrad, of course, had already made up his mind.

"Better to enlist on our own terms than wait to be drafted," he had argued. Infantry for him—no question. For Kurt, the decision felt more practical. With his mechanical experience, tanks made the most sense.

Both brothers enlisted.

June 1941, Rastenburg (Germany) Staging Area

Kurt stood firm on the small, swampy island, the air thick with heat and ash. His family—mother, father, brother, and sister—cowed behind him, their faces pale with terror. The swamp burned with fiery plumes; explosions erupted like miniature volcanoes across the murky water. The acrid smell of sulfur mixed with smoke as the chaotic dance of flames lit the dark horizon.

In his hands, Kurt gripped a sword—not just any blade, but one that glowed with an otherworldly energy. Snakes came in endless waves; their red eyes like embers. They hissed and lunged, venom dripping from their fangs, but Kurt stood unyielding. Each swing of his fiery blade severed heads and sent bodies writhing into the flames. Yet for every snake he cut down, two more rose in their place, their numbers swelled like a nightmarish hydra. From the sea of snakes, a monstrous red dragon emerged, its molten scales glowing like lava. The dragon coiled, preparing to strike, and just as its jaws opened wide, a serpentine creature shot forth from its throat— a snake more monstrous than anything Kurt even imagined. A hollow roar vibrated through the earth.

Behind him, his sister whispered a prayer, her voice trembling. His father murmured, "You are our last hope."

Kurt exhaled sharply, his grip tightening. The beast inched nearer. The death rattle of the creature morphed into the clanging of a Panzer's wheels and the rumble of tracks rolling past his field tent, as the morning sun began to rise.

The noise of the tank's approach pulled him back to the waking world. Kurt jerked bolt upright on his cot, a strangled shout escaping his lips: "Never." His forehead and shirt were soaked in sweat.

In the cot next to him, his friend Stefan shifted. "Hey, you okay?
"That damn dream again," replied Kurt.
"Snakes?" Stefan lit a cigarette.
Kurt replied, "Yeah, it was like before."
"I'm curious, did you ever kill the snake?" asked Stefan.
"Closer," replied Kurt. He popped a mint. He started packing his gear. He looked out over the assembly area, the crisp morning air carrying the distant clang of metal and the steady stomp of boots on packed earth. Training had been grueling, but he had taken to it quickly, determined to prove himself. Not just as a soldier— as a marksman. His father, a decorated sniper from the Great War, rarely spoke of the trenches. But the medals said enough—he had been a survivor, a soldier. A man worth remembering. Kurt wanted to be that kind of man. And maybe, more than anything, he wanted his father to see him as one. Being the shortest man in his unit only pushed him harder. His older brother never let him forget it. Kurt had grown up used to being underestimated—having to prove he was just as capable, just as strong. He couldn't tower over others, but he could learn to outshoot them.

Years of hunting in the forests of Sudetenland had honed his instincts, teaching him patience, precision, and the quiet art of waiting for the perfect shot. A rifle didn't care about height. A bullet didn't need reach. It just needed a steady hand and an eye that never wavered. War would be different—he knew that. But still, a bullet fired was a bullet fired. And Kurt had no intention of missing.

As a newly trained gunner in a short-barreled 75mm Panzer IV, Kurt absorbed every lesson drilled into him during training, knowing that soon, theory would become reality. His instructors had been relentless, hammering home that his role wasn't just about firing—it was about communication, efficiency, precision, and discipline under pressure. He spent hours on the practice range, learning the feel of the 75mm gun—its weight, its recoil, the exact moment it reached firing readiness.

He had to identify targets quickly, judge distances by instinct, and adjust for movement, wind, and terrain in mere seconds. He was to fire only upon the commander's order. The short-barreled 75mm gun was designed for infantry support, not tank duels, so if they encountered enemy armor, he had to aim for weak points—tracks, vision slits, engine compartments—and never waste a shot. Timing was everything. Fire too soon, and he might miss. Fire too late, and the enemy would fire first.

Inside the tank, Kurt breathed in the stifling, pungent mix of burnt gunpowder, oil, sweat, and scorched metal—a smell that clung to his skin, soaked into the black wool of his Panzer uniform, and became inseparable from the war itself. The confined space amplified everything—the distant rumble of engines, the metallic scrape of tools, the faint crackle of the radio. In that dark steel womb, even silence had weight.

Their black Panzer uniforms weren't for show—they were practical. Designed to hide the grease and grime of the machine, they absorbed the tank's filth as readily as its heat and noise. They had drilled him endlessly on crew coordination, reinforcing that a tank was only as effective as the men inside it. His loader had to work fast, calling "Up!" the moment a shell was chambered. The driver needed to position the tank for the best shot. The commander had to see the battlefield as a whole— choosing when to fight, when to move, when to escape. One mistake from any of them, and the entire crew could be dead in seconds.

His instructors had warned them how it would feel— the deafening roar of the main gun, the concussive force slamming through his body, the thick smoke filling the turret. Fear would come, they had said, but a good gunner didn't hesitate. He had to trust his training, focus on the target, and fire—when ordered—without second-guessing.

Kurt appreciated how the repeated training and firing on the range had built muscle memory. Locate the target, align the crosshairs, adjust for range, fire. The shockwave from the gun's recoil would rattle the entire tank, smoke blinding them for a moment, ears ringing from the deafening blast—but he had to stay focused, assess the hit, and prepare for the next round. His vision set him apart. While many gunners struggled with depth perception in the tight confines of a tank, Kurt had an almost instinctive feel for distance and depth. His years of hunting with his father built this innate awareness. His ability to judge speed, terrain, and range in three dimensions made him deadly accurate—a rare gift in a battlefield where seconds determined survival.

Now, sitting inside his assigned Panzer IV, Kurt ran his fingers along the edge of the gunsight, feeling the weight of what was coming. Training was over. Soon, the targets would shoot back. He thought of his father, the stories of his battles in the Great War, the weight of responsibility he must have carried. Did he feel this same tightness in his chest before going into battle? Did he ever feel ready? Kurt wanted to make him proud.

He reached into his uniform pocket and pulled out a small, creased photograph of his girlfriend, Nikol, tucking it next to the gunsight. He popped a mint, the sharpness cutting through the stale air, grounding him for a moment. The invasion was days away. Everything they had drilled into him would soon be put to the test. Kurt reflected on the first lesson in gunnery school: *Without a good gunner, a tank was worthless.* He felt the pressure intensely.

Ottmar, the loader, had the crucial task of getting a thousand pounds of ammunition—80 rounds—into the tank's ammunition racks. No small job. Kurt always helped him, and Ottmar never forgot it.

Stefan was the tank's driver, a role he had taken on with a mix of ease and indifference, leaning more toward the latter. Known for his lazy, chain-smoking habits, his reputation often preceded him. But for those who know him well, especially Kurt, there's more to Stefan than meets the eye. The two have been friends since childhood, their bond built on years of shared experiences and unspoken understanding.

Dietrich was the radio man. He was a handsome young man with a flair for fashion that stands out, even in the most unexpected places. On the other hand, Dietrich always methodically checks and fusses over his signal's equipment. The crew teased him endlessly on his self-absorption.

But Dietrich took it all in stride. He's developed a thick skin from years of teasing. Unfazed by their ribbing, he shrugs it off with a smirk, muttering, "They're just jealous." For Dietrich, a bit of style and confidence goes a long way—even in the midst of war.

Commander Marcus Decker, a seasoned Panzer officer in his late thirties, carried the weight of his experience from the highly successful Blitzkrieg campaigns across France, Denmark, Norway, Belgium, and the Netherlands. He realized that his new crew was inexperienced in combat, which was why he had been selected. A disciplined officer in the Regular Wehrmacht, Decker is driven by a deep desire to prove his value—not only as a German officer but as a tank commander capable of leading men through the chaos of war. His ambition for promotion was tempered by a pragmatic understanding of Wehrmacht military realities, and he knew that success on the battlefield would elevate him.

Though non-political and focused solely on his military duties, Decker was aware of the ever-present pressures of ideology and duty. He was not one to wade into political debates, but his sharp awareness of the changing tides of war and his ability to bend the rules, when necessary, made him a commander of both discipline and flexibility. His approach to leadership was not rigid; he understood the delicate balance between authoritative command and relational leadership, often walking the line between being a strict taskmaster and a soldier's officer, knowing when to push and when to pull back.

Currently commanding a platoon of four tanks, Decker's leadership was founded on practicality and efficiency. His leadership style was effective, but not without friction. His soldiers respected him for his competence but sometimes felt that his drive for advancement came at the cost of personal connection. To bridge this gap, Decker made an effort to share small, humanizing gestures, like offering his licorice stash to the crew on rare occasions or asking after their families during downtime. these moments, though brief, remind the crew of the humanity beneath Decker's hard exterior. To Decker, war was about survival and victory; anything else must be set aside—at least until the war was over Decker's thought for the day: 'I was in Paris last June. Now I am in Russia."

Meanwhile, miles north of Kurt's unit, brother Conrad and his best friend, Jan, were stationed in a different part of the front. Part of a four-man MG34 machine gun team, they, like Kurt, prepared their gear and weapons to move out. The area buzzed with activity—trucks, motorcycles, and halftracks being loaded with ammo and supplies, the noise and motion underscoring the urgency of the moment.

True to form, Conrad didn't like to be last. Soldiers instinctively stepped aside as Conrad moved through the ranks, a box of ammo on one broad shoulder and his MG34 machine gun slung on the other. He strode ahead, cutting through the crowd with an unbroken pace, his broad shoulders parting the chaos without hesitation. No one dared slow him down. Every movement was fluid, confident, as if the weight of the gear was nothing more than an afterthought. He didn't ask for space, didn't wait for anyone.

Recently, Jan had noticed a palpable change in Conrad since they had finished training and finally arrived at the front lines. An urgency now defined his demeanor— sharper, more dangerous. This shift was evident in Conrad's deliberate movements and razor-sharp focus, as if he were trying to outrun something unseen. Smiles had become rarer. Whether it was the weight of the MG34 or something deeper pressing down on him, Jan felt it in Conrad's relentless stride, as if he were now propelled toward some inevitable internal reckoning.

Chapter 2—Russia on the Border, May 1941

Not far away across the border, where Conrad's units had been assembled, Russian flags flew above primitive gray army barracks. Several Russian T-34 tanks were getting maintenance. Three rows of Russian soldiers were lined up, being inspected. Captain Marat reviewed the troop formation going from man to man. A winded messenger ran up. Marat looked over. The messenger, noticing Marat's rank, saluted. "A message for Captain Marat from Colonel Taranko".

Marat said, "You found me." He took the message. Waved the messenger away offhandedly. While walking slowly, he lit a cigarette and began to read the message. As he read, he shook his head slowly from side to side. He sighed deeply, frustrated.

He turned back to his men. Dripping with sarcasm, "Good news, ladies. No war... today. Dismissed." Troops broke for the barracks. Captain Marat stepped into his earthen and log command bunker, the heavy door creaking behind him. The dim space was decorated with Stalin posters glaring down from the walls. A large Soviet flag draped in the background. He strode over to the wooden table at the center of the room. With one hand gripping the message, he slammed it down onto the table so hard that two empty shot glasses toppled over, clinking as they hit the table surface.

The table was littered with maps, reports, duty rosters — and now, tipped shot glasses. What passed for strategy had long since blurred into ritual. He poured himself a generous measure of vodka. Rising from his chair, a glass clenched in one hand and the freshly delivered message in the other, he stepped forward, his gaze drawn to Stalin's towering red poster. The figure loomed above him—stiff, unyielding—his pointed finger seeming to land squarely on him in silent accusation.

It was just a poster, mere ink on paper, yet the image of Stalin still made Marat's chest tighten. A low, bitter chuckle escaped his lips, laced with dark irony.

"Today, Comrade Stalin," he muttered, his eyes fixed on the lifeless gaze of the poster, "in this message..." He shook the paper at the image of Stalin, his voice low and bitter. "...you told us, again, *not* to provoke the Germans... while they mass thousands of soldiers, artillery, aircraft, and Panzers on our very doorstep."

"Jesus, Mary, and Joseph," he spat, the irony slicing through his voice. "Even a blind fisherman can see the tide rising. But not you, Comrade Stalin. No, you still think you're Hitler's friend. Ever since you and Hitler signed the Molotov-Ribbentrop Pact, invaded Poland, and split it between you two like it was a loaf of bread, you think you will be married forever. Well, I'm telling you: time to wake up, Comrade. The romance is over. You got a divorce on the way."

His voice wavered with a mixture of anger, frustration, and fear. He turned back to the table. He took another long sip. Setting the glass down, he unrolled several maps across the table, tracing the ominous lines of likely German movements with his finger.

Marat downed the rest of his vodka, the fiery liquid fueling his contempt. The weight of looming war pressed down on him like the five feet of thick earth above his bunker. His knuckles whitened as he gripped the message tighter. His gaze didn't leave Stalin's rigid figure as he slowly drew his index finger down his scar on the left side of his face.

He remembered this scar too well. The sky was overcast, and the smell of wet earth hung to the air. His father, Dimitri, a grizzled peasant in his 50s, stood beside his farm horse. His face was weathered from years of hard toil under the sun and snow. His hands, calloused and rough, had worked a flask open, taking a deep swig before slipping it back into his pocket. With a grunt, he crouched down to clean one of the horse's rear hooves, dirt and muck caked deep into the hoof. His eyes, half-glazed from drink, darted toward his teenage son, Marat. "Boy, hold the horse steady. Tighten the reins," Dad ordered, his voice gruff, edged with impatience.

Young Marat stepped closer, cautiously gripping the reins. His eyes stayed fixed on the ground, trying to avoid his father's gaze. Both he and his mother had learned to fear the unpredictable temper that simmered just beneath his father's rough exterior, especially when he was in a drinking mood. Today is one of those days. Dad scraped the hoof with hard, deliberate motions, chipping away at the packed dirt. Suddenly, a hawk screeched nearby, its cry sharp and piercing through the yard. The horse startled, jerking violently. Dad was thrown off balance, lands hard in the mud. For a moment, he lay there motionless, before slowly staggering to his feet. His face twisted with fury as he wiped thick mud and manure from his arms and chest.

Nostrils flared, without a word, he stormed toward his son, rage boiling beneath his sun-scorched skin. Grabbing the boy by the collar, Dad yanked him close and made one fast slash across young Marat's left cheek with the still-filthy cleaning tool. The metal bit into his son's cheek, leaving a jagged cut that bled freely into the mud. Marat didn't cry, though the pain made his vision swim. His father's eyes, filled with alcohol-fueled rage, bore down on him as he stood, unyielding. Young Marat wipes the blood from his face with the back of his hand. Dad, still furious, glared at him, his voice low and dangerous.

"Think the world's going to care about your pain?" Dad spat. "If you are weak and show it the world will eat you up. No one will spare you for being soft." Marat swallowed hard, his chest tight. Too scared to speak. Too scared to move. The sting of the cut was nothing compared to the shame of his father's anger. Dad looked down at the boy, his lips curled in alcohol-fueled disappointment. "Get the horse back in the barn, and don't waste my time."

Back at the Russian bunker, Marat's finger lingered on the scar, the roughness of it pulling his thoughts away from the crumpled paper in his hand. The bunker was quiet—too quiet. The only sounds were the faint and random groans of the wooden beams settling. Like a tomb. The stillness pressed in on him like a weight, suffocating, as though the earth itself was waiting for something to happen.

The memory cut through the present tension, pulling him back to another time, another place. In a way, he thought, the bunker is not much different from his childhood barn if he's being honest. Not in the way it looks, not in the sounds, but in the way it feels. The stillness. The weight of waiting. He can almost smell the hay, the damp earth, the cold wood. The barn had its own rhythm, its own hum, but it was always quiet when the work was done. In those moments, there was nothing left but waiting for his father's next orders. Waiting for something to break the silence. And today Marat is waiting for the war to come to him. Marat sat quietly, frustration building as he thought about Stalin's refusal to recognize the growing threat from Hitler. Why was Stalin so blind? Hitler's aggression was undeniable—he was swallowing countries one by one, yet Stalin dismissed it, focused only on internal consolidation.

Marat's jaw tightened. How could Stalin ignore the obvious? The purges, the fear—everything pointed to a leader too focused on his own power to see the real danger approaching. Hitler's army was gathering

11

strength, and Stalin kept pretending they weren't a target. Was Stalin's pride the cost of Russia's survival? Marat felt the weight of it. They were about to be drawn into a war they weren't ready for, all because of a leader who couldn't, or wouldn't, recognize the threat.

But there was no turning back now. When the war came, he knew it would be up to him to face it, no matter the cost. He, and thousands of others, would have to pay the price of Stalin's pride. He knows what is coming— he's been trained to see the signs. Stalin may not believe it, but Marat does. The Germans will come, and when they do, there won't be time for hesitation. For tonight, all he can do is sit in the bunker, tracing the maps, imagining the routes their tanks will take, the fields they'll tear through, and the skies that will darken with the screaming Stukas.

Miles away, under the same looming tension, Kurt's unit, along with thousands of German infantry troops, artillery, and aircraft prepared for what was coming. At the staging area, the night was thick with restless energy, the air heavy with the smell of oil, sweat, and damp earth. Kurt, Stefan, Ottmar, and Dietrich gathered their gear beside their Panzer, the machine looming over them like a sleeping beast. The steel hull radiated the day's heat, but soon, it would run cold. As usual, they worked in quiet focus— checking equipment, securing ammunition, making sure every last detail was in place. But no matter how many times they had drilled, this wasn't training anymore. This was the last time they would prepare without blood on their hands. Kurt ran a hand along the side of the tank, feeling the rough texture of the paint beneath his fingers. Tomorrow, it would not be just a machine; it would be their lifeline. His lifeline. Decker's voice cut through the silence, firm but even.

"Gentlemen, it's official," Decker said. He let the words settle for a beat before continuing. "Daring ideas are like chessmen moved forward. They may be struck down, but they may also start a winning game." He paused, looking at each of them in turn. "We move forward tomorrow. June 22, 1941. 0300 hours."

A distant thunder rumbled, though there were no storms in the forecast. Just the storm of war. Kurt exhaled slowly, his fingers absently reaching for the dragon pendant Nikol had given him—a symbol of ancient wisdom, strength, and power—hanging at his neck. He wasn't superstitious, but he'd take any bit of luck he could get. By this time tomorrow, the world would be different. And so would they.

Commander Decker looked at each of them. "If you've got letters to write, write them tonight. If there are things unsaid, say them. Tomorrow, the world changes. The weight of his words settled over the crew. There was a quiet understanding between them. Tomorrow would not be just another day—it was the beginning of something much larger.

A few miles north, German infantry soldiers, including Conrad and best friend Jan, sat side by side in the back of a fully loaded truck, bumping along a dust-blown road. Their commander had given them the same news about the launch tomorrow. The air was thick with swirling dust, the late afternoon sun beating down. Conrad stares out the back, lost in thought, but not of the war that starts tomorrow. He has other issues. Jan nudged him. "Still moping about her?" Conrad didn't respond, his gaze fixed on the landscape behind them.

"I don't want to talk about it. I'm with Ericka now." But the name still echoed. Years ago, Nikol had been his fiancée—his claim, his prize. Because he betrayed her and lost her, she was the one who slipped through his fingers. And Conrad didn't take losing lightly.

Jan grinned. "Or maybe you're still jealous because of who she's with now."

Conrad tensed. He fought the urge to punch Jan—just for a second—then let it go. Instead of a fist, Jan got a flat:

"Fuck you."

He remembered the day Nikol caught him. "Damn you, Connie. We're engaged!" Her voice shook—fury and disbelief battling in her chest. The ring was off before she even realized. She hurled it at him. "*Were* engaged. Add it to your other trophies."

He turned to the dust-filled horizon, the swirling clouds mirroring the chaos inside him. Looking back, he felt like an idiot. He had mumbled lame excuses, but she'd cut him off, cold.

"I see what I see." And then she was gone.

And now, she was with Kurt.

After a long pause, he exhaled. "I guess a good war is exactly what I need right now," he muttered. laughed, oblivious.

Jan: "Well then, you're in luck. Your war starts tomorrow."
."

As Kurt and Conrad—each mile apart but marching under the same banner of Army Group North—prepared for the push toward Leningrad, both felt the weight of what lay ahead. The sky above seemed impossibly heavy, the ground beneath their boots vibrating with the thunder of an unstoppable war machine. Though separated, both brothers stood at the edge of the same storm, caught between the rush of anticipation and the looming unknown.

Chapter 3—Operation Barbarossa, 1941

Kurt couldn't sleep that night. The dawn of June 22, 1941, broke with an ominous sense of anticipation. Kurt, feeling destiny in his heart, watched as Germany's massive invasion force began its march into Soviet territory, destined to change the course of history. The roar of engines and the rumble of tracks drowned out all other sounds, as over 3.8 million German soldiers surged forward with terrifying speed and precision.

After the morning briefing, Kurt, the tank's gunner, climbed into his tank, the familiar scent of oil and metal enveloping him as he settled into the gunner's seat. His hands glided over the gunsight with instinctive precision; the motions as natural as breathing. Stefan, his driver, pushed open the left-side hatch, an unlit cigarette dangling from his lips. He squinted into the distance, where rising dust clouds signaled columnar movements ahead to the horizon. While Kurt was driven and serious, Stefan's laid-back, pragmatic outlook on life had always grounded their friendship, providing a counterbalance to Kurt's intensity. Kurt always knew Stefan was there when the stakes were high.

Commander Decker stood in his commander's cupola atop the tank, binoculars slung around his neck and a radio headset resting on one ear. He raised a gloved hand and ordered, "Start your engines!" Stefan nods and melts back into the driver's compartment.

Stefan's reasons for joining the army were simple. Unlike Kurt, who joined to follow in his father's duty-bound footsteps from the previous war, Stefan felt stifled by life at home with his parents and three sisters. The war offered him a chance to escape what seemed like the claustrophobic confines of small-town life. The allure of adventure was strong, and Stefan was not sure what he'd do if Kurt went without him. For Stefan, joining the army isn't about duty—it's about breaking free, exploring the world, testing his limits, and having a little fun along the way. In the tank, Stefan's competence quickly became evident. Though he carried the same casual attitude into combat, his instincts behind the wheel were keen. He had a natural feel for the machine, reading the terrain with uncanny precision and maneuvering the Panzer through tight spots as if it were an extension of himself. Watching him drive, it's easy to imagine Stefan on a racetrack instead of a battlefield. The way he coaxed every ounce of performance out of the tank—knowing when to push it to its limits and when to hold back—has earned him quiet admiration from the crew. "This beast drives better than my dad's old tractor," he joked, but there's a clear pride in the way he handled the controls. Despite his casual demeanor, his pointed focus behind the wheel makes him an invaluable asset, especially when the terrain or enemy fire puts the crew to the test.

One by one, the growls of idling tanks erupted into a roaring symphony as the four Panzer IVs of the platoon roll forward. Overhead, Stuka dive bombers shrieked, their payloads erupting in distant plumes of fire and smoke.

Dietrich hunched over the radio, frantically decoding battle chatter—weather, enemy activity, artillery, and road conditions. He was proud to be a radio operator. While all German tanks had radios, only command tanks in Russia were equipped with them, making the radio the vital link in Blitzkrieg tactics. This gave the Germans a crucial advantage in coordinating tanks, artillery, infantry, and air support once the battle began. Dietrich's meticulousness became part of the crew's routine, despite their teasing.

Farther north, Conrad and his Panzergrenadiers felt the weight of the same war machine in motion. The morning air bit at exposed skin, mingling with the faint, bitter scent of hot coffee, the clatter of clanking metal, and the bark of shouted orders. Dust rose, stinging their eyes, as thousands of Panzergrenadiers—clad in full battle gear—moved in disciplined waves. Their boots kicked up dirt that hung in the pale dawn light, mixing with the thick scent of gasoline and sweat. They waited for the order to advance, their eyes fixed on the horizon, hearts pounding with the unspoken anticipation of battle. The taste of metal and the grit of anxiety sat on their tongues, but their minds remained focused on the battle ahead.

Conrad strode purposefully at the head of his unit, a determined glint in his eye, his presence a steadying force amid the intensity of the assault. Beside him, Jan kept pace, his acute gaze scanned the columns of soldiers and vehicles that stretched endlessly along the primitive roads. Engines roared to life, belching black smoke into the crisp air as Hanomag half-tracks rumbled forward, each brimming with grim-faced troops and tightly secured weaponry. The road pulsed with movement—infantry marched in lockstep, vehicles groaned under their loads, and the unspoken resolve of men ready to face the trials of battle.

Likewise, to the south of Conrad's position, Kurt's tank pressed ahead with the overhead drone of aircraft adding another layer to this rising symphony of war.

Kurt was amazed to see the vast columns of like a long-armored snake. Kurt poked Ottmar and pointed out soldiers perched atop tanks hitching rides, their faces and helmets dust-covered, while Hanomags and support vehicles rumbled forward en masse. Kurt said, "At least we have seats".

Ottmar responded with a belly laugh. Ottmar, a bigger guy with broad shoulders, didn't balk at the loader's task, even though he was more cramped in the tank than most. Ottmar grew up on a farm as an only child, so he had major responsibilities all his life. At first, he found companionship with the horses. He talked to them every day. And they listened and loved the carrots he brought. He found long-term solace in his light banter with the animals and, ultimately, even with the farm equipment. The crew might have laughed at first when Ottmar talked to the tank and gun, but soon, they came to expect it. He never thought much about it. And now, in war, his tank had become the same.

Maybe even the crew relied on it too. Because in the chaos of battle, when steel groaned and death was a breath away, there was something reassuring about Ottmar's quiet words—like he was keeping the machine on their side. And coincidentally, although they would never admit it, his not-so-private chats with the gun and tank lifted his comrades too. "Happy loader, happy gunner, happy tank commander." It was more than just a saying—it was a truth Ottmar lived by. A smooth load, a clean shot, a tank that kept rolling—that's what kept them alive.

Dietrich adjusted his radio for the latest intel. As a boy, he had always been a spoiled by his mother, which had contributed to his attention to detail and self-presentation. Although not friends, he was from the same town as Kurt. They were acquaintances and ran in different circles. He had joined up due to conscription and had broken some hearts when he left. Though the turbulence of war surrounded him, he took care to look his best—adjusting his uniform with a careful touch, ensuring everything was just right.

As the Panzers pressed on the ground churned beneath the weight of thousands of tons of steel, throwing up miniature tornadoes in their wake. The army pressed forward, the horizon swallowed them, an immense lethal force headed into the unknown.

Commander Decker surveyed the scene from his cupola; his eyes scanned the expanse for signs of trouble. Decker's mannerisms reflected his dual nature as a leader who valued both order and adaptability. He was rarely seen without his clipboard and pencil, tools he understandably used obsessively to track inventory, troop movements, and fuel consumption. The crew joked that his pencil was sharper than most bayonets, though they knew better than to say it within earshot. Decker himself took quiet pride in his meticulousness; to him, details won battles as much as courage or firepower.

Despite his stoicism, Decker had a fondness for licorice—a habit he picked up during the Norway campaign, where a local farmer had gifted him a bag. He kept a stash tucked away in his tank, breaking it out during moments of heavy contemplation or stress. The sweet, biting taste serves as a strange comfort amidst the harshness of war, like a rich flavor cutting through a bland meal.

This will be his sixth country he has entered in the war. His voice cut sharply through the headset chatter, issued orders to his men with the calm authority of a seasoned officer. Under his command, the tank platoon rolled on, a spearhead of armored might poised to break the enemy's lines.

Later that morning their tank crested a small rise on a random dirt road. After an urgent message from Dietrich, Commander Decker held up his hand. "Stop."

The tank platoon halted. In a low but firm voice Decker, "Grenadiers report well-camouflaged enemy at one o'clock. At a stone wall and farmhouse... 200 meters. Load high explosive." Decker ordered the other three platoon tanks to come abreast at the crest. Just the idling Maybach 12-cylinder engines were heard in the warm mild breeze. The other three tanks began rotating their turrets to the target area.

Kurt peered through his narrow gun sight. Rifle muzzle flashes caught his eye as the Russian infantry opened fire revealing their positions. Next to him, in the driver's seat, Stefan had an unlit cigarette dangling from his lips, carefully scanning the terrain in front of the tank for the next advance forward. He noticed a muddy section to avoid. Their well-groomed radio operator, Dietrich, with radio chatter done, he now manned the forward machine gun. He ran his fingers over the trigger, testing its tension, before squeezing off short bursts with his sunglasses hanging in the V of his shirt.

Ottmar, the loader, as he gently retrieved the requested high-explosive round, cradling it in his hands as though it were a fragile child. Being a loader was not an easy job. The rounds were heavy, with a mix of high-explosive, armor-piercing, and smoke shells, and each one needed to be carefully stored in its designated spot to ensure quick access when needed. With practiced ease, he slid the round into the breech, patting it lightly before locking it in place. *"Go on, sweetheart— make it count."* With a final tap on the gun's casing, he called out, "Up!" It was the signal to Kurt that the shot was ready.

Kurt looked through the gun sight. A few seconds passed, the only sound was the idling of the engine. He could not fire without the commander's direct approval. Gently twisting the targeting dial, Kurt announced to the commander, "On target."

Decker replied immediately, "Open fire!"

Kurt slowly squeezed the trigger, just as his father had taught him when hunting feral hogs. The short-barreled cannon spat its fifteen-pound payload of high explosive death. Decker watched as Kurt's shot went high, striking the chimney pipe instead of the target. Frustrated, he pounded his fist on the hard turret.

A sudden renewed and concentrated blizzard of enemy small arms fire erupted, forcing Decker to drop down into the tank turret, slamming the hatch shut with a metallic clang. Ottmar quickly reloaded a shell while Kurt, frustrated with his first shot, re-adjusted his aim. On the bow machine gun, Dietrich continued his suppressive fire, forcing the Russian soldiers to duck behind the low stone wall. Decker watched through the slits of the commander's cupola, sizing up the chaotic situation unfolding before him.

Ottmar shouted, "Up!"

"On target, sir," Kurt called out.

Decker gave the order: "Fire!"

As Kurt slowly squeezed the trigger…. The farm wall erupted in a thunderous explosion, shards of stone spraying in all directions like lethal confetti. Kurt allowed himself a faint smile, his hand steady on the gun controls. Up top, Commander Decker grinned, his expression both satisfied and calculating.

Ottmar, seated beside Kurt, pats him firmly on the back, his smile broader than usual. To their left, the platoon's sibling tanks had gotten situated and now joined in the barrage. The air was filled with the deafening roar of their guns, unloading salvo after salvo into the enemy positions. On the ground, Ivan refused to yield easily. Despite the overwhelming firepower, Russian soldiers darted from cover to cover, braving the mayhem to return fire. Many were struck down, stubbornly trying to hold their ground despite the onslaught.

Bullets, grenades, and shells screamed through the air, hammering the earth and ricocheting off the tanks' armor. The ground quaked beneath the assault. The air now tasted like gunpowder, thick with the acrid smell of smoke. But slowly, the tide began to turn. Ivan's lines wavered under the relentless Panzer and infantry pressure. Their defensive fire had become more sporadic, their movements hesitant. Leaving their dead behind, one by one, they began to fall back, abandoning the walled perimeter—except for a thick, bushy section next to the farmhouse. Here, the enemy dug in, fiercely holding their ground.

Kurt felt the shift. The frantic pinging against the armor faded, and was replaced by an eerie stillness, broken only by the distant rumble of faraway explosions, like muffled thunder. The few seconds of silence hung heavy, unsettling, a stark contrast to the storm of noise that had surrounded them just moments before. The tension lingered, thick as fog, the calm before the storm. Kurt scanned the target area, his grip tight on the gun sight, as the seconds stretched out. From his driver's seat, Stefan called out, "They seem to be pulling back."

"Same here," Kurt responded, his eye pressed to the gunsight. The battlefield lay still, a frozen landscape of churned-up earth and shattered stone. Somewhere out there, the enemy was waiting—just as still, just as tense. It was like the silence before the clash, where the next move would show who had the will and the firepower to prevail.

Commander Decker, standing inside the cupola, scanned through the vision slits. His voice was calm and measured, but the faint smirk on his lips betrayed his satisfaction. *"That's better,"* he said. *"Much better."* He adjusted his headset and leaned forward slightly, surveying the stone farmhouse with a critical eye. "Now," he adds, his smirk widening, "let us redecorate. I have got a feeling they've left us a few surprises in there." The tanks' turrets swiveled to face the stronghold farmhouse itself. In the tense moments before the next barrage, the battlefield seems to hold its breath. "High explosive," Decker ordered. Ottmar jumped to it.

He picked up another shell and slammed the breech shut with a metallic clang, whispering, "In you go, baby—(louder) Up!"

Kurt called out, "On target." Kurt touched his dragon pendant.

Decker peered through the cupola slit. "Fire." The cannon roared, rocking the tank. The shell burst from the short muzzle, landing just right of the farmhouse. A miss. But it blew away a camouflage net, revealing a previously hidden anti-tank gun.

Kurt had been totally focused on the farmhouse. Stefan, peeking thru his driver's slit, to Kurt: "Kurt, check to the right of the house… antitank gun".

Decker's eyes widened. "What the… Where the hell did that come from?" He snapped into action. To Stefan, "Stefan, angle the tank better—hide our side or we're dead!" To Dietrich, "Report the anti-tank gun to the platoon. 200 meters. 2 o'clock, to right of farmhouse." To Kurt, "Sergeant, 25 degrees right. Get that Ivan gun."

Stefan jerked the tank to the right just in time, sliding into the mud. The Russian gun fired, the round smashing into the tank's thicker front plate near Dietrich's position. The impact jolted him violently, causing a bloody gash on his forehead. One lens of his dangling sunglasses cracked, pierced by a metal shard that had spalled from the inside wall of their tank. The Russian gunners frantically reloaded. Their gunner saw the turrets turning towards them. He yelled at his fellows to hurry.

With Stefan putting the tank into a violent directional shift, Ottmar had almost dropped the next round.

Kurt barked, "Ottmar I need you!"

Regaining his balance, sweat stinging his eyes, Ottmar forced the shell into the gun's breech. Ottmar, "Here you go baby." The deafening roar of the recent Russian blast against the tank had left everyone partially deaf, ears ringing. Ottmar shouted, his voice strained and louder than ever, but still barely heard by the crew: "Up!"

Realizing the crew couldn't hear, Ottmar slammed his palm against Kurt's shoulder. The contact was sharp, urgent. Blood trickled from Kurt's right ear, cutting through the grime on his neck as he fought to stay focused.

Ottmar's sharp contact jolted Kurt back to a memory from his youth. In the quiet woods, the campfire crackled softly. Conrad, Kurt, and their father sat close, shadows dancing on their faces.

Their father leaned forward, his voice low. "Take a long breath before you pull the trigger, boys. Patience and control—that's how you make the shot count."

Back to his gunsight, Kurt adjusted his aim, eyes narrowing with focus. He pulled back for a moment, brushing his fingers over the familiar touch of his Dragon necklace. Taking a deep breath, he steadied himself and returned to the sight.

"On target." Kurt called out to Decker.

Commander Decker: "Fire when ready."

The cannon roared, which launched the shell with a thundering blast. Half a heartbeat later, an eruption shattered the enemy position, and the Russian cannon crew were flung from their post. Smoke and debris rained down, filling the air with a sharp, pungent tang. A moment later two other rounds exploded into the position from their sister tanks.

Commander Decker exhaled, tension easing from his features. "Thank God, they hit us only with high explosive." He turned to Kurt, a rare smile broke through. "Good shooting, Sergeant."

The battle raged. German Stukas dive bombers, with their screaming Jericho Trumpet sirens, and Heinkel twin-engine bombers delivered their deadly loads on their Russian targets. Russian artillery explosions relentlessly fell on the German-held ridge area. Everywhere was the clanking of the metallic tank and assault gun treads and the loud roar of full-out tank engines. Kurt's four-tank platoon emerged dramatically over the contested ridgeline, perfectly orchestrated with the German artillery barrage. Commander Decker, atop the tank, shouted commands to the crew through his headset. Thick dirt, dust, and debris from nearby explosions rained down, spilling into the tank through the open hatch, causing Stefan, Kurt, and Ottmar to cough.

At his gunner's position, Kurt nervously popped a mint and touched his necklace, his fingers lingered on the cool metal. He glanced at Nikol's picture set beside the gunsight; his heart fluttered.

Stefan, with an unlit cigarette hanging from his lips, peered through his small viewport. "I can't see shit through this slit," he muttered.

Commander Decker, in his usual firm, low voice, replied, "Stop complaining. You just drive where I tell you. Just don't turn us upside down. You'll spill our gas."

The Russian Defensive Position is Assaulted: Conrad's Unit

At a Russian staging area beneath dark thunderclouds, a swarm of German fighters and bombers swept overhead, strafing and bombing the lines below. Fuel trucks and supply vehicles erupted in flame, their fire licking high into the sky like tongues from a raging inferno. The bombardment was so intense that even the Soviet command bunker's roof collapsed at one corner. The sky screamed with the whine of falling bombs while the earth shuddered under the rhythmic pounding of heavy guns—a deafening symphony of destruction. Suddenly, a jagged bolt of dry lightning split the sky, adding to the man-made chaos below, followed by a thunderous roar that shakes the ground. The air was thick with the stinging smell of smoke and the metallic taint of ozone, as if the very atmosphere was charged with the fury of the storm. The relentless barrage continued, each explosion igniting a flash of light and an instantaneous crack of thunder, amplifying the sense of impending doom.

In the Russian command bunker, Captain Marat gripped the radio receiver, shouting orders, his voice barely cutting through the rumble of nearby explosions. Dust fell from the ceiling like reverse steam, swirling in the oppressive air. The bunker corner is partially destroyed. Two more shells landed just outside the bunker, shaking the ground, and the reverberation sent a chill through Marat. The urgency of the moment pressed against him like a weight. Slamming the receiver down with a heavy sigh, Marat turned to Sergeant Trifon, his frustration now fully exposed.

"You won't believe this," Marat complained, his voice tight with disbelief. "Command doesn't believe the Germans have crossed our border." Sergeant Trifon, unfazed by his captain's rising fury, stood firm.

"Tell me what you need, Captain," he said evenly. His steady gaze met Marat's, offering not defiance—but something rarer: composure in the storm.

Marat glanced at the logs overhead and the corner damage, dust still drifted down, his thoughts racing as the ground trembled beneath another distant explosion. "Go straight to the depot. Tell them to move all our food, supplies, fuel, and ammo east, as fast as they can. Get them to the other side of the bridge immediately. We won't be able to hold them."

"Yes, sir," Sergeant Trifon responded with a sharp salute.

Without a flicker of emotion, he exited the bunker, leaving Marat alone with the weight of command. There was a brief silence as Marat took in the weight of his own words. He couldn't believe he actually had said that out loud. Sure, he had thought it but… to say it out load in front of the Sergeant. *Shit.* They were exposed…vulnerable. He looked across the bunker, where the sunlight streamed in from the gaping hole in the corner. The light fell on Stalin's stern portrait, offering little comfort in the face of imminent danger.

Then, his eyes fell on the half-full Stoli Vodka bottle sitting on the map table. Marat's mind briefly drifts, the hopelessness of it all creeping in. A short, bitter laugh escaped him, a reflex born of frustration. "I'll be lucky if I am able to finish this bottle." Marat's gaze shifted back to the map, his mind raced with strategies, possibilities, and desperate measures. His eyes fixated on the bridge. "Hell, might even have to blow the damn thing myself." The words were heavy, final.

Chapter 4—The Bridge and the Brewery, 1941

At the far end of the bridge, the cacophony of war engulfed Conrad, Jan, and their comrades as they hunched over the Russian bridge demolition charges. Conrad was working to disarm the charges. The cover fire from German Hanomag half-tracks and armored cars was relentless, but so was the barrage of small-arms fire from the retreating Russian soldiers. Every shot echoed across the river, the sharp cracks punctuating the shouts and chaos.

Sweat trickled down Conrad's temple, stung his eyes as he worked frantically to defuse the explosive charge the Russians had planted to blow the bridge. His fingers moved with the careful urgency of a man who knew that one wrong move or connection could mean instant death. He found it was hard to see the wires clearly in the shadows of the bridge pilings. The cold metal of the wires felt like ice against his skin; each strand vibrated with the pounding of his heart.

Beside him, Jan's expression was carved in stone, a mask of tension barely hiding the fear lurking underneath. His stare flickered between the chaotic demolition wires Conrad struggled with and the incoming Russian fire. Jan was torn between which presents the greater danger. The air was thick with the acrid scent of gunpowder and the clamor of shouts. The bridge groaned under the relentless assault, as if it understood what was at stake. Muzzle flashes tore through the battle haze, each burst carving smoke-shadowed streaks across the hardened faces of the men who fired.

A bullet zipped past, so close that Conrad felt as if the bullets, themselves, were actually hunting him. He even heard the famous 'Ivan hiss' of the bullet. He forced his breath to be steady, helping him block out the chaos, the screams, the thought of failure. Another bullet sliced the air past him on the other side. The world narrowed to his hands, the wires, and the life-or-death task before him. He focused.

He finally got the charge defused. He noted that the crystalline powder residue left a slightly sweet smell, like almonds, on his fingers. He briefly flashed to a holiday memory of *Christstollen*, the sweet Christmas almond flavored bread. Then a third bullet ricocheted off his helmet, snapping him back to reality.

The Russians retreated with resolute determination, they moved in a slow, methodical rhythm, firing with each measured step. The 7.62mm rounds sliced past with that high, dirty hiss they all knew too well—then came the thud, solid and final.

Conrad flinched as he saw two of his fellow grenadiers go down, their bodies crumpling onto the bridge deck, lifeless. The reality of battle seized his chest, but he forced it down, his eyes hardening. German infantry scrambled in a desperate push to cross the bridge and secure the far side, their feet pounding against the planks in a non-rhythmic, erratic pattern, like the chaotic spread of balls on a pool table at the first break. Sweating profusely, Conrad, Jan, and the crew hauled the MG34 and its ammo forward, muscles burning with each step. Bullets whistled around them, a deadly chorus that pushed them on. Conrad clutched the machine gun, drove forward, eyes locked on a patch of ground where the bodies of fallen Russian and German soldiers offered grisly cover for their position. Jan followed closely, the weight of the ammunition biting into his hands. Conrad braced to sprint, his body taut with urgency, but his boot caught on the outstretched leg of a dead German soldier. The stumble sent him hurtling forward, crashing hard onto the blood-soaked deck of the bridge.

The MG34 slipped from his grasp and clattered on impact as his helmeted head struck the slick, crimson-colored surface with a bone-rattling thud. The jarring blow pulled him out of time. The deafening roar of gunfire began to fade, softening unnaturally into a rhythmic, lulling sound—now like waves that crashing on a distant beach. The shift was disorienting, surreal, and Conrad felt untethered from reality, as though the battlefield had receded into some unreachable distance. Each second stretched impossibly, time unraveled into slow, deliberate beats, forcing him to confront every detail of his surroundings.

Blinking against the pain, Conrad's vision cleared. His senses surged with excruciating precision. Every sound, every movement was now somehow amplified, carved into his mind with impossible clarity. The blood that glistened on the deck looked darker—thicker—it's slow, deliberate seep defying logic. His own blood from his head wound seeped out as if to greet the Ivan blood. The metallic flavor of it filled the air, clawing at his throat and nostrils with every shallow breath. His pounding heart beat louder; it anchored him to that moment with an agonizing rhythm. Conrad was suddenly, unshakably aware—more present, more alive, than he had ever been in his life.

Then, as he opened his eyes fully, he came face-to-face with a dead Russian soldier. The man's head lay mere inches from Conrad, his grotesquely shattered face frozen in an eternal grimace. The back half of his skull was obliterated, leaving blood and brain matter pooled beneath the gaping void where it once was. But to Conrad, this was no ordinary casualty. An ominous weight seemed to hang in the air around the dead soldier, pressing against Conrad's chest and made each breath laborious. The soldier's closed eyes appeared unnervingly calm—too deliberate—as if waiting. The shadows on the bridge began to twist unnaturally, their edges flickering and stretching toward the corpse like grasping hands. The air grew heavier, colder, as if alive with a new unseen presence. The pungent scent of blood intensified, bitter and suffocating, and Conrad swallowed hard against the sour taste that rose in his throat.

Without warning, the dead Russian's eyes snapped open.

They were dull and glassy, yet disturbingly aware, as though they had stared straight into Conrad's soul. The lifeless stare pulled Conrad in, consumed him, dragged him deeper into the shadow nightmare. Conrad froze; his body refused to move as the soldier's shattered features contorted into an unnatural, satanic grin. Bloodstained lips curled back, exposing jagged, broken teeth in a macabre mockery of joy. And then, impossibly, the corpse's mouth began to move. The voice that emerged was guttural and raw, and vibrated through the air like a sound pulled from the depths of an abyss. The words, spoken in chillingly perfect, ancient High German, sliced through the unnatural silence:

"Du bist der Nächste." *(You are next)*

The phrase— "You are next"—hit Conrad like a physical blow. It reverberated through his mind as if he had been given a death sentence on the bridge by a dead Russian soldier. The words repeated, overlapping themselves, building into a haunting chorus that echoed from everywhere and nowhere all at once: "You are next. You are next." The blood pooled beneath the Ivan corpse started to stir. It rippled; it slithered across the deck like living tendrils. It seemed to reach hungrily for Conrad. The bridge beneath him tilted and warped, creaked and groaned, reality bent and splintered as the nightmare tightened its grip. The Russian's voice grew louder, the chorus rose into a crescendo as his glowing, glazed eyes bore deeper into Conrad's soul. Then, with a sudden, deafening snap, like the slamming of a great oak door, the Russian's eyes slammed shut. The grin crashed into nothing, vanished in an instant, and the figure collapsed back into lifeless stillness once more. Conrad's heart pounded furiously, threatening to burst from his chest, but his body remained paralyzed, locked in the terror of the moment. The final words— "You are next!"—lingered in his mind, pounded relentlessly with the weight of inevitability.

As the echoes faded, the rhythmic sound of the waves receded, now replaced by the sharp hiss of bullets screaming, in real time, overhead. The biting stench of gunpowder now invaded his bodily senses, mingling with the choking copper tang of blood. Gasping for real air, Conrad struggled to move, but the lingering terror bound him like an iron chain, and pulled him back into the now fading nightmare, refusing to let him go. Bullets screamed overhead like enraged hornets, their savage whine slicing the air inches above Conrad's head. A sudden hard slap on his head brought him back. Jan stood over him, violently shaking his shoulder.

"I saw all that blood and thought you were dead. You're really messed up, but you're not dead yet. If you're feeling up to it, let's go. No napping on the bridge. We've just started! Moscow's still waiting—you don't want to miss your war."

Getting up very slowly, Conrad said, "You were smart to be scared when I was working those demo wires."

"How so?" Jan asked.

Conrad, "Pretty scared myself. I'm red-green color blind." Adrenaline now surged through him. The fight wasn't over yet.

Further South: Zhiguli Brewery: Kurt's Unit

It was late afternoon. June 25, 1941. Four drab industrial buildings formed a semi-circle around a dirt depot area. Sign read "ZHIGULI BREWERY". Commander Decker directed the other three Panzers to select a building to park next to and bivouac overnight. With guards posted, Kurt and the crew relaxed and enjoyed a pale lager in the cold, roughhewn basement area. Stefan translated the sign on the wall: "Zhiguli Premium Beer". Electric lanterns cast a warm glow. Kurt announced, "Good fortune to liberate this brewery on only our third day in Russia." As Kurt took a long drink of the Zhiguli beer, he wiped his mouth with the back of his hand and glanced at Stefan.

"Not bad," he muttered, nodding as he raised the cool bottle. "It's no Pilsner Urquell, but after all we've been through, it hits the spot."

Dietrich, his head freshly bandaged, spread a map across the table. Noticing fresh blood seeping through, he paused to adjust the cloth, muttering under his breath. Finally satisfied, he leaned over the map, tracing a route with his finger. "Not bad... 202 km (125 miles)," he said, glancing up. "Leningrad is next." The crew quietly sang drinking songs and joked among themselves. Ottmar and Stefan locked hands in a rowdy arm-wrestling match, laughter rumbling around them.

Stefan lost. "Two out of three," he said.

"Don't blame me if you get hurt," replied Ottmar.

By lantern light, Kurt and Dietrich were soon joined by Ottmar. They cast shadow tanks with their fingers, battling fiercely on the wall. They also dueled with matchstick shadow MG34 machine guns, grunting and shooting as their tanks and machine guns fought to save the beautiful princess, dressed as a 9mm shell trapped in her tall tower—an upside-down potato masher hand grenade with the princess perched on top. The distressed princess was nearly taken by a shadow dragon, conjured by Ottmar's interlocking hands.

"Not on my Watch!" Kurt shouted. The winged dragon flapped and swooped, claws extended, attempting to steal her away. But Kurt and Dietrich's two shadow tanks fired a salvo in unison.

Boom. Boom.

With a dramatic 'death screech' from Ottmar—'I am slain'—the shadow dragon fell, and the shadow princess was saved. After another beer, they argued passionately over which hero she would now marry. But then Kurt, with a sly grin, ceded the princess to Dietrich with a deep, exaggerated bow, saying, "It's only fair since Dietrich is so tall, good-looking, and fashionable."

Dietrich confidently announced, "Of course I am."

Then, whispering in Kurt's ear, Dietrich added, "But I do think it really was your shot that got that evil dragon."

Kurt ruefully replied, "Of course it was." Their shared laughter filled the dim space—playful and fleeting. Gradually, the sounds dissolved into the night, leaving behind the soft glow of the lantern and the camaraderie of battle-hardened friends. Ottmar grabbed his pistol and took his turn on guard duty. For now, all was well in the basement of the Zhiguli Brewery on the third day of Operation Barbarossa. The next day, everyone was still relaxing and taking turns on guard duty.

They had coffee and cleaned their small arms. Commander Decker entered.

"Dietrich reported that our Panzer units are way ahead of schedule. Infantry is moving as fast as they can. That's bad news, boys, because we're now forced to wait another whole day for them to catch up."

The crew moaned in pretend disappointment. Decker continued, "But I have a surprise for each of you war heroes. It's time for a field inspection. Ottmar, go get Stefan. He's on guard duty now." The crew grumbled. Ottmar brought Stefan in. Stefan and the others holstered their pistols and put on their caps. They stood in line. There was absolute silence in the room. With a formal flair, Decker pulled a dented, dirty tin box from his side pocket. "As your direct field commander, I have decided that each of you has earned this one-of-a-kind battle medal. "Rest assured, no one else in the entire Wehrmacht has earned this very special badge of combat accomplishment." He strode confidently toward each man.

"Feldwebel (Sergeant) Knispel, you have some work to do. I commend you on your shooting so far. But I hope you can learn to hit your target in one shot," he sighed. "Not three. Our ammunition supply is limited, you know."

Kurt replied, "Yes, sir. I will do my best." They saluted, hands snapping to their foreheads, as the commander pinned a paper Zhiguli Beer label medal onto Kurt's uniform above his breast pocket. Decker stepped next to Ottmar.

Decker affixed the makeshift award onto Ottmar's uniform and steps back. "For outstanding service as crew morale officer, tank whisperer, and the only man crazy enough to sweet-talk a 20-ton beast." Ottmar offered a quick smile, then stiffened.

"Yes sir." He expertly saluted. They exchanged knowing glances. Decker moved to Dietrich.

"Now, Feldwebel Westfall. Despite your nasty forehead wound from that pesky Ivan high-explosive round, your handling of radio dispatches has been commendable. At least only one of your sunglass lenses was damaged, and not the rest of you. With you, I am assured we will win the war... with style."

Decker pinned the "medal" to Dietrich's chest. He approached Stefan, who fidgeted nervously, an unlit cigarette resting behind his ear. Decker said, "Now, Feldwebel Racy, you are my special project. Need

I remind you that our tank is not your personal ashtray?" Decker snatched the cigarette from behind Stefan's ear and ground it forcefully into the dirt floor. He stared intently into Stefan's eyes, who remained stone-stiff, staring straight ahead. Decker demanded, "Understood? Got something to say for yourself?"

Stefan replied, "But sir, if I may explain," glancing at Decker, who nodded for him to continue. "It was actually supplemental camouflage, making it harder for Ivan to see us, particularly from the air—from those damn Schwarzer Tod (Black Death) fighters—and… even if he did see us, he might think we were already blown up."

Decker said, "Tell that to your next commander. It's not regulation. And Feldwebel, given the volume of your smoking habit, the drifting ashes could compromise our vision slits, particularly near the bow machine gun, and hinder Dietrich's effectiveness." He glanced at Dietrich. "I'm sure Dietrich doesn't appreciate that." With a semi-muted cough, Dietrich nodded in agreement. Decker paused to let that sink in. Breaking his straight-ahead, at-attention stance, Stefan made quick eye contact with Dietrich, who winked. Then, in a more upbeat tone, turning back to Stefan, Decker added, "But… to your credit, you've done a good job so far. After all, you haven't turned our tank upside down—yet." He winked playfully, easing the tension with a smile. The whole crew stifled a collective laugh. "Dismissed," Decker said with mock formality.

The men broke into laughter, playfully pointing at each other's "medals." They teased each other about their mentioned faults, grabbed their beers, and burst into a spontaneous soldier's song. The singing rose and faded. The morning sun rose through the trees surrounding the brewery. Outside, the smell of wood smoke and coffee filled the air as the crew gathered around their small fires, boots crunching on the gravel beneath them. The light filtered through the branches, casting long shadows over the scene, where ammunition crates—with steaming coffee cups on top—and fuel barrels stood stacked in neat rows next to half-tracks and supply trucks. The men dug into their combat rations, unwrapping cans and packets with practiced ease.

Dietrich poked at the contents of his can with a skeptical frown, raising an eyebrow. "More of that flavorless *Wesselsuppe*, eh?" he muttered. "Named after that over-glorified SA Brownshirt fanatic."

31

The crew had come up with the sarcastic nickname for the thin, meatless soup—a jab at Horst Wessel, the Nazi martyr the dish was supposedly named after.

Ottmar, grinning, peered into his tin. "When I heard the SS got better food and more beer rations, I ran down to the enrollment office and applied to get in. Thought I could make myself look a bit more 'elite,' you know?" He took a bite, then shook his head. "But they took one look at me—no blue eyes, no blond hair, and definitely no confirmed Viking ancestors. Said I was too 'Polish' for their taste. And apparently, being 205 pounds didn't help either. They laughed at me when I told them that Odin was my great-great-grandfather. Guess I wasn't the 'perfect specimen' they were after."

Stefan raised an eyebrow, cigarette hanging from his lips. "Didn't know the SS was so picky about waistlines."

Ottmar laughed. "Yeah, just to make me feel better, they told me only four or five out of a hundred applicants made it. The rest of us? Looks like we were just stuck with this mystery meat."

Stefan, lit another cigarette and leaned against a box with a smirk. "They wouldn't have me in the SS either."

Kurt tilted his head, a faint smirk playing at his lips. "You applied?"

Stefan exhaled smoke. "Nah, I got the word. They would've taken one look at my name and my file and said, 'Nein.' Something about being too much of a 'Slav' for their liking." He tapped the cigarette ash. "Guess having a Czech grandfather didn't fit their mold."

Ottmar chuckled. "Guess we were both the wrong kind of 'German.' No wonder the SS got better rations."

Dietrich, stirring his can, chuckled. "Made me feel better knowing ninety-five percent of the entire army gets the same tasteless slop."

"I didn't apply because I had a fiancée at the time. She pampered me," he said, taking a spoonful from his tin, "in the right ways. But this *Wesselsuppe* certainly doesn't make up for it."

Stefan, cigarette dangling from his lips, raised a can with a mischievous glint in his eye. "I'll trade you my mystery meat for your *Wesselsuppe*. I'm in the mood for some soup seasoned with propaganda today."

Later, the platoon busied itself with resupply, hauling fuel and ammunition from the waiting Hanomags and trucks. The clank of equipment and the low hum of voices filled the air, but Kurt sat apart, leaning against the side of his tank, absorbed in his letter. His pen moved slowly over the paper, each stroke deliberate and heavy with thought. Another unopened letter rested on his leg,

Kurt's Letter

Nikol,

We were put out of action. We hit a road mine and blew out one of the track links. It's hard to fix. Those links are heavy. Stefan got a finger pinched. Took four of us to manhandle the track back over the main wheel sprocket. We used the jack handle to lever it into place.

Strange, though—I've only seen one Russian tank so far, and he was heading the other way. I've seen things I never expected to. I'll write more later.

I hope school's going well. I know nursing school isn't easy. I have confidence in you.

Miss you,

Kurt

He put a mint in his mouth and sealed the envelope, kissing it. Stefan came around the corner and pointed at the letter resting on Kurt's leg. "Whose letter is that?"

Kurt held it up. "This one is from Conrad. He's in the 12th Rifle Brigade, currently just north of here. Conrad wrote, 'Meet you in Leningrad for a Christmas beer and an Infantry vs. Tanker soccer match.' He reports that they are kicking Ivan's ass. He is quite optimistic. But that's Conrad. He sure loves being on the winning side. He plans to win the war all by himself."

"I thought you and Conrad didn't get along," said Stefan.

"It's complicated," replied Kurt. Reflecting, he remembered the talk he'd had with his brother shortly after Conrad's and Nikol's engagement breakup. It was then Kurt realized: Nikol had never really stood a chance with his brother—not because she lacked anything, but because Conrad didn't believe anyone ever could be enough. And yet, as Kurt watched her slowly gather the pieces of herself, something unsettled him. For the first time, he wondered—not as a friend, not as a confidant, but as something else entirely—whether there might be a place for him in the space Conrad had recklessly abandoned. Later, judging by the way Conrad behaved—even with Ericka—it became clear to Kurt that his brother had begun to question his own impulsive decision to betray Nikol.

Conrad Steps Up

Kurt's observation of his brother's aggressive nature was validated that same day, just eight kilometers north of Kurt's position. Under the harsh midafternoon sun, with a full load of soldiers, including Conrad and Jan, the German Hanomag was ambushed by Ivan machine-gun fire and came to a stop.

Conrad was the first out, saw the Russian gun flashes, and opened fire from his hip with his MP-34. That drew plenty of attention. Bullets whizzed around him, ricocheting off the still-slowly advancing Hanomag.

A bullet hit Conrad's helmet on the side and ricocheted off without penetrating. Stunned, he thought back to "You're Next. You're Next" for a few seconds, ears ringing, then he recovered.

The Hanomag laid down covering fire with its own MG34 machine gun, spitting tracers to suppress the enemy infantry. They began moving forward, providing cover from the slowly advancing half-track.

Conrad slapped himself across the face, steeling his nerves. Without waiting for orders, he barked, "Let's get moving!" and charged forward, Jan and the others close behind, using the rumbling half-track as cover. The men surged ahead in a coordinated rush, grit in their teeth and resolve burning in their eyes. Jan stayed close to Conrad.

Then, in a burst of Ivan machine-gun fire, three of them fell. Jan blurted out, "Oh Scheisse (shit), they just got Leo, Janis, and Markus."

Conrad brushed it off, his mind locked on the next objective. "We can't dwell on that now. We need to keep pushing," he said, his voice flat and mechanical. His eyes darted across the area, searching for any micro-movement of threat, his expression cold, momentarily numb to the losses around him. Fatigue and doubt washed over Jan, while Conrad's self-absorption and focus only intensified. The pressure mounted as the sounds of battle swirled around them. After a particularly close artillery round exploded, Conrad could barely hear the gunfire anymore—only the thudding of his heart and the creeping, suffocating silence of doubt. He remembered the dead Ivan's dark prediction echoing in his mind: "You're next. You're next." The sounds of battle faded.

Chapter 5—The Girl and the Gun

Days later, Kurt's tank was off to the side of a road with the platoon, under the cover of tall trees. The accompanying infantry chatted among themselves, nervously glancing around.

From the commander's cupola, Commander Decker spoke to his crew in the tank. "Gentlemen, stretch your legs for 10 minutes, but stay alert. The area has been swept but remember—we're in Ivan town."

With only a light breeze, the forest was eerily silent, save for the faint rustling of leaves and the occasional birdcall. Despite the German "sweep", meant to search for snipers, ambush points, and any signs of enemy soldiers still in the area, a diminutive female sniper, Yelena, barely out of her teens, had managed to remain hidden.

Crawling on her belly through the damp underbrush, her movements were slow and deliberate. Yelena, not yet twenty, was a graduate of the Russian Central Women's Sniper School near Podolsk—one of the thousands of Soviet girls trained to kill with patience, precision, and silence. She'd spent months learning to crawl on her belly a meter an hour, to wait motionless in the cold until her fingers went numb, and to fire only when the shot mattered. Her red-starred *pilotka* (cloth cap) sat slightly askew on her dark hair, a splash of crimson against the muted greens and browns of the forest floor.

Yelena peered through the scope; her finger poised on the trigger. Her crosshairs settled on the obvious prime target, Commander Decker, who stood, clipboard and papers in hand, in the cupola atop the turret, issuing orders. Just as she steadied her aim, he disappeared down into the turret.

"Damn," she muttered under her breath, annoyance flickering across her face.

She shifted her scope, scanning the scene, taking in the casual movements of the German soldiers. Her sights settled briefly on Ottmar, who was peeing by a tree, his back turned to the group. The image lingered in her crosshairs for only a moment before she dismissed him.

Nope. Tall and dumb, she murmured, deciding he wasn't worth the shot. Her scope glided to Stefan, who had lit a cigarette with an air of practiced indifference. His movements caught her attention—precise, self-assured. He had the look of someone who had seen too much and felt too little. But her interest was piqued only for a moment. *Maybe. A casual killer.* But something about him didn't hold her focus.

She scanned, her crosshairs pausing on the tall one (Dietrich). *Umm, tall, with an easy confidence*, she thought. *Like someone used to being noticed.*

To her, he moved with the kind of smoothness that felt more practiced than genuine—not the usual type of man you'd want covering your back in a foxhole. Her mind drifted. *He might even be nice on a date.* She caught herself and focused. Her crosshairs moved to the short soldier (Kurt) that the tall one was talking to.

Her thoughts followed:

Even with his back to her, she sensed the short soldier was different. His presence was quiet, deliberate, and strangely grounded for a frontline war situation. Unlike the rest of the close-cropped crew, the short one flaunted a full head of hair. Even from behind, she could tell he was growing the faint beginnings of facial hair—subtle, but there. Unusual for a German soldier, even in a combat zone.

She thought there was likely a reason he could get away with it. His posture was assured and relaxed. But he wasn't trying to impress anyone, and that impressed her. *Short man. Big threat.*

It was the kind of presence that reminded her of her father, whose silence, to her, always felt heavier than his words. Yelena knew his type—the kind that survived, the kind that could lead. Her father had been the local Chairman of the *Selsovet* (town mayor).

The short ones. Always driven, always with something to prove. They never backed down. In his stance, his quiet resolve, she saw herself—a side of her she wished she could embrace but didn't know how.

Her finger shifted slightly on the trigger as she narrowed her focus, studying both of them. *The tall one with the perfect hair? Not a warrior. Just another charmer. The short one? They were always the more dangerous ones.*

She could take him out with a headshot, maybe get the tall one too, if the angle was right. One shot, one bullet. She held her breath, waiting for the right moment, unsure if she could get them both in one shot. The angle was right.

As she watched, the short one bantered with the tall one, asking him something, gesturing to his pocket. The tall one smiled and nodded back. *Sure,* he nodded, holding out a hand.

She slowly steadied her hands. She settled the crosshairs on the back of the short one's head, her decision made. Now in her killer routine, her breath slowed, and her finger rested lightly on the trigger.

The short one reached into his jacket, fumbling with something he pulled out from his pocket. Through her scope, she watched closely, and for a brief moment, her focus shifted. *Looks like a candy mint.*

The small object slipped through the soldier's fingers and tumbled to the ground. For the first time in what felt like years, a flicker of a smile touched her lips. *I like candy too.* She hadn't had any since before the war, not since her father had brought home a bag of hard sweets after work. She caught herself. Her focus returned, and her finger tightened on the trigger again. It was just a momentary thought, but it pulled at something deep inside her—something she had buried for so long: *joy.*

Her finger slowly tightened on the trigger as the moment hung suspended. One shot, one chance. And then, in a micro second, a slip—something unexpected. The shorter soldier made a quick move downward to pick up something he dropped. Too late to adjust, her Mosin fired with its usual loud, authoritative bark.

The tall German was hit square in the chest. As he staggered, eyes wide in shock, the short one lunged forward, catching his tall friend and gently lowering him to the ground.

She peered through her scope, a flash of irritation crossing her face. *Damn,* she thought, *I missed the short one.* She clenched her jaw in frustration, watching his tall frame crumple.

Damn, sorry, she muttered inwardly. *Sometimes being so good-looking doesn't save you from death.*

Back at the platoon area, everyone scrambled. Stefan yelled and pointed to where the shot had come from. Decker emerged from inside the tank, grabbed the turret cupola machine gun, and opened fire in the direction Stefan indicated. The other three tanks followed suit, their machine guns cascading lead as trees, bushes, and dirt were shredded in a blizzard of bullets. Spent shell casings rained down like metal hail, clattering down the sides of the four Panzers. The seasoned infantry assessed the situation swiftly, divided into several search teams and initiated a systematic sweeping pattern to locate the sniper in the wooded area. With rifles ready, the German infantry split into a semicircle, advancing cautiously, eyes scanning for any sign of movement or the glint of a rifle barrel.

Yelena inhaled slowly, heartbeat steady as she cradled the Mosin. Her hands moved with practiced ease. *If I find the right position, maybe I can get another shot,* she thought—the idea snapping her focus back into place. She knew this dance all too well—the hunter was now the hunted. But then, her instincts took over. *No. These ones were moving too fast.* Their calculated movements and purposeful strides signaled lethal combat experience—soldiers she had learned to respect. Quiet as an evening shadow, Yelena melted into the underbrush, disappearing into the fading light. She shifted carefully, her crawling steps deliberate and weightless, each movement blending into the forest's rhythm. Around her, bursts of machine-gun fire shattered the quiet, rattling the trees and pulverizing the earth, but none found their mark.

She kept moving, slipping further into the dense cover, undetected. *Not today.* The words settled in her mind, calm and resolute. Survival wasn't about fighting every battle—it was about living to fight the next one.

Dietrich's body lay lifeless, a grim and painful testament to the cost of war. Commander Decker gathered the crew, his voice low and heavy.

"This is hard, men," he said, sharing the weight of their grief with quiet respect. The blood-splattered *Zhiguli Beer* medal pinned to Dietrich's chest fluttered slightly in the breeze, as if clinging to life. Another gust tugged at it, as though pulling it away from the fallen man. Each crew member wore their own medal, yet now, instead of pride, these small tokens felt like echoing reminders of what they had lost. Symbols of camaraderie and humor, once worn with a sense of unity, now seemed muted under the shadow of death, mocking this fragile line between life and the void.

Kurt glanced down at his own brewery medal, felt it weigh on him in a way he hadn't felt before—a pressing, painful reminder that no medal, no award, could ever bring back his lost comrade, Dietrich. The very thing that once bonded them now reminded him of the brother who was gone, the hollowness of it cutting deeper than any battle wound. Kurt reflected on the brutal reality of combat: it was the friendships, the brotherhood, that mattered most. In comparison, nothing else matters. No medal would ever fill the void Dietrich's absence left behind. Kurt ran his fingers over his dragon pendant, and his thoughts drifted to Nikol, remembering the simple, genuine comfort of her sharing bacon with him in the café—an innocent moment that now felt worlds away from the blackness of this war.

The wind picked up, tugging harder at the blood-splattered award until it tore free from Dietrich's chest. Kurt watched helplessly as the medal fluttered and tumbled through the air, vanishing into the dense brush—gone with the wind, as fleeting and intangible as life itself. Kurt now sat quietly beside Dietrich's still body. The chaotic noise of the battlefield had long faded, replaced by the oppressive weight of his inner silence. His gaze flickered over the bloodstained ground, lingering on the spot where Dietrich had fallen. The mint wrapper crinkled in his pocket as he shifted, and his jaw tightened. He didn't dare touch the wrapper. Stefan placed a hand on his shoulder, murmuring something Kurt didn't hear. He nodded anyway, his movements mechanical, detached.

Kurt knew that they would tell him it wasn't his fault—that it was war, that things happened. Soldiers died. But the words rang hollow, empty. His mind drifted back to the moment, replaying it, dissecting it.

The mint. The stumble. He exhaled sharply, as if trying to release the thought, but it lingered, unwelcome and heavy. The wrapper crinkled in his pocket again.

Stefan moved the tank next to a modest clearing where Dietrich's resting spot would be. He turned off the engine.

Kurt and Stefan grimly finished digging the grave a few feet from the tank. The weight of each shovelful of dirt felt heavier than the last, as though they were burying more than just earth. When they were done, Ottmar stepped forward, cradling the grave marker—a cannon shell— in his arms with unexpected tenderness. It wasn't just metal to him anymore—it was Dietrich's marker, a symbol of the bond they all shared.

As he knelt on one knee, Ottmar gently placed the shell on the ground, pointy end up. His fingers lingered on the cool metal; his usual easy demeanor stripped away. The battlefield had taken much, and this time, even the tank hadn't been enough. He ran a calloused hand along the tank's armor pitted surface, his touch unusually soft. The words felt strange, but Ottmar meant them. The tank had carried them through fire and fury, had taken hits meant for them more times than he could count. The tank had never failed them—not once. But it couldn't stop the sniper's fatal bullet that found Dietrich outside the tank's steel skin.

"Not your fault," Ottmar whispered, placing a gloved hand on the tank's scarred hull. "Easy now," he murmured. "Don't take this on yourself. Dietrich wasn't inside when it happened. You couldn't hold him then. It's not on you." With the engine metal cooling in the night air, the engine block clicked in reply. Ottmar nodded slowly, as if he understood. "You kept us alive in here. You did your part. He –Dietrich– knew that. He loved you too, you know. We all did." Another tick, steady, like a heartbeat slowing. Ottmar closed his eyes. "Rest now. We'll carry him between us. You and me." For a moment, loader and Dragon Tiger shared their grief — two survivors consoling each other in the silence after death. The engine ticked faintly in the cooling silence, metal settling with a groan, as if the machine itself was grieving—unable to protect its own. His hand rested against the steel for a moment longer.

Ottmar exhaled, then looked up at the crew, his expression strained for a moment. As if he got a message, Ottmar looked up the the crew and announces, "Goodbyes are hard, but we are to keep going." A promise, a quiet reassurance—maybe for himself as much as for the tank. No one responded right away, but they didn't have to. The weight of Ottmar's words settled over them.

Silently, he adjusted the shell, setting it upright—just a reminder. A mark of something that couldn't ever be undone. Ottmar finally stood, pulling his cap off as the others gathered. His eyes lingered on the tank, his fingers trailing once more over its worn armor, then shifted to the burial space where Dietrich would be for eternity.

Kurt watched as Stefan came forward and knelt, steadying himself as he reached for Dietrich's cloth cap, placing it carefully at the base of the shell. There wasn't any rush in his movements, only a quiet, steady purpose. With slow, deliberate, and respectful care, Stefan tucked two cigarettes into the cap, nestling them gently next to Dietrich's sunglasses, the one lens still cracked. Kurt handed him a couple of stick matches for the cap. The sunglasses—the ones Dietrich always wore, even when it was cloudy—were scratched and worn, a small but cherished part of who he was. Stefan's throat tightened as he wedged the cap at the foot of the shell. To Stefan, the grave marker felt like more than just a symbol; it was filled with pieces of Dietrich's life, pieces of their shared history.

Stefan's tough exterior cracked as the weight of everything hit him. A single tear escaped, trailing slowly down his cheek. He didn't wipe it away. Instead, he let it fall onto the grave—a quiet, unguarded moment of grief for a fallen comrade who was more than a soldier.

Dietrich was family.

Kurt stepped forward, the memory playing back in brutal clarity— the mint slipping from his fingers, the crack of the sniper's shot, the instant that had cost Dietrich his life. His chest tightened as he pulled out the same crinkled bag of mints, his hand trembling. What had once been a small comfort in a world gone mad now felt like a monument to guilt. With a heavy breath, he scattered the last of the mints over the grave, watching them fall onto the freshly turned earth. Each one seemed to carry the weight of things left unsaid. He let the wind take the empty wrapper. For a heartbeat, he thought he could still hear the sniper's shot—an echo stitched into his memory, a moment he would never outrun. The wind rose, stirring the dirt into swirling eddies around the grave, as if the earth itself mourned the loss.

Stefan and Ottmar approached Kurt in silence, their shared grief pulling the three of them together without a word. Stefan silently offered Kurt a cigarette. Kurt hesitated, the small gesture feeling heavier than it should in the weight of the moment. He hesitated again, then accepted it, and Stefan lit it for him.

Kurt drew deeply, the smoke burning his throat as he coughed, his eyes mirroring the raw, unspoken pain they all felt. Stefan handed Kurt the pack, and Kurt took it, inhaling again—more slowly this time. He exhaled, watching the smoke twist and swirl into the air, carried by the solemn breeze. Above them, a hawk circled, its cry piercing the stillness. With a beat of its wings, it soared higher, disappearing into the mist. The three men stood, rooted in silence, their grief heavy, their bond unspoken but unbreakable.

Chapter 6—The Cross and the Snake

Kurt's tank, with Decker up top in the cupola, was on a dusty dirt road. They were the lead tank of the usual four-tank platoon. They were followed by several infantry-laden Hanomag halftracks. They approached a village. They heard machine gun fire. They rounded a tight bend, directly adjacent to where an SS *Einsatzgruppen* death squad was finishing up after shooting 30 or so civilians. An SS soldier with a flamethrower methodically ignited houses and buildings one at a time.

An officer, Major Berndt, sat with detachment in the snake-logoed armored car with the door half open. Decker halted the tank. He climbed down from the tank and approached. Kurt got up to the cupola to watch.

Decker said, "Major, is this necessary? Unarmed civilians?" From his seat, Major Berndt looked dispassionately up, a cigarette dangling from his mouth with a clipboard and pencil in hand. He gave an emotionless sigh. The smoke from his cigarette curled lazily in the air.

Looking directly at Decker, "As you might guess, these are partisans," he said, spitting the words like venom. "Communist partisans. Jews. Retards. Gypsies. We have our orders direct from Reichsführer Himmler." He glanced up at Decker, then let his gaze shift to Kurt.

Without waiting for a response, he turned away, still seated. His voice, now devoid of humanity, grew quieter as he adjusted the camera strap on his shoulder. He jotted a note on his clipboard, then turned to his driver and silently held up what looked like the day's itemized tally of the dead—each line as neat and casual as a shipping invoice.

Major Berndt looked at Decker. "I assume you have your orders," he said, pointing patronizingly with his pencil down the road. The Major turned to his driver. "We got all the photographs we need. Let's go." The Major left without another word.

Kurt felt a chill crawl through him—and it wasn't from the wind. The words hung there: *We got all the photographs we need.* Cold. Indifferent. Like a death sentence whispered by someone who had long stopped seeing the dead.

The SS Major had spoken them as if the bodies were nothing more than fallen timber, just another task checked off his list. Decker remained momentarily frozen, the smoke from the burning buildings drifting into the sky, mingling with the bitter taste of his own powerlessness. The wind shifted, carrying with it, the thick, putrid stench of death curled through the air like an unseen specter. It clung to them—impossible to escape, impossible to ignore.

From the cupola, Kurt asked Decker, "Permission to come down?" Decker gave a short nod. Kurt climbed down and fell into step beside him as they began walking toward the killing ground—a stretch of churned earth now quiet between volleys. The sharp crunch of dirt and gravel under their boots filled the silence between them. As they drew closer, the sounds of shouted orders and the mechanical click of rifles being reloaded drifted through the air. The distance closed fast, but each step felt deliberate, drawn out by the weight of what lay ahead. A low fire crackled somewhere behind the execution line. Smoke curled above the scorched roof of a barn, blackening the morning sky. Then came the stench—burnt wood, blood, something sickly sweet beneath it all.

When they reached the clearing, the scene opened like a wound. Bodies lay in rows, naked, arms tangled and legs twisted, discarded like rubbish. Their clothing had been stripped before death—piled behind a nearby truck, guarded casually by a soldier smoking a cigarette. The dead were robbed not just of life, but of dignity—stripped of everything, down to the rings on their fingers and the gold in their mouths. Stepping nearer, Kurt's stomach tightened. His breath came slow, deliberate—his body caught between rigid stillness and the urge to act, though against what, he couldn't say. He forced himself to look down. Lifeless forms, tangled in unnatural stillness, stripped of identity except for torn clothing, a random shoe, and blood-streaked faces. The metallic scent of death pressed against his senses, and bile threatened to rise in his throat. Then—something familiar in the chaos.

A girl, half-obscured beneath another body. Dark hair. A slight frame. The angle of her jaw, the curve of her cheek—something sharp and intrusive, slicing through him like a blade.

Commander Decker noticed. "What's the matter, Sergeant?"

Kurt's voice came out low, almost a whisper. "That one looks like... my sister." The words slipped out before he could stop them—reflexive, unfiltered. *His sister?*

No. It couldn't be. Katrina was home. She had to be. She was safe. Wasn't she? Katrina, in many ways, had been like him—too bold for her own good. She questioned many things that didn't look right, even when she wasn't supposed to. She challenged their father on the war,

44

pushed back when their mother told her to hush. If she had been born a man, she'd probably be standing in his boots, staring down at this same horror. Had she spoken too freely? Had she trusted the wrong person? A wrong word in the wrong company—that was all it took these days. And she would never hold her tongue, not even when she should. His legs refused to move, as if stepping forward would make it real. He wanted to look away, to dismiss it as a trick of the mind, but instead, he found himself staring harder, searching for the flaw in the resemblance, willing it to appear. A sharp wind kicked up the dirt, swirling it over the bodies like a cruel mockery of movement, but the girl remained still. Too still.

Kurt's fingers curled into fists, his nails biting into his palms as if pain could ground him, force logic back into his mind. It wasn't her. It wasn't her. Then logic kicked in, she's home with father and mother a thousand miles away. But the chill sank deeper into his bones, gnawing at something more primal, more terrifying than the battlefield ever had. Because if it wasn't Katrina this time, it could be next time.

And that thought—that creeping, unrelenting truth—settled in his chest like a weight he would never be rid of. SS soldiers continued inspecting bodies, with single shots ringing out at random. They looted the bodies. One soldier was removing gold fillings from a corpse with pliers. It was all routine for the Major. The flamethrower soldier torched another building.

Kurt's jaw tightened, his breath slow and deliberate, though every instinct screamed at him to turn away. His voice, when it came, was low but sharp, cutting through the silence like a blade.

"This is not war," he said to Decker, his eyes locked on the carnage before them. "It's naked murder." The words sat heavy between them, unchallenged. Decker said nothing. There was nothing to say. The truth of it hung in the air, undeniable, like the blood-soaked earth beneath their boots.

That night, the snake dream returned for Kurt again. He felt the snake wrapping around his chest, tightening with slow, deliberate pressure. Its scales were cold against his skin, each coil pulling tighter, each breath harder to take. The voice that followed wasn't entirely his own—nor entirely human. It was a nightmare voice, low and cruel, whispering directly into his soul. "This is war. This is who you are. You are your family's last hope." The words burrowed deep, coiling in his mind just like the snake—inescapable, ancient, and true.

Over the next days and weeks, Kurt and the platoon rumbled forward toward Leningrad on the narrow, forested roads, with heavy bushes on the sides, winding tighter as they pressed deeper into enemy territory. A handmade sign, in Russian, with a crudely painted arrow reading "Leningrad", stood crooked by the roadside, half-buried in weeds. Kurt's tank, leading the column of four Panzers, rolled ahead in single file.

Decker, as usual, was perched up top, scanning the tree line for any sign of danger. The encounter with Major Berndt still weighed on him, a lingering shadow in the back of his mind. Behind them, two Hanomags followed close, their tracks clattering over the uneven, dusty terrain. They rounded a sharper corner. Out of nowhere, Kurt's tank took a hit in the tracks from a hidden gun. The tank lurched to a sudden stop. Twelve seconds later, the second round impacted on the lower, far side of the turret.

Decker, thrown off balance, had to grip the cupola edge for support, his head spinning for a brief moment. The rest of the Panzer column halted just around the bend, leaving Kurt's tank exposed out front, alone on the narrow road. Decker's instincts kicked in. He grabbed the radio.

"All tanks, hold position," he ordered. His eyes narrowed as he scanned the tree line, trying to locate where the shots had come from. He could feel their eyes watching him. The forest was silent—too silent. Inside the tank, chaos reigned. The impact had ignited a signal flare in the cramped space, sending thick, suffocating, acrid smoke and sparks swirling. Ottmar, with frantic intensity, opened Stefan's driver's hatch. He shoved the flaming flare out with his gloved hands, muttering curses under his breath.

"Bad naughty flare!" he growled, shaking his fist as it fell to the road. "Don't come back—ever! You're dead to me and our tank!" Despite the brief moment of dark humor, the tension remained. Minutes passed. There was no follow-up gunfire, just the sleepy drone of the idling engines and the dark silence of the forest.

The now-dismounted Hanomag infantry moved up and fanned out, weapons ready as they scanned the dense tree line. Decker gave a quick, measured order. "Find out what we're up against here. I don't want to bring the rest of the platoon up if it's a trap." The soldiers disappeared into the underbrush on both sides of the road, their movements careful, deliberate. The minutes stretched. The only sounds were the distant rustling of wind through the leaves and the occasional crack of a branch underfoot. Finally, one soldier returned from the tree line. "Nothing for a hundred meters," he reported. "No movement, no tracks—just silence." Decker ordered the soldier to coordinate a defensive line.

Decker exhaled, then turned to the tank. "Stefan!" he called. "I need you on this." Stefan climbed out, dropping to the ground beside him. Decker gestured to the damaged track, where the sheared links lay twisted and broken. As the infantry fanned out and saw nothing close by, Decker and Stefan had no choice but to begin replacing the damaged track links to get the platoon moving again.

In the tank, Ottmar and Kurt were now alone. The engine idled. "Damn. Track is shot. This is not good. We are sitting ducks. Worse than that, we are sitting smoking ducks!" Kurt coughed from the smoke. "What hit us? (hacking cough) I don't like this one bit." He nervously rubbed his pendant.

Ottmar coughed. "Nothing we can do about it now." They threw open all the hatches, letting the smoke billow out. From his gunner's seat, Kurt climbed up to the cupola hatch, eyes scanning the direction where the enemy round likely came from. His jaw tightened. "Where the hell is he?" he muttered. Ottmar glanced up from below.

"Probably didn't want to mess around with the rest of the platoon," he said, his voice steady despite the tension. Kurt dropped back down to his gunner's position inside the tank, frustration mounting. He searched by traversing the turret, the grinding whine filling the cramped interior as he scanned the forested and bushy terrain. Ottmar pulled a shell from the rack, running his hand along its smooth casing, as if reassuring it before its moment arrived. He held it up slightly, turning to Kurt. *"This one's ready to do her job,"* he murmured, his tone half-serious, half-affectionate.

"Not yet", Kurt replied, his voice distant, his mind locked on the hunt. Kurt didn't look away from the gunsight. His jaw tightened, muscles rigid, breath slow and measured. His eyes scanned the landscape, every shadow, every jagged edge of wreckage a potential threat. The silence pressed in, thick and suffocating. His pulse pounded in his ears, tension coiling in his chest like a wound spring. The enemy gun was out there— waiting, watching.

47

A bead of sweat traced down his temple, but it wasn't just his forehead—his armpits were damp, the fabric of his uniform sticking to his skin. The heat, the nerves, the waiting—it all pressed down on him, heavy and relentless. Ottmar gave his shell a final pat before sliding her back into her berth. "Be patient, girl. Your time's coming."

Suddenly, Kurt stiffened. A shadow burst from the tree line—a tank, emerging from the woods at an angle, just 200 meters away. His heart raced.

"Ottmar, Ivan at 11 o'clock!" he shouted. "That's the bastard that hit us. Damn. Fuck, it's a T-34! He's closing in—coming to finish us off!" Kurt's mind raced. There was no time to waste. Kurt snapped, "Switch to armor-piercing. Make it quick!"

It was kill or be killed.

Startled by the hidden tank, Kurt thought back to a time before the war, on a hunting trip at a wooded campsite. The soft crackling of a fire filled the quiet evening air. A tent stood to one side, and Kurt sat close to his dad, the warmth of the flames casting flickering shadows on their faces. His father, with a serious expression, spoke with the weight of experience.

Dad: "Wild pigs are tough and smart. Don't underestimate them, or you can get ugly hurt—or worse. When they come at you, it's fast and sudden. You've got to be ready." He stared into the fire for a moment, letting the lesson sink in.

Gunfire brought him back. With a blast, the advancing Russian tank opened fire with its bow machine gun, pinning Decker and Stefan down outside. Ottmar jammed an armor-piercing round into the breech with a loud clang. "Ready, boss—send them some made-in-Germany love," Ottmar growled with a sinister chuckle.

Kurt adjusted his aim, fingers trembling. He fired, but the round bounced off the T-34's thick frontal plate. "Bounced. Another round, Ottmar!" Kurt barked, pulling back from the sight momentarily. He took in a deep breath, then returned to his position. The T-34 gained speed, angling down the slope toward Kurt's immobilized Panzer. Its front machine gun spat lead, keeping Decker and Stefan pinned outside in a ditch next to the tank.

Ottmar, growling with frustration, slammed a fresh round into the breech. "Up!" he shouted. The T-34 fired while advancing, and the shot hit the dirt, splattering Decker and Stefan with dirt. The Russian tank crashed through the bushes and mud, bobbing like a cork in water as it closed in.

Kurt's aiming point shifted as the turret painfully tracked to the Russian tank. His hands tightened on the controls, struggling to keep the sights on the T-34. The turret's traverse was agonizingly slow. The Russian tank ground closer, its machine gun still blazing, sending a hail of rounds toward them.

Kurt gritted his teeth. He needed to get this shot. Time was running out. Finally, his sight aligned with the T-34's turret ring. He held his breath, his mind clear, focusing. With a measured exhale, he pulled the trigger. The shell punched through the turret ring with a deafening roar, ricocheting inside the Russian tank, exploding with force.

BOOM.

A flash erupted as the T-34's ammunition cooked off, sending the turret flying skyward. The flaming, turretless hull lurched forward before coming to a jerky stop about 20 meters from Kurt's tank. The T-34 driver, totally engulfed in flames, desperately tried to climb out of his forward hatch. German infantry fired, and he slumped down, half hanging out of the hatch, still twitching as flames consume him. Kurt rose from his gunner's seat and goes to the cupola, head emerging from the commander's perch. The sight of the burning tank and the smoldering, twitching body hit him like a sledgehammer. They were downwind a bit of the burning hull. The raw stench of scorched flesh filled his nostrils, overwhelming him. He stared, frozen in horror, before the nausea surges. Kurt turned and vomited, unable to hold back the physical and emotional revulsion.

Later, Decker and Kurt stood in the dense woods, not far from the tank. The rest of the crew worked diligently on the damaged track, the sound of metal clanking and tools scraping against the armor filling the air. Decker turned to Kurt, a serious yet encouraging look on his face. "Sergeant, you're a good man. That tank you just took out wanted to kill you—and all of us. Ivan would have danced on our dead bodies if he had the chance."

The words landed with weight, cutting through the lingering tension. Decker wasn't just giving praise; he reminded Kurt of the reality they lived in. It's kill or be killed, and today, Kurt made sure they lived to fight another day. Kurt, still pale and shaken, shifted uncomfortably, his mood heavy with the weight of what he has done.

Sensing Kurt's inner turmoil, "I need to remind you that this is your first tank victory. Against an invincible T-34, too! Very impressive work. You hit him exactly where you needed to with our little gun," said Decker. Kurt just stared into the distance, struggling to process the gravity of his actions. The praise felt distant, almost hollow against the backdrop of the day's very real horrors. He forced a faint smile, but it doesn't quite reach his eyes. Decker clapped a reassuring hand on Kurt's shoulder.

"You did good, Kurt. Remember that. You survived, and you fought back. We all need to keep fighting if we're going to make it through all this."

Kurt nodded, appreciating Decker's attempt to lift his spirits, but the darkness lingered, a shadow over his victory. Decker looked discreetly at the necklace on Kurt's neck. "Sergeant, I have an idea. Perhaps it would help, just maybe a little bit, if you put a dragon tattoo on our tank turret. It could bring good luck and remind us of why we are all here."

Kurt, startled from his stupor, echoed, "A dragon tattoo?" He instinctively touched his pendant, thinking of Nikol. He thought for a minute. "Yes, I think you are right, sir. The whole crew has earned a tattoo for our first tank victory."

Decker replied, "I like that. After seeing you in action with just you and Ottmar, you don't have to convince me that there is something very special in your dragon pendant."

Later he finished the dragon "tattoo" on the turret. Pleased with his artwork, he smiled and turned to the crew who had gathered to see the finished work. "It pleases me to share my good luck charm with the whole crew! This will now give us extra strength in the hard times. I christen thee… 'Dragon of War'".

Ottmar nodded approvingly, running a hand over the fresh paint. "And like the dragon, we strike fast and burn everything in our path."

Stefan, a lit cigarette in his mouth, came up to Kurt. "How about a smoke? You earned it." Stefan lit one up for Kurt. Thinking of Dietrich, Kurt took it.

"I'll write my brother, Conrad, and let him know to keep an eye out for our Dragon Insignia." Kurt took a drag on the cigarette and coughed. The crew chuckled and shared in the light moment, their spirits lifted as they rallied around the newly painted symbol of unity and resilience and Kurt's new smoking habit.

The crew gathered around, Stefan taking a long drag from his cigarette. Kurt stood back and said, "I'm adding this for a few reasons. It started with my girlfriend, Nikol—no secret there. She gave me this note with my dragon pendant." He took a piece of dog-eared paper from his pocket. Kurt read the paper, his fingers brushing the necklace:

"A spark ignites, the path unfolds, a legend born beneath the skies. You're not just walking a path, my love—you're forging one. Wear this, and remember who you're becoming."

Stepping back once more, Kurt smiled—a different smile this time, filled with pride and purpose. He literally beamed with love. He turned to the crew, his voice quiet but firm. "This isn't just for luck. It's a reminder. Every time we go out there, we fight to come back. Back to not only base but also to our homes and our families."

Stefan, with a cigarette between his lips, gave a nodding grin. "I like it. It's a dragon with heart."

"… And a gun," Ottmar added. "Don't forget the gun."

Conrad's Position North of Kurt

A couple months later, the morning sun filtered through the dense trees, casting dappled light across the bustling staging area in the forest. The air was thick with the smell of gasoline and the rumble of engines as Hanomag halftracks splashed through the mud. Motorcycles zipped by, their riders weaving through the chaos, while Panzer Grenadiers swarmed around, loading supplies and ammunition with urgency and precision. Kurt's brother, Conrad, stood by the back of a truck, heaving boxes of ammunition alongside Jan. Sweat trickled down his brow, but he barely noticed, his mind racing with the news he had just received.

"I got a letter from Kurt this morning," he said, straining as he lifted a particularly heavy box. "They lost Dietrich, but apparently, my little brother finally got his first official tank kill. Because of his pendant his commander even had him put a dragon logo on the turret." The instant the words left his mouth, his thoughts bolted to that moment when Nikol had burst in on him and Ericka.

Jan, only half-listening and caught off guard, blurted out, "That's from Nikol, isn't it?" Conrad froze, the weight of the ammo box momentarily forgotten. His fingers tightened around the rough edges of the crate, knuckles whitening. For a moment, he was somewhere else—

somewhere far from this box of 500 rounds of 7.92mm ammunition in his hands, or even Jan. Around them, soldiers barked orders, motorcycles kicked up mud, and halftracks rumbled in and out of the staging area. Everything was in motion—everyone moving forward, preparing for the next battle. But Conrad? No. He was stuck, like the ammo crate he now held too tightly, unable to move forward.

Conrad's face darkened. A wave of aggravation washed over him, his jaw clenching as he forced down the surge of emotions threatening to rise. The rage passed. Then, in a voice barely more than a growl, he muttered, "Mind your own business. Let's just get this shit loaded. We've got orders," he snapped, his tone low and tight.

The atmosphere shifted between them; the weight of Jan's words hung in the air. In silence, they continued loading the truck, the forest and military preparations providing a pulsing backdrop to the unspoken burdens and fears they all carried deep inside.

"Sorry," Jan muttered, his voice thick with regret, barely audible. The apology drifted into the noise of the staging area, carried off like as if it was never meant to be heard. Conrad said nothing and hurled two crates of hand grenades into the truck with more force than necessary.

Alarmed, the Master Sergeant in charge barked, "Hey, soldier, those are hand grenades. Take it easy."

Conrad gathered himself before responding, "Jawohl, First Sergeant," his voice clipped. Two days later, the air was thick with tension as Conrad's grenadier unit prepared to assault a Soviet bunker complex that had been stalling progress in their sector. The plan was straightforward: six of the twelve men would advance on a key machine gun position, a crucial target to suppress enemy fire.

As they moved through the heavy brush, the dense foliage offered both cover and concealment. But it wasn't long before disaster struck. The sharp crack of gunfire erupted, followed by the deafening blast of a Russian hand grenade. Two of Conrad's men fell immediately, their bodies collapsing to the ground. Chaos erupted as shouts filled the air. "Ambush!" one soldier yelled; his voice barely audible over the intense gunfire. In the commotion, Conrad noticed that one of his men, Manfred, was seriously injured from the grenade, lying behind a cluster of larger rocks about six meters away. Blood seeped through his uniform, staining the ground beneath his leg.

Conrad exchanged a glance with Jan, whose expression mirrored the turmoil swirling within him. "I've got to get him," Conrad said, his jaw tightening with determination.

Jan was stunned to hear Conrad say this. Jan scanned the area for any new signs of enemy activity. "Too dangerous. We're in a really bad position,"

"I told you," Conrad snapped, his voice hard, anger flashing in his eyes at being questioned. "I'll get him. If you want to join me…" Their eyes locked … the tension thick between them. Jan could see it—Conrad was ignoring the odds. This Conrad wasn't asking permission; he was already in motion.

Jan just shook his head, a weary sigh escaping him. "I want to live at least one more day, Connie. I'll wait here."

Conrad wasn't waiting. He had already sized up the terrain, spotting a path through the thick underbrush. "Give me your pistol. Here's the machine gun. You cover me—pin down those two Ivans on the right. I'll bolt to the rock and bring him back. Just keep firing, and if you run low, use the grenades." His voice was crisp, no hesitation, only focus. "Remember short bursts or my barrel melts and that makes me mad." Without waiting for a word, Conrad shoved the grenades into Jan's hands, his movements swift and precise. He grabbed Jan's Walther pistol, jamming it into his belt, then gripped his own with a steady, determined hand. Jan hesitated for a heartbeat, the insanity of the plan sinking in, but after a tense moment, he nodded.

"You're out of your mind," Jan muttered, his voice low but resolute. "But I'll cover you. If you make it back in one piece, beers are on me for the next two years." Conrad didn't respond. His eyes locked onto Manfred, just six meters away, his leg badly wounded. There was no time for hesitation. Conrad exploded forward, pistols raised, firing as he ran straight toward his fallen comrade.

Jan's MG34 screeched to life behind him, its tight bursts punching through the air like a metal cough—spitting nails, sharp and mechanical. Each three-second volley acted as a moving shield, forcing the enemy to drop behind cover. At great cost, the Soviets had learned to fear the angry scream of this German machine gun. Conrad sprinted forward, legs pumping, pistols barking in rhythm with his breath. After two bursts and a pause, the air cracked again—Jan's fire tearing through smoke like a buzz saw against bone. Conrad pushed harder, closing the distance to Manfred. He ran hard, both pistols firing in rhythm—each step a shot, each shot a step closer to Manfred.

Jan's machine gun kept up its buzz-saw suppressive burst fire, the enemy pinned down just long enough for Conrad to get across the open ground, heart pounding in his ears, and reach the rocks and Manfred. Without hesitating, he hoisted Manfred over his shoulder, grimacing at the weight and the urgency of their situation. While Jan's MG34 bursts ended, enemy fire now resumed and whizzes by, but the primal instinct to survive kept Conrad moving.

Just as he made it back to their position, Jan tossed his first grenade, and the explosion resonated through the air as dirt and debris flew. He was pleased with himself, relief evident in his voice as he saw Conrad and Manfred safely return.

Breathing heavily, Conrad collapsed to the ground beside Jan, the adrenaline fading, and the weight of their actions settling in. A little later, now off the front line, Manfred, pale and trembling, called weakly to Conrad. "Thank you for what you did." Looking back at Manfred, Conrad's usual hard edge softened. Manfred, his hands still trembling slightly, said, "I want to show you something."

Conrad raised an eyebrow, curious. "What?" he asked, with a bit of a Conrad edge to the tone. Slowly, Manfred reached into his breast pocket and pulled out a worn photograph, handling it like a delicate relic. He held it out, and Conrad took it, studying the faces in the picture. The photograph showed a woman and two small children. One of the children sat on a bike, grinning widely, while the other stood beside her, their smiles radiating warmth and love. In that moment, Conrad's heart sank. He thought of Kurt, Nikol, Ericka, his sister Katrina, Mom, and Dad. He looked from the photo to Manfred's gashed leg—a brutal reminder of the war's cost. *This is no soccer game,* he thought. For a brief moment, Conrad's usual hard expression softened, and he gave a nod, his face serious, with a hint of unspoken insight—his first vague feeling of empathy as a soldier.

Manfred's voice was barely a whisper. "Conrad, you are a good man. And my family says... thank you." Conrad looked at him, the bravado gone for once. "Look, we're in this together, Manfred," he said, placing a hand on Manfred's knee. "Couldn't leave you there." His voice was low and steady, almost as if he surprised himself with the words. A faint, sincere glimmer of humanity surfaced in his eyes. He clapped Manfred on the shoulder, almost embarrassed, and with the slightest grin, added, "We're both lucky that worked."

As he stood, Conrad glanced back at the photo of Manfred's family. It wasn't just a picture—it was a reminder of what all this was really for. Not the fight in front of him, but the life waiting behind it.

Some distance south of where Conrad and his unit were engaged, Kurt stood with his team and the assembled four-tank platoon. The air was thick with anticipation; the mechanical rumble of the tanks idled in the background. The sixteen men stood, eyes fixed on their platoon commander as he glanced at the paper and map in his hands, the weight of new orders bearing down on his shoulders.

Kurt asked him, "What are our orders, sir?"

Commander Decker began, his voice steady but with an edge of urgency, "We are now to bypass the direct northbound assault on Leningrad. We are to march east to a town called Shlisselburg, a village with an important linking rail hub to Leningrad. We secure that and then our next target is south to a town called Tikhvin."

Decker scanned the rest of the orders quietly to himself: *Press east to Shlisselburg, a town of about four thousand. It's 35 kilometers directly east of Leningrad, on the southern shore of Lake Ladoga. Your mission is to take and hold it. Intelligence reports suggest there are no significant defenses left, as the heavy weapons have been pulled to defend Leningrad.*

He paused, letting the weight of the next part settle in. *Once you've secured Shlisselburg, push southeast to Tikhvin—about 220 kilometers. It's the only major rail hub for all of Russia's Northern Armies and Leningrad.*

Decker let out a sharp breath. "Ultimately we are to march to Tikhvin. Given its central crossroads position, that will no doubt be a brutal fight." The men shifted, exchanging quiet glances. They understood. Decker's eyes scanned his men, gauging their readiness. The men nodded in agreement, silent but resolute. "This is a pivotal moment, and we won't be alone. Command expects solid resistance, but we've proven ourselves before, and we'll do it again."

Decker continued, "We're getting a new radio operator tomorrow. Kris Korson," Decker said, allowing a slight smile to break through his usually stoic demeanor. "Besides being proficient in radio operations, he brings something else with him—his harmonica. Says he plans to fill our tank with music."

There were a few quiet chuckles among the men, a welcome break from the tension that always lingered before a mission. Music, especially in the bleakness of war, was a rare gift. "You'll like him," Decker added, his tone softening for a moment. Then his expression turned somber. He took a deep breath. "Dietrich... would have expected that." His voice lingers on the name; the recent loss still a shadow in everyone's mind.

Chapter 7—Welcome to Shlisselburg

As Commander Decker's platoon approached Shlisselburg, he stood in the cupola, headset on, and informed his men, "Not far now, men, just six kilometers." They completed the journey without encountering resistance.

But as the journey grew closer to its destination, Kurt's hands tightened around the gunsight controls. His senses were alert, even though the landscape outside remained quiet. It had been a long time since he'd felt quiet like this. The tension that had once felt like a constant companion now felt more like a weight—a weight that pressed on him, whether he wanted it or not. On October 16, 1941, upon entering the outskirts of Shlisselburg, Decker directed the accompanying Hanomag half-track to advance and assess the situation while the tanks remained behind. The infantry dismounted and flanked the half-track, discovering only townspeople engaged in their daily routines. Kurt sat in the stillness, his thoughts a quiet hum, waiting for the signal. The quiet outside felt strange and unsettling. It didn't match what he expected.

An hour later, the radio crackled with a report: "No sign of Ivan, sir. No heavy weapons or built-up defensive positions. It's really spooky strange. The townsfolk are just carrying on like it's any other day. We've checked all the obvious places for snipers—nothing."

Kurt's fingers tightened on the controls, and he tried to push the unease away. Maybe it was nothing. Still, the thought gnawed at him— Was this the calm before the storm? Or were they just being set up for something worse?

Commander Decker ordered another sweep of the buildings, this time door to door. The men moved methodically, clearing each structure with military precision. Kurt remained in his tank, eyes fixed on the scene outside, the stillness gnawing at him.

Minutes ticked by. The crew waited in silence, the rumbling of the engine filling the void. No sounds of conflict. Nothing. The longer the silence stretched, the more it felt like something was wrong. Kurt's grip on the turret crank handle tightened. He knew the score—*this* was too quiet.

Decker, frustrated but maintaining his calm, posted guards at the major intersections and in a few high vantage points. "Just to be sure," he muttered.

Kurt glanced at his crew, then at the distant horizon. There was something about the emptiness around them that unsettled him. It felt wrong. They had been here too long without resistance. Maybe this was the lull before the storm.

Satisfied, Decker ordered the tanks to proceed to the central town square to await resupply. Kurt's tank halted near a cluster of dull municipal buildings, and Decker gathered the crew in a loose semi-circle outside the tank. He scanned the square, watching civilians as they shopped, chatted, and wandered about, as oblivious as ever, like they see Panzers every day in the market.

"It's bizarre." he muttered, his voice tinged with a mix of caution and disbelief. To Decker, it seemed the town was clueless about the war. "I think it's time for some well-deserved R&R, but take your pistols with you," Decker added. "Return here in an hour." He turned to Stefan with a smile, adding, "Since we didn't hit a mine while you were driving, you can now get your smoke break. But stay away from our tanks and vehicles."

With guards posted, the soldiers dispersed, some idly turning into "tourists," heading off to buy sweets and trinkets from the nearby market. The tension of the moment ebbed slightly as the men, still on edge, relaxed in the lull. Stefan lit a cigarette and wandered over to Kurt, who, in turn, lit his own.

As they walked toward a nearby candy shop, Kurt's appearance struck Stefan more than usual. His once-youthful features were now sharper, his face framed by a mustache and a goatee. His hair, longer than before, fell uncombed. There was a darker transformation to him— a heaviness in his gaze that Stefan couldn't ignore. It wasn't just the war that had worn him down; it was the weight of everything he'd seen, the things he had to do that were now carved into him like a permanent scar.

Kurt's eyes, once more hopeful and wider, now held a shadowed awareness that spoke volumes—a quiet understanding of the world's cruelty. No longer the fresh-faced man who had stepped into this war, he now exuded a kind of weary competence. His posture had changed too—hunched, like someone who had learned how to carry a burden that could never be put down.

They reached the shop, where an older woman stood behind the counter, her face lined with years of hardship. The bell above the door jingled softly as they entered. Kurt nodded in her direction, stepping up to the counter. He pulled a couple of items from the shelf—a packet of licorice candy and a postcard of a dragon he'd found tucked away in a corner.

With a cigarette hanging from his lip Kurt asked in Russian, his voice steady but slightly flat, "How much?" The exchange was brief and businesslike. He wasn't there to talk, just to get what he needed.

"100 rubles or 8 cigarettes." The clerk replied.

Kurt huddled with Stefan, who gave him some cigarettes. Kurt, in Russian, says, "Here are 10 cigarettes." The clerk smiled and took them, satisfied.

It was clear now that Kurt had grown into his role—not just as a soldier, but as someone who had seen too much and no longer cared for the pleasantries of civilian life. He could go through the motions of normalcy, peace, but his mind was always elsewhere—back in the tank, in the fighting, or in the memories of battles past. Despite the soft atmosphere of the shop, there was still a weight to him, one that couldn't be shaken off by a simple transaction. This quiet town unsettled Kurt in a way he didn't expect. The silence pressed inward, stirring a tension he couldn't name.

Stefan glanced at him, noticing the change in his friend. A few years ago, Kurt would've laughed off serious moments—cracking jokes just to keep things light. But that was before the war. But now, there was only silent resolve and a flicker of something else—a weary detachment. Stefan wasn't sure if it was the war that had shaped Kurt or if Kurt had shaped the war around him, but either way, Kurt wasn't the same man who had first entered this conflict.

Stefan then stepped forward. "I'll take 10 licorice sticks. Here are 5 cigarettes," he asked in Russian. The clerk frowned and held up both outstretched hands, signaling that the price was 10 cigarettes. Stefan, already irritated, stepped back, his fingers inching toward his pistol, his patience worn thin.

But for Kurt, standing beside him, it wasn't the transaction that struck him—it was everything else. The weight of the war, the brutal memories that never left him. It was the damn war gnawing at his every moment, stripping him of any sense of peace. The senseless death, the endless slaughter, the endless lives lost, crushed, and forgotten. The moments flashed in his mind—the cries, the bloodshed, the hollow eyes of the fallen. He had witnessed too much, and the weight of it all was suffocating.

With Stefan placing his hand on his pistol Kurt's chest tightened with a startled fury that shot through him like fire. He hadn't felt this way in a while—the pure, unfiltered rage. His body, already tense from the invisible weight of the battlefield, snapped. Without thinking, his body moved, and the words exploded from his mouth like an untamed force. "Stop it! Just… stop it!" The shout cracked the air between them, a thunderous roar that shattered the stillness of the shop.

The female clerk, startled, took a step back, her eyes wide in alarm at the raw power in Kurt's voice. Her hand instinctively moved to her side, as though expecting some kind of immediate threat. What had been a peaceful atmosphere in the shop cracked under the intensity of Kurt's emotional outburst, the tension palpable.

Stefan recoiled, eyes wide, unsure how to respond. The force of Kurt's explosive rage had caught him totally off guard, leaving him momentarily speechless. Kurt, his chest heaving, glanced at the clerk, who now stood frozen, her posture rigid with surprise. The moment hung in the air, charged with a raw energy that made the shop feel small and suffocating.

Stefan, still trying to process, stammered, "But Kurt, you paid too much—10 smokes for some licorice and a postcard?"

Kurt's breath came fast, ragged, as he fought to rein in the chaos inside him. His chest tightened—part anger, part something deeper. "How the hell can you be arguing over this, Stefan, after everything we've seen?!" His voice cracked, but he didn't care. The grief, the guilt, the sheer injustice spilled out, louder than the noise around them. "How can you not see what's wrong with this?" He stepped forward and put a firm hand on Stefan's, pushing it away from the pistol on his hip.

The clerk swallowed hard, her eyes darting nervously from Kurt to Stefan, unsure of how to react. Kurt was no longer just angry—he was unraveling, and it was clear that the weight of the war had come crashing down on him in this small, insignificant moment.

Stefan, now realizing it wasn't about the cigarettes, took a cautious step back. His gaze softened, a flicker of understanding crossing his face as Kurt stood there, trembling with the force of his emotions.

Kurt, still caught in the storm of his thoughts, took a deep breath. Regret and shame washed over him, his body sagging as the fury drained away. "I'm sorry," he muttered, voice low, unsteady. "I shouldn't have... I don't know what came over me." He glanced at the clerk, who hadn't moved—still standing there, her eyes wide, mouth slightly open, hands clutched tight around the edge of the counter as if bracing for something worse. The tension in the room was suffocating.

Kurt ran a hand over his face, trying to steady himself. "I just... I can't take it anymore. This war—it's tearing us all apart." The woman didn't speak, but her breath caught—just loud enough to be heard—and she took a small, instinctive step back, her shoulders tight with fear and confusion. Kurt saw it, and it hit harder than any word. He looked away, ashamed. The tension eased.

Stefan, offering a quiet apology with a quick glance, pulled out more cigarettes, counting out 15. He handed them to the clerk, who smiled faintly, clearly relieved to avoid any further escalation. The exchange was awkward, but it marked a small truce, a moment where the world outside the shop seemed far away.

They took a long walk and then returned to the tank. They saw that there was a white-haired bearded policeman in a fancy colonial-style uniform with a tall fur braided hat with his bicycle. He was writing on a clipboard.

Kurt, in Russian, "How can I help officer?" Kurt, Stefan, and the policeman talked. Stefan helped on interpretation. Kurt knew some but Stefan is well versed. The policeman pointed to a sign and then to the city building behind the sign. Kurt slapped his forehead in a "how stupid of us" way. The sign said (in Russian) "No Parking."

With the commander inside the tank, buried in paperwork, Kurt approached and climbed up to the top. He tapped lightly on the edge of the commander's open hatch.

From inside, Decker's looked up, headphones still on, slightly askew, "What is it?"

Kurt briefed him quickly, his tone low and direct. Decker listened, his face neutral at first. Then, with a sigh, he pulled off his headset and climbed up and out of the hatch. Standing on the back deck of the tank, he scanned the small group gathered nearby—a mix of curious villagers, a very formal-looking policeman, and a bicycle leaning on a tree.

Decker rubbed his chin, narrowing his eyes at the scene. He turned to Kurt. "Now tell me what he said again."

Kurt repeated the constable's message verbatim. As the words sank in, Decker shook his head in disbelief, his lips curling into a faint smirk. A chuckle escaped him as he muttered to himself, *"I can't believe this."* He winked at Kurt, amused by the absurdity of it all. Stefan just shrugged. Kurt lifted both hands, palms up, in perplexity.

Kurt gave Decker the "You're the boss" look. With that, Decker disappeared back into the tank. A few moments later, he emerged holding a modest canvas sack. He climbed down, the sack slung casually over his shoulder, and handed it to Kurt.

"Ask the constable if a carton of French cigarettes might smooth things over," he said, a sly grin tugging at the corners of his mouth. Kurt took the policeman aside. They talked.

The policeman folded his arms, his clipboard across his chest that emblazoned with medals, and slowly but firmly shook his head. "No." He gestured to Kurt, pointing at the building and the parking space where their tank was parked. Stefan helped fill in the words Kurt did not understand.

Kurt went to Decker. "He says the cigarette donation handles the two minor city ordinance violations. But being the mayor's personal parking space is a whole different and more serious matter. It's apparently a respect thing, sir. I think we need to make this right."

Decker scratched his chin. "Sounds like it's a public relations issue, even if we are invading their country. Hang on, I got another idea that might do it."

He ducked back into the tank and emerged with another, slightly larger canvas sack. After a brief conversation with Kurt, Kurt took the sack to the constable.

The constable opened it, and his eyes widened in surprise. He nodded approvingly. Kurt talked with him and placed both sacks in the constable's bicycle basket. The policeman shook Kurt's hand, tipped a salute to Decker, and dramatically tore up the tickets. "You gave him his favorite beer—Zhiguli," Kurt said to Decker. Kurt reached into his bag and gave Decker five licorice sticks from the store.

Decker laughed. "You know too much, Sergeant. Licorice in Russia is something I never thought possible! Haven't had any since Norway. Thank you. In resolving this situation, I've always believed in the

Goethe saying, 'The way you see people is the way you treat them, and the way you treat them is what they become.'"

Regarding the constable, Kurt said, "He says he wishes to see us again on our way home. I'm not sure if that's was a good or bad wish." The crew began to gather around, and the tension evaporated into an unexpected moment of levity. Ottmar and Kris, clearly enjoyed the break, had chocolate smeared across their faces. Kurt smiled as he surveyed the scene.

"You see, in the good times, the dragon brings us treasures and sweets—and double-wide VIP parking," Ottmar quipped.

Later that afternoon, Kurt sat on the front deck of the tank, wrote a letter to Nikol. His words came slowly, a mixture of news and sentiment poured onto the page.

Back home, Nikol sat in the gymnasium bleachers, still dressed in her workout clothes, reading Kurt's letter.

Kurt's letter
Nikol,

I have some exciting news. With my first tank victory, my Commander suggested I put our dragon tattoo on the tank turret- like the one we got for me at the lodge. I promised him and the crew that the dragon will bring them strength and good luck too. I also wrote Conrad to keep an eye out for us, as his unit is in our area. But there's sad news. We lost Dietrich. His family will be devastated. The cold is setting in fast now.

Miss you
Kurt

Kurt sealed the envelope with a kiss. Lighting a cigarette, he opened it once more and reread the words slowly, as if holding on to each line might bridge the distance between them. The smoke curled upward, mingling with the faint scent of ink and paper, a fragile tether to a world that felt farther away with every passing day.

Nikol's Letter

Dearest Kurt,

I'm doing my best not to worry about you, but you know me—always a little too much on that front. Please, be Knispel-careful. And whatever you do, don't get yourself blown up in one of those tanks, alright?

Things here are a bit dull, though I suppose that's better than the alternative. The rationing isn't terrible yet, but I've become an expert at stretching what we have. I started nursing school, but it's been a bit of a mess lately. They've cut back on classes because there aren't enough teachers, so now I help father at the hospital whenever I can. The place is packed with new patients, and I've already learned a lot about how much difference a nurse can make. It's a lot of work, but it feels incredibly important.

I miss our rides in the woods. It's strange how something that felt so simple is now something I ache for. But I'll hold on to those memories. Don't worry.

Oh, and by the way—here's a mint I stole from you last week. I couldn't resist. Consider it a little reminder that I'm still keeping an eye on you. Don't get too used to it.

Stay safe, Kurt. And whatever you do, don't do anything stupid (I mean it this time). I need you back in one piece.

Love,

Nikol

Kurt noticed something in the envelope, cigarette hanging from his mouth. As his eyes landed on the mint inside, he couldn't help but smile despite the weight of everything pressing on him. He fished out the mint, turning it over gently, pretending it was some small part of her he could still touch. For a moment, he thought of her, her cheeky sense of humor, and the way she would probably be laughing at him for making such a big deal out of a stolen mint. He chuckled softly under his breath, the smoke curling around his fingers. She was so damn bold, even in her

64

letters. He wasn't sure if it was the mint or just her words, but for the first time in days, a piece of the tension in his chest eased. As he read the rest of her letter, he felt the familiar pull of longing, and a bittersweet ache twisted in his gut. She was so far away, yet so close emotionally. Kurt sighed, his grip tightening on the letter. She was still keeping track of him, even if it was in small, playful ways. It made him feel alive, despite the cold, desolate world around him. With the letter in one hand, Kurt took a deep drag of his cigarette, stared out at the horizon as though the world outside the tank could somehow match the warmth of Nikol's words.

After some time in Shlisselburg and with the platoon resupplied and rested, Commander Decker received permission for the next leg of his mission. It was clear: proceed to a small feeder rail station, Kostrinsky, north of Tikhvin. Command expected a major fight in Tikhvin, and as a precaution, they wanted the rail station secured—just in case Tikhvin, itself, became a contested problem. Having this rail junction would help ensure the supply lines to Leningrad could remain cut off.

***

On the Russian side, a half-buried log-and-earth bunker pulsed with lamplight. Two soldiers in frost-crusted winter gear leaned over a map-strewn table, their breath fogging in the cold. Stalin's portrait stared from the wall, the mustached gaze a reminder of what failure meant.

Captain Marat stood rigid beside them—older now, tempered by gunpowder and loss. Commander Vitaly Taranko, gray at the temples and educated in Europe, briefed him in a low, steady voice, the kind men used when the next move could cost lives.

Neither Marat nor Taranko were in a good mood. They both understand the grim reality: the Germans had penetrated deep into Russia in a shockingly short amount of time.

Commander Taranko spoke; his tone measured but tense. "Captain, the Nazis have rolled through Schlisselburg and now threaten Tikhvin. We should have defended Schlisselburg, but Stalin had moved all available units to protect Leningrad. Tikhvin is our only land railway junction to provide Leningrad with food, fuel, and ammunition. And we've got over 2 million countrymen there."

Marat met his gaze. "What's the plan, sir?"

Taranko pointed to the map. 'This village, Kostrinskiy, is a rail station just outside Tikhvin. You, Captain, need to stop the German southerly advance from Schlisselburg here. You understand, Captain?'

He took a long drag on his cigarette. 'I chose your unit because you have fresh replacement T-34 tanks. And I chose you because your mixed record shows you hit hard and take what you want. I need a man like you.'"

Taranko continued, 'But you have to hold Kostrinskiy station. If we fail there, it will be absolutely critical that we hold the Tikhvin bridges. If you fail, it's very likely that we'll both be re-educated—or worse, sent to the gulags. This year alone, Stalin has executed seventeen generals for failing to stop the Nazis.'

Marat, "Understood, sir. So, we're looking past that 'roughhousing' incident with Chief Polykauf?" A forgotten memory stirred in Marat's mind. He thought back to a dimly lit, smoke-filled bar, where he, heavily intoxicated as usual, had raised his voice above the din. 'You don't like the look of my scar?' he had challenged, his tone sharp and dangerous.

Across the small table, Major Polykauf had smirked, his eyes lingering on Marat's facial scar for a moment before he took another sip. "Well, scars are common in farm families, aren't they, Captain? Some are worn on the outside, while others... well, they stay beneath the surface where they belong." The words struck deep in Marat's memory, cutting through him like a razor-sharp edge. His eyes narrowed as the insult sank in, demanding retaliation. Without hesitation, Marat lunged at Polykauf, unleashing a brutal assault that left the man barely conscious. For a split second, Marat saw the Major as a reflection of his own younger self, the victim of his own father's violence. But the irony hit him just as quickly—he had become his father, now the one standing over the victim. Blood had splattered across the table as Polykauf collapsed to the ground, gasping for air. Marat drew his bayonet, the cold steel glinting in the low light.

With a deliberate slash, he cut across Polykauf's left cheek. He felt the thrill of power that his father must have felt. Major Polykauf, barely conscious, could do nothing but tremble at Marat's cruel gaze. His voice dropped to a growl as he spoke to the prone bleeding Major with sickening calm. "There. Now you earned your very own farm scar. You look much better now—though still not quite as handsome as me." He threw his head back and gave a full belly laugh, relishing the moment.

Back in the bunker, Commander Taranko leaned back in his chair, smoke curling from his cigarette. "Yes, I remember that incident." He eyed Marat sharply before softening, just a touch.

"The Major Polykauf incident ... not yet, Marat," he said, the tone heavy with meaning. "It hasn't been easy on anyone since the Nazis started this war. But if you get this done..."

He paused deliberately, taking a long, slow drag. Smoke escaped his lips as he exhaled with weight, each word carefully chosen. "I'll speak to the people's committee. See if we can clean up your 'shit list' — including that ugly Major Polykauf incident. He's a party commissar, which is touchy enough, but you really messed him up good. Gave him a facial scar, as I recall."

Marat stiffened but stayed silent.

Taranko continued, "And that *village girl* mess? Turns out she was the local commissar's daughter. That still hangs over your head, comrade." Taranko stood, his back now to Marat as he stared at the stern face of Stalin on the wall. The silence lingered, oppressive.

Taranko continued: "But if you hold that town... things might start looking better for you, particularly if you make yourself a hero." Slowly, he pivoted, his gaze hardening as it locked onto Marat. "You know how much Stalin loves his *heroes*."

Marat puffed out his chest, full of brash confidence. "I'll make those fascist dogs sorry they ever set foot in our motherland!"

Taranko, unimpressed, let the bravado hang in the air for a moment before continuing. "One more thing." He lifted a shot of vodka, swirling it in his glass as his tone shifted colder, sharper. "I've got a report of a particular Panzer that's been a real *pain in my ass.*"

"How so?" asked Marat.

"It's easy — even for you — to spot this tank." Taranko downed the shot and set the glass down with a deliberate thud.

Missing the not-so-subtle barb, Marat bristled. "How easy?"

Taranko's expression darkened, anger flickered in his eyes like a live wire. "That damn tank has a dragon painted on its turret."

"A dragon? So what?" Marat raised an eyebrow.

Taranko leaned in, the room seeming to shrink around him. His voice was low and biting. "Not that it's any of your damn business, Captain, but that damn *Dragon Tank* blew up my brand-new heated command car." The words hung in the air like a death sentence.

"Do you have any idea what it took to get that car? I waited four months for it — four *months* — in this freezing hell!" He straightened; voice sharp as steel. "I want that dragon on my wall. Do you understand me, Marat? Get it done."

Marat, chest still puffed, saluted stiffly. "Consider it done, Commander." Taranko turned without a glance. "Dismissed." The word hit like a slammed door.

Chapter 8—Fire, Love, and Ghosts

At the village square of Kostrinsky Station, 19 kilometers northwest of Tikhvin, Captain Marat stood before his assembled men. The 40 Red Army soldiers, wrapped in their winter coats, huddled together, their breath rising in clouds against the early winter chill. Behind them, four T-34 tanks loomed like silent steel sentinels, their metal hulls frosted and weathered, but still poised for battle. On the outskirts of the village, two anti-tank guns were positioned, manned by crews as tired and worn as the land itself. The stillness in the air was suffocating, broken only by the occasional creak of metal in the near freezing cold.

Marat's voice cut through the air like a whip. "We're going to stop the Krauts here." He jabbed a gloved finger toward a map pinned to the side of a truck. "Word is, they're holed up 60 kilometers (37 miles) away resupplying and waiting for their infantry. Given the muddy road conditions, that gives us two days, maybe less, before they're on us." He paused, scanning the faces of his men. "Tonight, I want defensive positions established. The tanks," he gestured sharply toward the square, "stay here in reserve. The anti-tank guns cover the main approaches. The two machine guns are positioned nearby—one on each side of the anti-tank guns, about 30 meters away. Trucks and supplies are hidden behind the square, out of sight. As for the rest of you—set up defensive trenches, barricades, anything that can hold and provide cover." Marat's tone shifted, a flicker of a smile breaking through. "Today is Red Army Day, comrades. We are required to celebrate—*after* all preparations are complete, of course. Vodka will wait until then. Post guards with the machine guns. Now get it done!"

The men nodded, a mix of resolve and weariness etched into their faces. Some muttered to each other as they moved to their tasks. Drivers coaxed reluctant engines into life, sending puffs of black smoke into the chill air, breaking the silence, as the tanks took their positions in the square. The troops hefted ammo, tools, and crates, trudging to their designated positions. The two anti-tank positions were decided, and the guns were moved into place. Branches and shrubs were used to camouflage their positions. The crews cut wood to reinforce the positions. The two machine gun positions were set up and guards posted, flanking the anti-tank gun positions.

Marat lingered for a moment, his gaze drifting toward the forested horizon. The wind howled through the trees, but it wasn't the coming storm he was listening to—it was the tension building inside him. Somewhere out there, beyond the trees and the cold, he could feel them—the enemy. It wasn't a rational thought, but a primal sensation, one that stirred in his bones and twisted in his chest.

His scarred face tightened as the evening cold bit into his skin, the old wound itching, sending a sharp-edged tingling through him. For a brief moment, his thoughts flickered to his father—those brutal years of suffering under the weight of his cruelty. The scar, the physical reminder of that time, seemed to burn anew, the pain not just from the cold but from the years of rage that had marked him, inside and out. Then, on that fateful encounter, Chief Polykauf's words sliced through the memory: "Not a battle scar, but a farm scar."

The sneer that had spread across Polykauf's face—the way he'd reduced him with that single remark—still made Marat's blood boil. It was meant to diminish him, to brand him as something less.

A farm scar? That's what Polykauf saw? As if everything Marat had endured—his pain, his survival—was nothing more than the mark of a peasant. A simpleton. Something beneath the dignity of real combat wounds.

But the irony wasn't lost on him. He knew the truth was that scar wasn't from war. His father had given it to him—and then blamed a screeching hawk, as if cruelty needed an excuse. The message had been clear: suffering was to be borne without question. Yet here, amid fire and ruin, Marat was finally deciding who he was—not through his father's violence, not through Polykauf's arrogance, but through the weight of his own choices.

With a sigh of total acceptance, "Let them come," he muttered to himself, the words a quiet defiance in the face of the storm. He dropped his hand from his scar, the tingling still simmering under the surface. The soldiers behind him continued with their preparations, unaware of the inner struggle taking place. He exhaled deeply, a cold mist rising into the early evening air, and forced himself to focus. War, Marat realized, was a different kind of scar—one that never healed, carried for life, and could not be seen.

As the sun dipped below the horizon, long shadows stretched like dark fingers over the village. The air grew colder, the first stars piercing the twilight. Inside the village's modest hotel, the dim lighting flickered against the cracked wallpaper, and the scent of wood smoke lingered in the air.

Marat pushed through the heavy front door, leaving a trail of dirt and mud in his wake. He pulled off his gloves, tucking them into his coat pocket, and like a dog, he shook the excess dirt off at the doorway. His pistol hung low on his belt, and his PPS-41 submachine gun sling rested across his right shoulder. The weight pressed against him, a constant reminder of the war he was entrenched in—an assurance of protection that offered little comfort in the emptiness that gnawed at him in quieter moments."

As he noticed the woman at the desk, his mind flickered momentarily—a dull ache stirring as he realized his weapon had been his only companion in this war-torn world. Promises shattered, men fell like the snow outside—sometimes faster than the snow itself. The PPS-41 gave him the comfort of something reliable—steady, familiar, and a daily source of physical safety. In a world where emotional safety only mattered when a soldier was killed and a letter needed to be written to his family; it was all he had.

The slender, older hostess looked up from her ledger. Her silver-streaked hair was tucked neatly into a bun, but there was weariness in her eyes as she scanned the imposing figure before her. She had seen men like him before—soldiers, hardened by war—but there was something different about the way he carried himself. Then she noticed the rank. He was an officer.

Marat stepped up to the counter, the creak of the floorboards beneath him barely audible. He looked at the woman behind the desk, her expression polite but distant, as if accustomed to the steady flow of tired travelers. He gave her a quick once-over, his gaze lingering on her face, his voice low and tinged with playfulness.

Marat: "I sense we're getting an early snow for this time of year. What's your name… darling?" he asked, the pause lingering in the air.

The woman looked up from her work, her eyes narrowing for a moment before offering a practiced, soft smile. She hesitated, unsure whether to indulge his boldness or maintain the professional distance, but something in his gaze made her pause. Curiosity flickered in her eyes.

"Gwenyth: 'Gwenyth Christensen. And you are...?'" Her name slipped from her lips like a soft breath. She scanned him briefly, unsure of his intentions. *Was he flirting? Being rude? Or just testing the waters?* The way he looked at her—intense, piercing—made her heart race faster than she was comfortable with.

Marat leaned against the counter, a slight smile curling at the corners of his lips as he noticed her unease. He was skilled at unsettling people with a glance or a word, but her calm restraint made him pause, something about it holding his attention.

"Marat. Just Marat," he finally responded.

There was a moment of silence, thick with unspoken tension. Gwenyth processed the encounter, her eyes lingering on him for a moment longer than necessary. She wasn't sure if she was caught in a game or if there was something more to this soldier—something beneath the hardened exterior.

With a sudden shift, Marat spoke again in a more official tone, as though shedding his previous casualness.

"No, Gwenyth, on second thought, just call me Captain Marat."

Gwenyth reached for a room key and slid it across the counter. Gwenyth: "Your key, Captain. You staying long?"

Marat took the key but didn't meet her gaze. "That depends on the Germans. And the damn weather."

She looked out the window, watching the activity outside begin to settle. With the temperature drop snow was beginning to fall. Gwenyth: "Well, I want you to know, Captain Marat, I feel safer already with you as my hotel guest."

Marat glanced up at her, a rare, almost imperceptible smile tugging at the corner of his mouth. Her attempt at levity caught him off guard, and for a fleeting moment, he found himself responding in a way he hadn't expected.

Gwenyth, surprised by his response, tried to hide the flush that crept onto her cheeks. The humor she had been trying to mask was unexpectedly returned by a man she had presumed to be cold and distant.

Thinking for a moment, Marat quickly grabbed his gloves and turned as though to leave, pretending to change his mind.

Marat: "Actually, I've changed my mind." He adopted a mock angry tone as he took a few steps toward the door.

Gwenyth (concerned): "Everything all right, Captain?"

Marat turned back toward her; his eyes steady as he met hers. He returned to the desk, his tone dropping slightly, this time laced with a hint of playfulness.

"Call me Marat, Gwenyth. That's what my friends do."

Gwenyth, taken off guard again, scanned him carefully. An officer, competent... yet something about him left her uncertain. Her cheeks flushed as she looked up, the start of a smile playing at her lips. Gwenyth: "So, I'm a friend now?" she asked, her voice light, though an edge of uncertainty lingered. Was this just the usual soldier's game?

Marat took the keys with his bare right hand. His fingers brushed against hers for a split second—an intentional touch. She didn't recoil. His dark eyes lock onto hers, a look that held her in place. The air feels thick between them, charged with unspoken words. A shadow of hesitation crossed her face as her gaze dropped to the pistol at his side, then to the machine gun slung over his shoulder.

Marat winked at her, but something shifted—the edge in his face gave way; softer now, his voice low and tired. "The war won't last forever, Gwenyth." The words came slow, as if drawn from a well he rarely let anyone near. They carried weight—not just sorrow, but truth—something he'd kept buried beneath armor and orders.

There was a moment of silence that stretched between them, the only sound the wind rattling against the windows, as if the world outside were as uncertain as the one within. The weight of his words settled between them—an unspoken truth. Death was everywhere, and in moments like these, nobody was safe.

Gwenyth hesitated, her breath catching for a moment as the weight of his words settled in. His sorrow was palpable, and for an instant, she no longer looked at a soldier, but a man who had been broken by this war—like so many others. She looked into his eyes, searching for the truth behind the mask. Slowly, her lips pressed into a thin line, and then, almost reluctantly, her lips curved slightly, betraying a soft smile. It's a smile born of curiosity... and something else. Something softer, maybe even hopeful.

Her decision was made, though it was not entirely without hesitation. He seemed like a good man, one who carried burdens like she did, and in this fractured world, that's enough for now. It's been a while since she had allowed herself to feel anything like this. But a lingering feeling made her want to believe it. Her smile deepened, and for a fleeting moment, she wondered if it was the start of something new. Without a word, she walked to the front door and flipped the "Closed" sign across the glass. The soft click echoed in the room, a quiet acknowledgment of what she had chosen. Turning back, she felt the shift between them—unspoken, but clear. Marat didn't move, but neither of them needed to say anything more. The choice was made.

Elsewhere, the war had other plans.

***

Meanwhile, not far north on a muddy, now freezing, railroad service road just outside Kostrinskiy Station Commander Decker stood in front of his men. By October 1941, the weather had taken unexpected historically rare turn for the worse. The temperature plummeted without warning, and what had started as a cold front intensified into a sweeping winter storm that blanketed the entire front near Kostrinskiy.

Commander Decker: "We really have no idea what is in the upcoming village." He signaled with two fingers to the lead Hanomag. "I want two scouts to recon the station and report back." Two soldiers dismounted from the Hanomag. Just then, Kurt dragged Stefan forward.

Kurt said, "We both know some Russian." Stefan rolled his eyes. Kurt, "It makes sense you send us also."

Decker gathered his thoughts for a minute. He addressed the two Hanomag volunteer scouts. "Do any of you know any Russian?" They shrugged. "No." He turned to Kurt and Stefan. "If you two are so eager, go with them. Shove off at midnight."

At the rail service road staging area, Kurt and Stefan checked their watches and coordinated with the other two soldiers. It was midnight, and they cautiously entered the woods to approach the rail station village. Three hours later they returned and reported. Kurt stepped forward, pulling a folded piece of paper from his pocket and handing it to Decker. "Sir, they're all drunk. It's Red Army Day, and they've uncorked every bottle they had. They're celebrating like they've already won the war." He gestured to the paper. "Here are their numbers and positions. Given two 3-ton trucks, I would guess about 30 or 40 men, four T-34s in the village square, and two anti-tank guns covering the main road. Two flanking machine guns with guards. Trucks are staged behind the square. No signs of patrols outside the village. They act like they have no idea we are here."

Decker scanned the paper quickly, his brow furrowed as he processes the report. After a moment, he nodded and folded the paper, tucking it into his coat. "Good work, boys. And as Goethe said, 'Knowing is not enough; we must do.'"

As if on cue, the wind picked up and the snow was beginning to blow. He stepped back, addressing the group with a commanding tone. "Here's what we are going to do. We'll conduct the 'squeeze and squirt' tactic. One tank, one squad, and the MG34 team will take up an ambush position on the far side of the village. The remaining three tanks and two Hanomags and infantry will push Ivan from this side, driving them straight into the meat grinder. The two trucks and four guards will remain behind well out of sight." The men nodded in understanding, the tension thick in the air as Decker's plan began to take shape. He gave them a final glance, his voice softening slightly. "Get some rest while you can. We move before first light."

The group began to disperse, their gloved figures occasionally swallowed by the swirling snow. But Stefan lingered, muttering to Kurt under his breath, "Drunk or not, they've got four tanks. T-34s are no joke."

Kurt adjusted his position, exhaling slowly. "Yeah, they've got tough skin. I've bounced enough shells off them to know." He paused, his tone lightening slightly. "But everyone's got their weaknesses."

Stefan smirked faintly, with a head nod towards Decker, who was still speaking quietly with another soldier. "Yeah, well, we've got him. I heard Decker's fought in six countries since the war started—five of them now are part of the Reich. Weakness doesn't even show up in his playbook." Kurt allowed a faint smile, the cold wind biting at his face. He said nothing more, the unspoken understanding between them filling the silence. The two shared a brief chuckle and a knowing glance, their eyes briefly meeting in mutual understanding of the weight they both carry. The sound of their boots crunching against the now frozen ground filled the otherwise silent night, the cold pressing in from all sides. The stillness of the night felt almost suffocating, yet the heavy weight of the coming battle pressed against them like an invisible force. Each man carried it in his own way, his own thoughts clouded by the anticipation of what's to come.

By early the next morning, Kurt noticed the weather had turned even more brutal. The storm arrived in full force, its fury sweeping across the landscape like a white winter beast unleashed. The wind howled as snow began to fall, swirling into a cold, blinding blur. Kurt squinted through the haze, the icy sting biting at his skin. He pulled up the collar of his coat, wishing for even the slightest scrap of shelter.

The ambush team had already moved out to the far side of the village, buried in the snowstorm, their progress silent and ghostlike. Kurt and the crew went to their tank. From his narrow gunner's sight, Kurt could barely even make out even tree lines. His breath fogged his gunsight in the cold, and he had to keep wiping it clear.

He adjusted his other gear, eyes scanning the distance, waiting for the signal. His heart pounded in his chest—not from fear, but from the tension that had been building since the previous night. The soldiers—his men—had all done their part, and now it was just a matter of time.

Commander Decker ordered the main assault unit to advance, concealed by the storm's relentless veil, moving with storm-muffled stealth. The German infantry soldiers slipped through the fresh snow with a predator's grace, their movements calculated and deliberate. There was no wasted energy, no sound of boots in the fresh light snow. At the forward infantry guard positions, knives flashed in the dim light, swift as shadows. The sentries barely had time to react before the steel sliced, silencing them in an instant. The muffled sound of their bodies hitting the ground was completely swallowed by the wind and packed snow, their lives taken without a sound. By noon, the bodies would be nothing more than frozen shapes, rigid and unmoving, no longer feeling the cold but having become the cold itself, frozen statues in the snow.

The machine gun nests were next. The Germans infantry advanced with precision, slipping through the storm like whispers on the wind. From his position in the tank, Kurt could only imagine the movement outside—each soldier's steps calculated, their actions measured as they crept closer to the unsuspecting Russian crews. The air inside the tank felt suffocating, a tight knot of anticipation building in his chest. Every passing second stretched on, thick with the uncertainty of what might happen next. Would the Russians notice? Would chaos erupt at any moment? Kurt's grip tightened on the controls, unable to shake the tension, knowing they were close, but not knowing when everything would erupt any minute.

Every soldier knew exactly what needed to be done. The Soviet nests fell swiftly, the gun crews silenced without a sound, dispatched without a shot being fired. Kurt's fingers locked around the controls, his pulse steady despite the silent and deadly drama unfolding outside.

Hungover and half-aware, the Russians were easy prey. Death slid through the camp like a mist on morning ground—unseen until it was too late.

Kurt's eyes stayed locked on the gun sight, ears alert, waiting for the signal. His body was tense, but he had no part in this immediate action—yet the knowledge that his unit was executing the plan with deadly efficiency filled him with grim satisfaction. The rare early-season storm outside became the perfect cover, hiding their approach until the trap had already sprung.

The lead assault soldier crouched low behind a snowbank, the wind battering his face as he pulled out his radio. His voice was low but steady, cutting through the static. "Both guards and the hornet nests are handled. Anti-tank guns are next."

From the other end of the line, Commander Decker's calm, voice crackled through the static. "It's important to let us know when the Ivan anti-tank guns are handled." There was no hint of concern in his tone— only the cold calculation of a man who has seen it all and knows what comes next.

"On it, sir," the soldier responded with clipped intent, there was no time for hesitation. Every second counted. At the first Russian anti-tank position, the Germans struck with brutal efficiency. The soldiers moved quickly, neutralizing the crew with a series of swift, lethal moves. The northern gun was rendered useless before the Russian gunners even had time to react.

The lead soldier ducked into cover and reported via radio, his voice low. "Got the northern anti-tank gun treated. The southern gun's wide awake and remains a problem." The situation was fluid, but the soldiers were relentless, just waiting to press on to their next target.

There was a pause before Decker replied, his tone measured. "We'll deal with it." The main German assault team braced themselves, their faces stung by the wind and snow, every muscle taut with anticipation as they awaited their next move. The storm raged around them, a relentless backdrop to the tension thickening in the air.

Decker's voice crackled through the radio, sharp and decisive. "Advance." The order was simple, but the weight behind it was undeniable. The machine gun nests were next. The Germans infantry advanced with discipline, slipping through the storm like frost-glazed phantoms. The infantry and two Hanomags moved forward, the cold certainty of battle settling in as they pressed on through the storm. It seemed the storm itself fueled their progress.

The tanks were next. With a jerk, Stefan, unlit cigarette tucked behind his right ear, started the tank toward the anti-tank gun target area. Kurt's hands tightened on the controls, the familiar hum of the engine beneath him grounding him in the moment. The tank's movement made the air inside feel less suffocating, and a wave of relief washed over him. They were moving again, back in the game.

But then Decker's voice cut through the radio, snapping Kurt back to full attention. "High Explosive." The target was clear—anti-tank guns first. Ottmar was already in motion.

Ottmar moved with practiced ease, selecting the round with smooth, efficient movements, his hands steady despite the pressure of the situation. As he picked out a shell, he talked to it "You got a date, girl. Let's get going". With that, Kurt rolled his eyes.

Ottmar slid the high-explosive shell into the breach, the cold steel biting against his fingers. Not a flicker of doubt, just the steady rhythm of something rehearsed to perfection. The breach closed with a soft click, and Ottmar's voice rang out, calm and steady: "Up."

Kurt's pulse quickened, a bead of sweat rolling down his forehead despite the cold. Inside the tank, the air felt suffocating, thick with the urgency of what was finally underway. His mind raced—every scenario running through him, the uncertainty gnawing at him, but his body was still, like a coiled spring, waiting to unleash. He re-tightened his grip on the controls, forcing himself to concentrate on the task at hand. The next move could decide everything. Kurt focused through his gunsight but couldn't see anything due to the snow and low light.

Snow continued to accumulate as the three Panzers and the two Hanomags advanced towards the station village; the trucks stayed behind. The tanks emerged from the tree line, moving abreast along the road. In the fury of the storm, the Germans tanks readied to unleash their power, making their presence known like a second storm inside the first. The three Panzers converged on the southern Russian anti-tank position.

Decker said: "Anti-tank position 2 o'clock. 50 meters."

Kurt's hands moved instinctively, cranking the turret to the designated position. He found it. His eyes locked onto the target, cold and focused, scanning through the sights. The world outside was a blur of snow and chaos, but inside the tank, for Kurt, there was nothing but the target. "I see him," Kurt reported, his voice steady. He adjusted the sight settings, his fingers sure and fast, dialed in for the shot. "On target."

Decker's command was simple, yet heavy with intent. "All tanks, open fire."

The sound of his voice was the signal, and in an instant, the tanks roared to life. Machine gun fire rattled in the air, sharp and relentless, while the cannon unleashed a thunderous blast. Kurt's shot cracked out, deliberate and clean. The shockwave from the gun's recoil rattling his body, the flash of fire lighting up the storm-soaked battlefield.

The anti-tank position crumbled in seconds, reduced to rubble under the sheer force of the onslaught. Russian soldiers never got off a shot. The assault was over almost before it had begun.

Meanwhile, as the three tanks did their work, the 2 Hanomags and the German soldiers pressed forward, cutting through the snow and advancing into the town, each step pushing them closer to victory. The German infantry entered the village from the west, firing as they advanced. As the Russians had been caught completely by surprise, panic quickly setting in as they scrambled to return fire. Upon seeing the tanks coming up behind the infantry, they began a hasty retreat toward the other edge of the station village, firing as they went. Machine gun and cannon fire now echoed throughout the small village square; the sounds of chaos and desperation filled the air.

Back at the hotel a panicked Russian soldier had burst into Marat's darkened room. Marat and Gwenyth lay naked in bed, the dim light casting shadows over their forms. The soldier stammered, "Captain, the Nazis have entered at the west end of the village."

In his drunken stupor, Marat jolted upright, knocking over an empty vodka bottle with a clatter. He rubbed his eyes, struggling to focus. "What? They were reported to be two days away."

"Their unit is mechanized, sir. Three Panzers and at least two half-tracks."

Marat cursed under his breath, swung his feet over the side of the bed. "Damn, they never give us the important details." In less than an instant, the soldier disappeared.

Marat pulled on his shorts, shirt, and pants, his movements rushed and almost frantic. With a forced wink, he kissed Gwenyth before heading to the door. Wrapped in a sheet, Gwenyth stepped into the corner, retrieved his Pepesha machine gun, and handed it to him with a wry smile.

"Now, Captain," she teasingly said, "you might actually be more of a threat with this..."

Marat freezes, suddenly self-conscious. For months, the Pepesha has been his only source of comfort—cold, unyielding, and a constant reminder of survival. But since last night, something unfamiliar stirred within him. Her affection kindles a primal longing he's long suppressed.

She hands him the machine gun, and as she does, the sheet "accidentally" slips from her shoulders, pooling at her feet. Marat takes the gun, his grip instinctively tightening, as if trying to steady himself.

"I wouldn't mind if you stayed another night, my dear," she murmured teasingly, knowing full well he couldn't, bending slowly and seductively pick up the sheet.

Marat hesitated, then sighed with exaggerated regret, "Truly sorry, my kitten." He grabbed his coat. "The motherland calls. My job today is to kill some Hitler-worshiping fascist pigs."

At the door, he paused, hand on the handle, and glanced back. His grin was teasing, a flicker of something deeper in his eyes. "It may take a few more days." He winked once. His voice holds a hint of mischief. He grabbed an extra drum of ammo, still buttoning his coat, he is down the stairs

Before he leaves the room, she said, "By the way, I think your scar is sexy, Captain." He grinned upon hearing this.

The words hang in the air for a moment, then dissolve instantly as he steps out of the hotel into the now stinging cold. The weight of his Pepesha settles back, almost comfortably, onto his shoulders, a harsh reminder of duty. His grin shut like a prison door, and in its place, the full reality of who he was now—and who he must be.

Outside there was total chaos. Some of the Ivan tank crews are just now climbing into their tanks. Several tankmen slipped trying to get on the now ice-slicked tanks. Once on the street, Marat saw a Panzer emerge into the opposite edge of the square.

Kurt's tank also entered and stops a block away from the other tank, not more than 30 meters from where Marat stood. Marat immediately ducked behind a stone and brick wall next to some ammo crates, peeking out.

Decker called out "Armor Piercing".

Ottmar loaded the canon as smoothly as a race car driver shifts gears. "Up." Marat's eyes bulged when he saw the dragon on Kurt's tank turret.

He thought out loud, "It's him!"

The Dragon Panzer turret started it's traverse towards the Russian tanks in the square. Kurt's eyes locked onto a T-34 as it powered up and began pivoting toward his tank. His heart rate quickened; his focus sharpened. His tank's movements were slow. As the turret traversed, he adjusted the sight, his hands steady. Once on target, Kurt to Decker: "On target."

"Fire," Decker's voice rang through the radio, and Kurt didn't hesitate. His finger squeezed the trigger, the tank's cannon roaring to life. The shot hit a bit low, the T-34's track flying off, the tank now immobilized.

Kurt watched as the Russian crew scrambled out of the disabled tank, panic in their movements, desperately trying to escape. But his gaze never wavered. He saw a soldier crouching behind a wall in the distance. That Russian opened fire with his machine gun, aiming at the Dragon Panzer's vision slits. The bullets bounced off the turret with a sharp, hollow "tap tap," like a hammer pounding metal. Kurt didn't flinch. He knew the armor would hold.

The remaining three T-34s began to pull back, turning to leave the square, but Kurt wasn't about to let them slip away. His turret swung, lining up with the closest enemy. Upon command, he fired, his shot perfectly timed with one of his sister Panzer's. The T-34's engine exploded in a burst of flames; the inferno on the rear deck lit up the snowy street with dancing shadows.

Kurt felt the T-34 explosion shock wave even inside the Dragon Tank. Knowing full well that the tank was freshly loaded with fuel and ammo, the T-34 tank crew bailed out immediately. Two of them fell to the ground, cut down by German infantry. The other dashed for cover, running between buildings.

Back to the Russian soldier behind the wall, Marat was now out of ammo having used up both his drums. "That damn fascist Dragon Panzer." German machine gun and rifle fire stitched the buildings and shells explode near Marat. Russian soldiers scurry past him. Marat screams, "Stay and fight! Hold the line!"

A fleeing Russian soldier yelled, "Half our men are dead. Too hot for me. They're all yours, Captain!" He kept running. Marat felt he had to do something. He looked around and saw the ammo boxes. He reached down into an open crate (marked "RPG-40 Anti-Tank Grenades"). Grabbed one. Steps out. Aimed for the Dragon logo and hurls it. It bounces off the dragon turret and thunderously explodes on the front deck of the tank. Inside the Dragon Tank, all the crew covered their ears from the concussion and ringing of the shock wave from the anti-tank grenade.

Commander Decker, "Kris, that crazy Ivan needs some MG34 attention before he hurts somebody." Kris covered his ears, the blast of the grenade leaving him temporarily deaf, his mind struggling to catch up. He didn't respond. Frustrated, Decker delivered a sharp kick to Kris's shoulder, jolting him back into the moment. Kris blinked before he realized what Decker expected. With blood still dripping from his ears, Kris opened fire.

To the crew, the usual machine gun chatter sounded distant, like being submerged underwater. Kris's MG34, now sounding muffled, unleashed a stream of tracer rounds that lit up the air, ricocheting off the street and the buildings around Marat. The tracers exploded in flashes of light, but Marat somehow remained unscathed. One of the tracer rounds slammed into the already open ammo crate, igniting the dry hay-filled wooden box. Marat stopped in his tracks for a split second as smoke began to curl from the crate. Then, primal self-preservation kicked in, and he bolted down a narrow alley, his boots almost skating on the now icy ground.

Twenty seconds later, the crate detonated in a deafening roar, unleashing a cascade of explosions. Shards of wood and metal transformed into tiny, deadly barbed spears, slicing through the square with lethal precision. The ground buckled with the blast. For a heartbeat, the war went still—then came roaring back.

The other two retreating T-34s moved east, loaded with soldiers hitching rides. They ran right into the pre-placed, hull-down, camouflaged Panzer, the infantry, and the MG34 team. One of the two retreating Russian tanks was immediately hit by the Panzer. Hitchhiking soldiers are blown off like a broom knocking icicles off a gutter. The T-34's turret was jammed to one side. Smoke fills the tank with an internal fire. The crew bails.

The other T-34 turned sharply south, losing some soldiers off the deck with the violent and sudden maneuver and headed into the forested area in at full speed blindly knocking down trees and bushes. The other retreating Russian infantry ran headlong into the German ambush. The MG34 machine gun unit opened up with its devastating 800 rounds-per-minute bullet blizzard, decimating them.

Meanwhile in the village, Kurt's tank, the other three Panzers, and the two Hanomags slowly advanced, with their infantry. The battle was over in 15 minutes.

Later, Stefan, on his hands and knees on the front deck of the tank, a rag in his hand, swept grenade debris off the hull and vision slits. The tank still reeked of burnt metal and smoke from the earlier blast. Nearby, both Kurt and Kris pressed bandages to their ears, blood seeping through from the concussion.

"That was too close," Stefan muttered, tossing a shard of metal into the snow. "My ears are still ringing."

Kurt grimaced, adjusting his bloody ear bandage. Pointing to Kris, "At least your ears aren't bleeding."

Stefan paused, glancing at Kris, then back at Kurt with a smirk. "Look on the bright side—now you'll have a perfect excuse whenever you pretend not to hear my complaining."

Kurt snorted, wincing at the movement. "That would be a nice improvement."

Even Kris, despite the pain, chuckled quietly, muttering under his breath, "Damn Ivan and their grenades."

Commander Decker strode toward the tank, his boots crunching over turned stones and debris. His face, uncharacteristically bright, carried an expression of satisfaction.

"Men, we did damn well this morning," Decker declared, his voice carrying across the group. "Not a single casualty. Not one! For once, everything went as planned." His tone shifted, softer now, with genuine earnestness. "Be proud. What we achieved today was nothing short of textbook tactical operations."

Decker's gaze landed on Kurt, a glint of approval in his eyes. "And Kurt," he said, "it was generous of you to give Alfred the credit for that second kill. I know the two of you teamed up on that T-34 in the square."

Kurt shrugged, brushing a streak of soot from his sleeve. "Alfred's a good gunner. Besides, he deserved it—he hit the weak spot before I did."

Decker nodded once, the look in his eyes carrying a trace of mischief. "That kind of teamwork keeps us alive. Keep it up."

As Decker walked away, Stefan glanced at Kurt, raising an eyebrow. "Generous of you, huh?"

Kurt rolled his eyes. "Don't start, Stefan."

Stefan went back to scrubbing. "Might need a bigger tank—just to fit your ego."

Kurt snorted, shaking his head. "Fine. I'll take the bigger tank for my 'ego'—if you agree to a smaller mouth. Fair trade?" He looked over at Kris. "Right, Kris?"

"You bet." Overhearing everything, Kris let out a faint chuckle, still clutching his bandaged ear, blood seeping through.

Stefan, standing nearby, couldn't help but echo the chuckle under his breath—a small, shared moment of camaraderie in the tension of the day.

As Kurt's platoon advanced further southward, their four tanks rumbled past a battered, weather-beaten sign that read Tikhvin. The sounds of battle soon reached them. The tanks pressed forward, joining a fight already well underway against entrenched Russian troops, machine guns, and anti-tank positions. They tore over snow-buried bunkers as explosions rattled the ground. Russian soldiers began to fall back, firing scattered bursts and lobbing grenades in retreat. Behind them, German infantry methodically swept the complex, clearing it with pragmatic precision.

Among the Panzergrenadiers, Conrad and Jan—now ragged and dirt-streaked—worked to set charges to blow a large wooden dugout. Kurt's tank rumbled over a line of trenches and shattered bunkers. Hunkered down and appreciating the Panzer support, Conrad looked up and spotted the Dragon Tank. Kurt's tank is now just 50 meters (164 feet) away, had its iconic Dragon insignia clearly visible. His breath caught, and a rush of emotions surged—relief, pride, and something almost like awe. He nudged Jan sharply, his voice rising with a rare note of excitement. "That's the Dragon Tank! It's Kurt!"

Jan glanced at the tank, squinting slightly before smirking. "Surprised a T-34 hasn't turned that short-barreled Panzer IV into a mantelpiece trophy yet. Those things don't have much of a life expectancy out here against those forged-in-hell steel cockroaches—T-34s."

Conrad's eyes stayed fixed on the tank, his usual hardened demeanor softening into something resembling a grin. "He made it," he muttered, more to himself than to Jan, his voice tinged with disbelief and a hint of admiration. "That short little bastard actually made it this far. He's tougher than I thought."

Jan chuckled, shaking his head. "Guess the kid's lucky—or else he's a damn good shot."

The two stood up in their trench, waving and shouting. Their antics, however, caught Ivan's attention, and a flurry of gunfire forced them to drop back down behind cover. With a grinding rumble, the German tanks pushed forward, leaving Conrad and Jan to continue their gritty infantry work amidst the smoke, broken ground, and scattered gunfire.

Later, Conrad turned to Jan, a rare smile cracking through his normally icy demeanor. "I think I might've underestimated my little brother," he admitted softly, his words nearly swallowed by the wind. "I do miss giving him a hard time," he chuckled quietly. "Maybe I should've thrown a match or two his way."

Jan tugged his coat tighter as the wind bit. "Tough it out, big boy. Just another perfect day on the Eastern Front."

***

Meanwhile, already a couple of kilometers away, Commander Decker's Panzer platoon—resupplied and ready—pushed southeast, carving tracks in the deepening snow toward Tikhvin. It was November 1941, and the cold gripped them with relentless force. Temperatures had dropped to between 14°F and 5°F, and heavy snow blanketed the entire area.

Midway through the advance, orders came down: Kurt's platoon was to break off and conduct a recon sweep toward a nearby feeder rail bridgehead—one that could determine whether they could take and hold Tikhvin itself.

By late afternoon, the cold gnawed at the men as the four Panzers—followed by two Hanomags and two trucks—approached a short railway bridge. Decker signaled the column to halt, raising his binoculars to scan the area. The bridge and surrounding terrain appeared still... too still.

"I've got a bad feeling about this," Decker muttered under his breath. Switching to his radio, he relayed orders to the other tanks. "I smell an ambush." Decker instructed the lead Panzer to advance ahead of the group, scouting the path forward. He positioned the remaining three tanks abreast on the road, his own tank in the center flanked by the others. "Infantry, move to the flanks. Spread out and cross the iced river," he commanded.

The column repositioned swiftly, the lead tank creeping forward while the three Panzers held the line behind it, side by side. The formation was tense, every man on edge, the cold air thick with the expectation of an attack. Decker radioed, "Go ahead slowly." The lead tank crossed solo. The crossing was eerily quiet—until the Panzer cleared the far end of the bridge. Then a T-34 broke cover, fired, and de-tracked the Panzer. A second round from the T-34 struck, igniting an engine fire. Finally, spotting the T-34, the crippled Panzer fired back, but its round bounced harmlessly off the T-34's frontal armor. Moments later, a second T-34 emerged, fired, and detonated the Panzer's ammunition, blowing it apart in a fiery eruption.

Along with their infantry, two more T-34s emerged, their guns blazing. The remaining Hanomag troops dismounted and joined the firefight. The German tanks returned fire, but facing the T-34s' strongest armor fronts, their shells had little effect. Kris and the other Panzer gunners opened up with their bow machine guns as Russian infantry charged forward with their tanks. A T-34 shell ricocheted off Kurt's turret.

Another German tank, to the left of Kurt's, was hit and burned. Its crew were cut down as they attempted to flee. Two of the T-34s adjusted their positions to fire on the German grenadiers crossing the ice to flank them. Through his secondary vision slit, Kurt watched in shock as his comrades were decimated. "We've got real trouble—a nest of T-34s. They got Osterman's and Olaf's tanks." He steadied himself. "Ottmar, armor-piercing, NOW!" Out of habit, Kurt kissed his dragon pendant.

Like a shoe into a shoehorn, Ottmar glided the armor-piercing round home. "Up!" Ottmar called.

Kurt lined up his sights on the closest enemy tank, which had turned to take on the German infantry crossing the frozen river.

"Ready, sir," he reported to Decker.

"Fire," Decker commanded.

His shot landed exactly where he aimed, smashing into the rear of the turning T-34, which burst into flames. The Russian crew bailed, one of them completely engulfed in flame, writhing and rolling on the frozen ground in a futile attempt to extinguish the flames with snow.

On the second tank, avoiding the strong frontal armor, Kurt targeted the ammo area in the lower midsection.

"Up!" Ottmar called.

"On target," Kurt reported to Decker.

Decker ordered, "Fire."

Kurt hit his mark on the second T-34, and it exploded with dramatic pyrotechnics, its turret flying through the air. The Hanomag infantry followed the two remaining, slowly advancing Panzers. One soldier got into a good position and fired his Panzerfaust (bazooka), de-tracking the third T-34.

"Up!" Ottmar called.

"On target," Kurt answered.

Decker shouted, "Fire," and by now, the disabled T-34 had started burning. On the frozen river the German infantry advanced in their flanking maneuver, crossing it and gaining the far side. Down to one tank and with the element of surprise lost, the remaining T-34 and its infantry withdrew.

Once across the bridge—and over a mound of corpses—the Germans secured the immediate bridge area. The sounds of battle faded.

The crew and groups of grenadiers gathered in the lee of their tank. The frigid wind bit at their exposed faces. Smoke from the battle still drifted through the air, mingling with the sharp scent of diesel and scorched metal. Commander Decker surveyed his men, his usually stoic face softened by a rare hint of approval.

He pointed to Kurt, his voice carrying over the muffled silence of the blood- and snow-covered battlefield. "Sergeant, pretty good... three." That brought Kurt's total to twenty-two.

Kurt, his face streaked with soot and weariness, shook his head modestly. "Make today's tally two instead of three, sir. Our brave and crack-shot grenadier, Olaf over there"—he gestured toward Olaf, who was leaning on his Mauser with a faint grin— "he took the shot that stopped the Ivan tank. If he hadn't crippled that tank with his Panzerfaust first, I would have missed my mark. He gets the credit."

Without hesitation, Kurt strode over to Olaf, wrapped him in a huge hug, and slapped him on the back. Despite the biting cold, Olaf's cheeks flushed red, and he managed a sheepish smile, his breath misting in the frosty air.

Still leaning on his Mauser, Olaf waved a hand with a modest shrug. "Just doing my part, Sergeant... like you and your crew."

"And if it wasn't for Ottmar being the fastest loader in the battalion..." Kurt said, throwing an arm around him.

Ottmar grinned. "Fast hands win battles," he quipped, earning a few frozen chuckles from the group.

"What about that driver?" Stefan asked, pointing to himself.

"Correct," said Decker. "Let's see... our able driver didn't flip us upside down. I'll call that a win."

His lips twitched into the faintest smile. "Fair enough. Look, any way we look at it, it was a team effort." He glanced over the group, taking in their weariness and the familiar rhythm of camaraderie returning.

Ottmar's voice dropped a note. "What about Helmuth—the one who had Olaf's back?" Olaf's best friend, Helmuth, had taken a fatal bullet from Russian infantry while covering Olaf as he operated the anti-tank Panzerfaust. They all saw it.

"Let's get him," Kurt said.

The snow was already hard-packed when they dragged Helmuth's body free of the brush where he had fallen. He was still warm an hour ago. No steam from his breath anymore. No one said anything at first. Kurt glanced at Decker, who looked away. Stefan began clearing a spot behind a burned-out structure, scraping at the frozen ground with a mess tin, cursing softly when it bent.

"Don't bother," Kurt said. "We'll mark him and come back."

After the others attended to the other two tank crew bodies, Kurt reached beneath Helmuth's collar, pulled out the dog tag, and split it cleanly along the scored line. One half slid into his pocket to give to Decker. The other, still on its chain, he slipped back over Helmuth's neck. It was safer there—tucked inside his shirt, resting against his chest, where even the hated Russian wind couldn't steal it. "The graves detail will find him," Kurt said quietly. "It's what they do."

Stefan paused, still hunched from the cold. "If we hold the line," he muttered. Kurt didn't answer. He stepped back, scanning the tree line—thinking, for just a moment, that Helmuth might still be there, moving among the shadows with the rest of them. They left him just off the path, in the lee of the broken shed, under a tarp weighted with rocks, alongside the other bodies. A stick marked the spot. Not much more. When the platoon rumbled back to life, only Olaf looked back. He and Helmuth had just celebrated Helmuth's nineteenth birthday two days ago, with cigarettes and a pastry scrounged from the cook. What he saw now was his friend, receding beneath a rock-laden tarp—no helmet, no rifle, no future, no past, the snow settling on the tarp. The engines faded as they went further away down the forest road.

Helmuth was just gone. Like all soldiers in a tight unit, Helmuth and Olaf had grown close. Two years of backing each other up in almost daily firefights, bad jokes, shared meals, whispered plans for after the war—all erased in a single shot.

Now Olaf was just another face in the column. The one person who had truly seen him was under the tarp. The wind picked up again—restless, endless—flapping the edge of Helmuth's tarp as the snow began to fall harder. Olaf did a double take, rubbed his eyes, for it looked, just for a moment, like the tarp was waving goodbye. By midnight, Helmuth would be frozen solid. And by morning, the world—and the war—would move on without him.

***

Decker addressed the crew from inside the tank. "Our victory was, however, costly. Rest up while you can. We've got the rest of Russia to conquer."

They nodded—their breaths formed clouds in the freezing air. Despite the losses, a flicker of pride wove through the group. They had survived another brutal engagement in harsh, unforgiving weather.

For a couple of days, they remained at their newly secured bridgehead position, awaiting reinforcements, ammunition, and fuel.

Chapter 9—Taken by the Wind

Tikhvin, November 1941

Kurt's tank and the other remaining Panzer lay hidden in the forest, camouflaged with heavy branches and snow. In the razor-sharp cold, the crew struggled with even routine maintenance, their frostbitten fingers stiff and clumsy. Still in summer uniforms and whatever jackets they could scrounge, they were woefully unprepared for the intense Russian winter.

Frostbite spread among the men, their pale faces and sluggish movements a stark reflection of the toll the freezing weather had taken. The promise of a quick victory had become a cruel memory, replaced by the harsh reality of their shivering bodies beneath the heavy, gray Russian skies. Kurt could feel the cold creeping into his bones as he worked his controls, the chill biting even through the thick improvised layers of his uniform.

Once the supplies and fuel arrived, the platoon headed south to join the main German force. Heavy fighting followed, but despite the horrid conditions, the combined German forces finally captured Tikhvin on November 8. The air was thick with the weight of exhaustion, the men too weary to feel the victory they had won. Kurt's hands ached as he gripped the turret controls, his fingers stiff from the cold. Even the snow smelled oily.

The brutal winter of 1941 and 1942 was unlike anything they had expected. Temperatures dropped to the coldest in fifty years, and by December, frostbite had claimed nearly half their men during the battle for Tikhvin. The Russians were better equipped for the freezing conditions, their clothing and supplies superior to anything the Germans had. Kurt's tank shuddered as the engine sputtered—just another reminder of how their weapons were affected in the biting cold. The Russian soldiers, however, had an edge. While the Germans used gun oil, the Russians used a thinner lubricant—kerosene—it kept Ivan's weapons firing when the world froze around them.

Kurt grimaced as he watched the tank crew struggle to start the engines each morning, the engine-to-engine cold-water exchanger now their only means of getting them running. They had to keep one engine running overnight to pump warmed coolant into the others—an exhausting and makeshift solution, but the only one they had devised. Even with that, they still lagged behind the Russians, whose tanks, like the T-34, had wider tracks better suited for snow, ice, and mud. But the Germans would continue to fight—because that's what they had to do.

Supplies eventually arrived by horse-drawn wagons, trucks, and half-tracks. The units refueled and rearmed with precious ammunition. Two replacement Panzers also finally arrived, coated in jackets of ice and frozen mud. The men used cardboard, leaves, newspaper, and straw to crawl into and sleep in and under the tank.

One morning, the crew woke to Stefan reading aloud: 'God—it's minus twenty-five.' Cold enough to kill a man in hours. Because at -25°C (-13F) its cold enough that your skin would freeze to the metal if you touched it."

Kurt, blowing snow off his gloves, approached Commander Decker. "Sir, given these conditions, I would like your permission to fire at will without your order. Sometimes we lose a few seconds that could really make a big difference."

Decker replied, "You are good, Sergeant, but at this stage, no." Kurt was disappointed. In the midst of this chaotic and frozen hell, Kurt and the crew continued to fight, in spite of the elements. The cold gnawed at them, but they pushed on, their breath clouding the air inside their steel turtles as they rumbled through the snow-blanketed forests. Kurt's tally of destroyed enemy tanks grew with each passing engagement. The Dragon Panzer's surface was now scarred with hundreds of indentations—like measles—from machine gun fire and bounced anti-tank rifle shots.

By the time the harsh winter finally relented, Kurt barely recognized himself. His hair had grown longer, and a thick goatee framed his face, a rough testament to the months that had passed. His appearance now mirrored the wildness of the land they fought on—untamed, hardened by the elements. His skin, once youthful, had been ravaged by the relentless winds and biting cold, each scar a memory of battles fought and won, each mark etched deeply by the Russian winter. The lines on his face had deepened, not just from the passage of time, but from the unyielding weight of survival.

Kurt had faced two ruthless adversaries, both of whom had stripped away pieces of the man he once was: the Russian Army and the merciless Russian winter. But beneath the physical changes lay something far heavier—emotional scars etched into long-term memory, ones that would haunt him with nightmares for life.

It was dark now, and Kurt retreated into the tank to break the wind. The vehicle was heavily camouflaged, snow-packed tree branches draping over it like a blanket. He checked Nikol's picture next to his gunsight and smiled, then laid down. Like most nights, his mind raced. The snake dream had come again that night.

As a boy, Kurt had always admired the medals and honors adorning his father's office walls—relics from his father's time as a sniper in the "glory war to end all wars" of WWI. Those gleaming symbols of courage and victory had captivated him, just as his older brother Conrad's athletic trophies had sparked a mixture of envy and awe. Surrounded by his father's battlefield accolades and older brother Conrad's undeniable physical prowess, Kurt grew up under the weight of self-imposed expectations. Strength, heroism, triumph—they weren't just ideals but demands. But the war he now fought offered no such glory, no relief. Victories, as fleeting as sunlight through storm clouds, were quickly buried beneath the crushing weight of hunger, frostbite, death, and despair. Each triumph was undone, and the pattern began again—an endless, grinding cycle of suffering, as if the war itself were a cruel machine, devouring lives without end.

In the morning, Kurt sat in the tank, reflecting over his coffee. Out here, in the icy wastelands of the Eastern Front, the idea of glory now felt like childish fantasy—naive, empty rubbish. The memory of Dietrich surfaced again, sharp and unrelenting. Kurt had dropped a mint—then the sniper's shot rang out. Dietrich took the bullet meant for him.

"He's Mine"

The wind was rising. It sliced through the trees and rustled the tank's camouflage branches, making *scratching* sounds—like claws raking against steel. The dried limbs dragged and scraped over the turret, as if something wild and unseen circled the tank, testing for a way to get in. It crept around every hatch, every seam, curling like a living thing hunting warmth or weakness.

At times he dozed, then came the voice—faint but unmistakable, cruel and taunting. Kurt stiffened. The wind was whispering: *"Remember, Dietrich is mine."* The words cut through him like frost in his lungs. He clenched his fists, trying to shake the thought. No matter how many times he replayed that moment, he couldn't undo it. The once-bright ambition in his eyes had faded, replaced by a grim resolve born of necessity. His duty was far from over. Winter was nearly past, but the war raged on. There would be no rest until the final shot was fired—or until no one remained to fire it.

Despite the horror pressing in from all sides, Kurt pushed forward. He had no choice. Behind the front lines, fear spread like a disease. The Eastern Front had become a twisted nightmare: mass executions of innocents and prisoners, the brutality of forced labor camps, the hunting and summary execution of partisans, the deliberate starvation of civilians and prisoners, and the silent complicity of those who looked away.

Fear was no longer just a shadow of war—it had become a living thing, merging with indifference until it consumed everything. It gnawed at their souls and numbed them to the truth. Here, in this frozen world, the first casualty was truth. The next was courage. As the war dragged on, Kurt felt the quiet erosion of his spirit. The silence of inaction was deafening—but it was the only language anyone seemed to speak. He wanted his father to be proud. But deep down, he knew what the Russians would do if they ever reached Germany. Amidst this frozen hell, Kurt's tank crew continued to fight, undeterred by cold or conscience. His confirmed kills now stood at twenty-four.

The Russians struck back furiously, retaking Tikhvin a just a month later on December 10. Desperate to keep the rail lifeline to Leningrad open, they pushed the Germans back and reinforced their defensive lines. Tikhvin had become a keystone. The Soviets held it, and with it, the fate of the starving city, Leningrad.

By January 1942, Kurt's unit was ordered to regroup farther west. His four-tank platoon moved out in single file, crawling along a snow-covered dirt road that traced the edge of a winding river. They reached a tight bend where the river curved against the road—a narrow stretch, no more than ten meters across. The current was too strong for the surface to freeze solid. Ice clung to the barrel and dripped from the commander's turret machine gun.

Commander Decker: "Men, this looks like a good crossing point."

Kurt: "Don't take that chance. We only have a meter of clearance or our engine will flood."

Decker: "This is the narrowest spot we've seen since this morning. Are you volunteering for a swim?"

Kurt thinks for a moment. "I can do this."

He climbs out of the tank, stripping off his boots, pants, and shirt. Now in just his shorts and socks, he grabs the fuel tank measuring stick and heads toward the river. He enters the ice-choked water slowly. Step by step, the frigid current climbs higher up his legs. After about three meters, the water is already at his waist. Just ahead, he feels a steep drop-off.

Kurt: "It's no good. There's a large drop-off after this."

He turns and carefully retraces his steps, taking baby steps to maintain balance.

Decker: "I'm beginning to appreciate you more, Sergeant."

Kurt, frozen and blue, is quickly wrapped in blankets by the crew and hustled out of the wind and into the tank. After drying off and putting on dry clothes, he sits beside the engine—the only source of heat. His teeth chatter as he clutches a bottle of schnapps and his dragon pendant.

Kurt: "I guess I'm having fun. Did this duck hunting once... but not on purpose."

Stefan: "Screw the ducks, Kurt. You just saved the tank, man. If it wasn't for you, we'd be building igloos till spring. That took balls."

Kurt: "Those balls are very blue now."

By mid-1942, the Leningrad front had stabilized. But the price was steep. The raw truth remained: the Russians had replacements. The Germans did not. As part of Operation Blue, the German Army pivoted 1,200 kilometers (745 miles) south toward the oil-rich Caucasus Mountains—modern-day Russia, Georgia, Armenia, and Azerbaijan.

In May 1942, after his twenty-seventh tank kill, Kurt was granted leave to go home. His crew, equally worn and battle-hardened, watched as their war brother departed, leaving them behind at the front. But Kurt carried the scars of that brutal winter with him—a permanent reminder of the Winter War in Russia.

Chapter 10—I have a War in my Pocket, 1942

In a vehicular parking area trucks drive up. They stopped for supplies and fuel. Kurt and other soldiers got out to stretch. Kurt lights up a cigarette. There is random shooting going on behind some warehouse buildings. Kurt went to see what is going on.

Turning the corner, Kurt saw an SS Einsatzgruppen unit preparing to machine-gun a line of Russian peasants—men, women, and children. Several hundred bodies already lay stacked in a burial ditch. Another group was being herded forward. As the execution resumed, a black command car started up and rolled slowly down the road—heading straight toward where Kurt stood.

At first going at speed the car approached and then ground to a fast halt, its engine rumbling low. Wearing his black Panzer crewman uniform, Kurt glances up and immediately recognized the passenger stepping out—a tall figure with an unlit cigarette dangling from his lips and a compact Leica camera hanging on his shoulder— Major Berndt. The same SS Officer Kurt remembered Decker had run into last year.

Berndt surveyed the scene with the entitled ease of a man used to deference. His eyes locked onto Kurt—standing still, a lit cigarette clenched between his lips, unflinching.

"I stopped as I was out of matches. Got a light, tanker?" Berndt asks, his tone official yet deceptively polite. Kurt didn't move. He took a slow drag from his cigarette, exhaling deliberately, the smoke curled between them. There was a long pause, heavy with unspoken defiance. Berndt's eyes narrowed as he gave Kurt a once-over, his gaze lingered on the tank battle badge on his uniform. "You know we're on the same team, don't you?" His voice carried a subtle threat beneath the surface.

Kurt tilted his head slightly, holding Berndt's stare. Kurt took a drag on his cigarette. "There's a difference," he said finally, his voice even but loaded. He exhaled. He let the words hang in the air before adding, "Sir." Another pause. "My team shoots armed soldiers who are trying to kill us. You however, after we do the real work, you wait a couple of months and then drive up in your armored Mercedes staff car and have your people gather up every unarmed civilian you can find and shoot them and their families… sir."

Berndt's jaw tightened; his composure faltered for a brief moment. He took a step closer, leaned in close to Kurt's face, his voice dropped to an icy murmur. "Careful, Sergeant. That attitude of yours might get you into trouble one day."

Kurt didn't flinch. "Trouble? I've already been in it since this war started. But at least I can sleep at night as I'm not the one pulling the trigger on women and children. It's been my experience you get back what you put out... sir."

The words struck home. Berndt's face hardened, his expression tightening into a barely restrained mask of cold fury. For a moment, he looked ready to lash out—until a distant shout shattered the tension.

One of his aides jogged toward the car, shouting, "Major! We got more film and the prop trucks waiting at the checkpoint!" Berndt glanced toward the aide, seizing the excuse to end the confrontation. Without a word, he checks his camera and he spins on his heel, strode back to the car, and climbs in. The door slammed shut.

Unlit cigarette in his mouth, "Move," he snapped at the driver, his voice cold and clipped.

The heavy Merecedes lurched forward, its engine growling as it disappeared down the road. Kurt stood motionless, the tension still crackling in the air. He took another drag from his cigarette, his eyes narrowed as he watched the armored vehicle vanish down the road.

"He'll die," Kurt said flatly, eyes still locked on the vanishing Mercedes. "Maybe not by my hand. But someone's. Men like that don't ever make it to the end—especially out here."

He flicked the cigarette to the ground and crushed it under his heel with a slow, deliberate twist. The moment passed, but its weight lingered. Berndt was gone—for now—but the sickness in Kurt's gut stayed behind. There were things you saw in war that never left you. And men like Major Berndt... they didn't just haunt the enemy.

Hours later, he hitched a ride on a supply truck bound for Narva. The vehicle jolted over the rough road, its tires crunching through deep ruts. Kurt braced himself against the side of the truck bed. The hum of the engine and the rhythmic bumping beneath him he found to be were almost comforting in their predictability. The cold gray Estonian landscape stretched before him, and Kurt's unease deepened. His duty wasn't finished. He was a soldier—and he would do his part. But the truth was clear now: the army itself wasn't broken, only the regime that commanded it—savage, cruel, and demented beyond belief. The words he'd exchanged with Berndt still echoed, a grim reminder of the inner conflict he now carried. Every jolt of the truck, every mile behind him, pulled him further from the brief peace he'd once known. There was no calm—not now, not with madmen leading the war. There was no peace—there never had been—and there would be none until the war had run its course.

The late afternoon sun filtered through the curtains of the family living room as Kurt burst through the front door, his boots loud against the wood floor. His parents rose from their chairs, their faces a mixture of surprise and relief, and Kurt immediately strode toward them. He wrapped them in a tight embrace, his arms encircling them both. His father clapped a firm hand on his back, a gesture of pride, while his mother clung to him, tears streaming freely as she whispered, "You are home... you're finally home." For a brief moment, the burdens Kurt carried seem lighter.

Then, across the room, his eyes met Nikol's. She had stood near a window, giving Kurt's family space, her hands patiently clasped in front of her, the golden light of the setting sun cast a glow around her form. She had her dragon necklace on. Her eyes locked onto his, without a word emotions surged between them. Sunlight caught the dragon pendant around his neck—the matching one she had given him—and its shimmer seemed to cast a bridge of light between them.

Kurt took a couple of steps. Nikol stepped forward too. They both paused, caught in the moment, visually taking each other in from head to toe. Her lips trembled as she exhaled shakily. Her eyes scanned his face, braced for the changes she knew to expect—but hoping to find pieces of the man she remembered still intact.

She wasn't naive. She understood war didn't just wound bodies; it rewired souls. And yet, she searched his expression not with fear, but with quiet courage—wanting to help carry whatever truths his eyes could no longer hide.

The shadow of weariness in his eyes, the deepening lines on his brow, and the raw, windburned texture of his skin told the story—bitter cold, searing heat, sleepless nights, and the kind of hardship that didn't fade when the shooting stopped. Kurt was no longer a young man. His face had aged beyond its years. Even the edges of his ears bore the pale scars of frostbite, silent testament to nights spent entombed in steel, his body numb with cold. She could sense the remnants of softness still in him—not just raw endurance, burned deep into muscle and memory by the unyielding rhythm of the Eastern Front. Somewhere deeper still lay the silent, coiled strength of the dragon that hung around his neck... and in his soul.

The wind may have taken Dietrich, but Nikol's flame had reclaimed Kurt. And in that moment, as she looked at him—not with pity, but with knowing—he understood that something fragile and human had survived.

Nikol took it all in. And in the sacred silence between them, she saw more than just what the war had done—she knew there would be things he would likely never speak aloud. The things he had buried. And though her heart clenched at the sight, she did not look away. She never would.

Kurt took in Nikol, his chest tightening as he looked her up and down. She's more beautiful than he remembered, though it's not just the way the light plays on the contours of her face or how her hair gleams like spun gold. There's something deeper—an inner radiance, a quiet strength in her eyes that wasn't there before, cultivated perhaps, by the same months of waiting and hoping that had tested them both.

He exhaled deeply, the faintest smile broke across his face as his roughened hands twitched at his sides, aching to reach for her. In that moment, he realized that not even the war could dull what she meant to him. If anything, it has made her presence more precious, her beauty more vivid.

His voice, hoarse and barely above a whisper, escaped before he could stop it: "Nikol." Her name on his lips was all it took. His boots moved softly toward her. She stepped into his arms, and he wrapped her in a fierce embrace—holding her like she was the only real thing left in a world gone mad. For a moment, the war, the pain, the distance... all of it dissolved. What remained was the now—the raw, grounding comfort of her touch. Now was truly a magic moment.

Nikol buried her face against his shoulder, her breath hitching as emotion overwhelmed her. Kurt pressed his cheek to her hair, eyes closed, breathing in her familiar scent—anchoring himself in the steadiness of her presence.

From across the room, his parents watched in silence. The intensity of the moment—so vulnerable, so intimate—made them both shift uncomfortably. It was the kind of love they had rarely witnessed, let alone expressed themselves. His mother dabbed at her tear-streaked face with a handkerchief, a quiet gasp escaping as she clasped a trembling hand to her chest. His father, ever composed, cleared his throat and looked away briefly, the sheer force of the emotion almost too much to bear. He silently grasped his wife's hand. And yet, neither of them could turn from it.

She glanced at her husband, her eyes shimmering. "It's like they've been waiting for this forever," she whispered, her voice soft with awe and a touch of embarrassment.

His father nodded—just slightly—a quiet recognition of something powerful, something undeniable. Though his posture stayed firm, his gaze had softened. They both stepped back, instinctively giving the couple space. And in that shared stillness, they watched as Kurt and Nikol anchored themselves in one another—grounded in a love that had survived the storm of war.

***

Later, around the table, Kurt spoke. But he left out the gut-wrenching daily fear of snipers, the memory of burning a Soviet soldier alive in his first tank battle, the constant hunger, the repeated nightmare snake dreams, the smell of smoke and blood, his frostbitten ears, the lack of fuel, the searing heat of the Leningrad summer, the undeserved guilt he carried over Dietrich's death, the cries of the wounded, and the deep, bone-biting cold of the Russian winter—with its harsh winds and their tattered uniforms.

He chose not to mention his fiery victories over twenty-seven enemy tanks—and the 108 men sealed inside their steel tombs, most of whom had no time to escape and never return to see their families again. Some were torn apart instantly by the blast; others burned alive, pounding on hatches that had jammed shut from the inside. A few managed to climb halfway out before being swallowed by the fire. He said nothing of their screams, their arms reaching through smoke, or how their bodies sometimes kept moving, even after the flames and infantry bullets had done their work.

Instead, he told them about the time his crew had celebrated a victory with a shared beer—complete with song and merry harmonica music. He spoke of how they played shadow tanks in a brewery basement, how his commander had suggested painting a dragon, touching his pendant, on their turret for luck, and how their tank once received a parking ticket in Shlisselburg—where, for an hour, they got to be tourists again.

His mother listened intently; her hands folded tightly in her lap. Her face was a blend of pride and quiet concern. Her eyes flicked to the faint frostbite scar on Kurt's jaw and the deep weariness etched into his features. She didn't dare ask about the things he wouldn't say, but her silence stood as quiet testimony to a mother's love. "I'm just glad to be home," Kurt said softly. He remembered something Decker had said before he left the front—how battalion records showed he was one of the top gunners on the Eastern Front. Precise. Unshakable. A quiet asset. But numbers didn't mean much to him anymore. Not the kill counts. Not the medals. Not the silent nods from higher-ups.

What he wanted—what he *ached* for—was something the war couldn't give him. He just wanted to be home. To sit at a table without scanning for shadows. To wake without frostbite in his bones or smoke in his lungs. To hear her voice and not wonder if it would be the last time.

After a while, Kurt's father stood and motioned for him to join him outside. Kurt grabbed his jacket, and the two walked to the woodpile behind the house. The chill of late afternoon bit at their faces as his father picked up the ax and began chopping wood with practiced ease. After a few logs, he handed the ax to Kurt.

"Man-to-man, how's it going?" his father asked, voice steady.

Kurt took the ax and began chopping. He said nothing. The rhythm of his swings filled the silence.

"Son, talk to me," his father pressed.

Kurt chopped harder, wood chips flying, the sound of splitting wood growing louder.

"Surely the Knight's Cross...?" his father ventured, his tone both firm and probing.

Mid-swing, the ax handle snapped in Kurt's hands. The sharp crack echoed through the cold air. Splinters and steel fell to the ground as he looked up, chest heaving, eyes blazing with caged-up fury. He stood there gripping the broken handle, breathing hard.

"Damn it, Dad! Forget the Knight's Cross," he exploded, voice raw.

"This war is nothing like I imagined. In Russia and Poland, we've become monsters. Our own SS death squads are murdering unarmed men, women, and children behind the lines. Both sides are executing

102

prisoners. And those we don't kill—we starve. Just like the Russians do to our men."

He paused, jaw tight. "It's pure hell. I was trained to endure the cold, the hunger, the wounds, the pain. I was ready for all of that. But I wasn't ready for this. I wasn't ready to see my country sink so low—committing acts so utterly inhuman."

Kurt took a step back, gripping the broken ax handle in both hands in front of him. "I want you to be proud. I want to do my duty. But none of this is right. Murdering innocent people isn't what we were trained to do. We were trained to fight armed soldiers. Not this."

His father didn't interrupt. He simply watched as Kurt's words poured out—each one heavy with anguish, and long overdue.

"Look, Dad." Kurt paused, his tone shifting as he steadied himself. "Man-to-man," he added, the weight of what he was about to say clear in his eyes.

"What matters to me now is really simple: my crew, and the team who keep our tank going. We survive because we value each other—nothing else matters. We keep each other alive. We don't do our duty because of some damn medal or bow to the totally delusional Nazi mythology. There are some truly evil men in power, holding intimidating positions. People are scared—really scared. They look the other way, afraid to speak up. They stay silent, thinking it'll save them."

His grip tightened on the broken handle, knuckles whitening as his voice hardened. "Seeking personal glory? That's a fool's goal. It gets you nowhere but dead. Dead like Dietrich." The name landed hard. The weight of it hung in the cold air between them, cutting deeper than any words. Kurt's chest heaved as he stared at his father, waiting—for acknowledgment, for understanding, for anything that might help untangle the chaos burning inside him.

Kurt's voice softened, the rage giving way to something steadier. Firmer. He looked his father in the eyes, a flicker of quiet determination breaking through the storm.

"I don't need the Knight's Cross to know who I am, or what I stand for. So, if you're asking about that, Dad—this is my answer. I'll keep fighting. But not for their medals. Not for glory. Not for their ideology. I fight for my crew. And to protect my family—by keeping the Russians out of Germany, if I can."

He paused. "For the people who deserve a chance to live… even in a country gone mad."

He exhaled slowly, a subtle but unmistakable resolve settling into his features. "Maybe that's the kind of thing worth being proud of. Maybe that's the real answer to all this."

His father shifted slightly, the depth of his son's pain sinking in— but he didn't break the silence. He just watched, the unspoken and uncomfortable truths between them louder than any words could be. For a moment, the only sounds were Kurt's heavy breathing and the faint rustle of wind through the trees. The weight of his words hung between them, undeniable and heavy. Finally, his father stepped forward and placed a firm hand on Kurt's shoulder. Then he quietly took the broken ax from Kurt's hands.

He said, almost to himself, "Your mother and I... we've heard the rumors. This war—it's not like the last one."

Kurt extended his arms, palms up. "What the hell, Dad…?" He waited, needing something real. His father met his eyes. "Look, son, your mom and I raised you right. Yes, you're a soldier. But first and always, you're your own man." He bent down and picked up the rest of the broken ax handle from the ground.

"In life, there are things you can't control—no matter how much you try. But remember this: you always have control over what you choose to do. Be smart. But do the right thing. If you don't… you'll never be able to look yourself in the mirror and believe you're a good man. And that, son—that will crush your soul."

He paused, the wind tugging at the edge of his coat. Then quietly: "If you listen hard, you'll know when it's time to make your stand."

They walked back toward the house in silence. "Now," his father said, with a faint smile, "you and Nikol need to go to the mountains for a few days. Just breathe and relax."

***

The next day, Kurt and Nikol sat by the window at a bench table in a quiet lodge high in the mountains, a light snow swirling outside like a frozen curtain. Ski scarves and gloves lay casually on the table. Two frosty mugs of beer sat between them, untouched for now, as the crackle of the fireplace filled the room with warmth. The faint murmur of other guests drifted in and out like ghosts.

Kurt smiled. "You really take the cake with these reservations."

Nikol grinned. "One of my friends owed me. But you mentioned... things?"

Kurt lit a cigarette and took a long drag. At the sight of the cigarette, Nikol's face shifted—surprised, wounded. His smile faded. He looked away, the light gone from his eyes. "Smoking," she said, with a dry edge. "Damn that, Stefan. I'm sorry. Go ahead."

Outside, the wind battered the window. It rattled faintly in its frame. Kurt stared into the snow. "Dietrich," he said quietly. "You remember him. We used to fish and hunt together... had so much fun."

He trailed off. Mumbled. Couldn't finish. After a long pause, he added, "Sniper got him."

"I'm so sorry," Nikol said softly.

Kurt's voice was low, bitter. "Nikol... that bullet that killed Dietrich had my name on it."

She turned toward him. "Why do you say that? Soldiers get killed in war."

Kurt shook his head. "I was giving him a mint. Dropped it by accident. And when I bent down to pick it up... in that instant, the sniper's bullet hit him. Just missed me."

He didn't lift his head. Kurt inhaled deeply and let it out slow. "It should have been me." Nikol said nothing—but she understood instantly.

Kurt continued, eyes still low. "Other things... they're really ugly. I told my dad." Then he told Nikol what he had told his father. As he spoke, his emotions surfaced—frustration, shame, anger. The more he described, the more animated he became. His hands moved. His voice cracked. The weight of it all came spilling out. When he finished, Nikol sat quietly for a moment. Then: "So the rumors are true."

Kurt nodded. "It's worse in Poland. My duty is to my country, but my country... is doing truly evil things. They lie about everything. To everyone. Nobody trusts anybody. I just don't know anymore..."

The hostess arrived and placed their food on the table. Neither moved until she left. Kurt stared into his beer, then pushed at the edge of his plate with his fork. "Yesterday," he said quietly, "I showed my dad my Iron Cross Second Class. You know what he said?"

Nikol turned toward him fully. "What?"

"He asked when I'd get the Knight's Cross."

"And how did that make you feel?" She asked.

"It upset me." He looked away. He thought of Conrad. Thought of how easy it had always come for his older brother.

"I told my father that I don't suffer from a sore throat—that I don't fight to claim disputed or shared victories as my own. I share everything with my crew and my platoon mates. Always have."

Nikol smiled faintly. "Your sister told me you were that way."

He looked at her, a little surprised. "What way?"

"That you're not interested in the fame or the medals," she said. "She said that's who you are."

Kurt shrugged. "Just shiny things for the chest." He took a sip of beer. His eyes grew distant. "It's the bond we shared out there..." He drew patterns with his fingertip on the side of the cold mug. "...The job was getting everyone we could home in one piece."

Touched, Nikol reached across the table and placed her hand gently on his. He met her touch. His voice quieted. "I try. But sometimes I wonder..." His words drifted off. He thought of the differences—between himself and his father, between himself and his brother. Between who he'd been, and who he was now. Nikol sensed his sibling insecurity—the way his father's approval still haunted him, the unspoken rivalry with Conrad.

"Your dad loves both you and your brother," she said gently. "Conrad's easy to like, as we both know. But he doesn't compare to you." She looked at him—steady, sure.

"Kurt, you're more than enough. Don't let anyone—*not even your father*—make you think otherwise."

Outside, the snow drifted on. Wind occasionally rattled the windows. The warmth inside the lodge seemed to deepen. Kurt's shoulders relaxed slightly as he looked at her, her unwavering support a quiet balm to his doubt.

"To us," he said, raising his mug. She smiled, lifting hers to meet his. He finally smiled back. Their mugs clinked softly. The warmth of the fire and their connection pushed back the chill of the world outside. Morning came at the lodge. Kurt and Nikol lay together naked in bed, their bodies tangled in warmth and comfort. They kissed softly, then rose. In that quiet moment, they felt the weight of its specialness. No words. Just presence. They embraced once more before dressing, and a few minutes later, headed downstairs for breakfast.

106

Later that day, they slipped into a small tattoo parlor tucked in a back alley of the city—quiet, discreet, far from the eyes of the authorities. The kind of place that didn't advertise. The kind of place that kept its head down. In those days, tattoos weren't fashionable. They weren't mainstream. They belonged to people who lived on the fringes—outlaws, different, misfits. People who didn't quite fit the mold.

The tattoo artist, too, operated on the edge. He was a quiet older man with dark eyes and steady hands. A man used to work in silence, outside the system, under the radar of regime's control.

For Kurt, there was a strange draw to that world. The war, the uniforms, the endless orders—it was all suffocating. This place, this act, felt like a breath of something real. Getting a tattoo wasn't just rebellion. It was *relief*. A small, defiant piece of freedom etched into his skin.

He looked at Nikol and smiled. "When I check the time, I'll think of you."

"Let me see," asked Nikol.

He lifted his arm and checked his watch—resting just beside the small dragon inked into his forearm.

"I thought tattoos were forbidden." Nikol commented raising an eyebrow.

Kurt: "If they don't like it, hell, they can cut my arm off." He now offered Nikol a mint. With her coy smile, she accepts.

Nikol: "Mints are a treat."

Kurt smiled back at Nikol with affection. "With you around, I'll take sweet to smoke any day." He tossed his pack of cigarettes into a trash can and walked to the lodge shop to grab a bag of mints. Slipping them into his pocket, he gave her a final lingering look, knowing their time together was running out.

After their goodbye, Kurt set off for the journey ahead. The days of travel felt endless, filled with the rumbling of trains and the steady click of the tracks beneath him. It wasn't until several days later that he finally arrived at the Panzer Training Center, just south of Berlin, where his next chapter awaited. He met up with his mates, and the real work began: training on the new Panzer IV F2, equipped with the new long-barreled 75mm gun. The gun's increased muzzle velocity made it far more effective against the T-34's thick armor, something Kurt knew would be critical in the battles ahead.

The training was intense, but it wasn't long before the call came to head to the Caucasus front, where the battle awaited them. As they boarded the train, the atmosphere was thick with anticipation of the coming fight. The train yard was alive with the sounds of industry—grinding metal, clanging tools, and the rhythmic hiss of steam escaping from nearby engines. Towering above the chaos were four new Panzer Mark IV tanks, their gleaming 75mm long-barrel cannons reflecting the harsh summer sun. Loaded meticulously onto flatbed railway cars, two tanks per flatbed car, the tanks stood like newly born steel beasts, unaware of the challenges that lay ahead, their cold, unscratched metal frames still and dormant, yet destined for the savage trials of war.

Kurt stepped back from the turret, eyes tracing the contours of the dragon, now fully formed on the metal surface. He stood there for a moment, taking in the power of the symbol he had created—its metal-like scales gleaming, the wings unfurled in a fierce, silent flight. A quiet breath escaped him, and in that stillness, the name came to him from deep inside without thinking...

"Dragon of War," he whispered to himself, his voice thick with conviction. It felt right, as though the name had always belonged to the beast now painted on his tank. A symbol of their strength, their resilience—his, their crew's, and the machine that would carry them into battle side by side

He glanced at his forearm, where his tattoo peeked from beneath his rolled-up sleeve. He lingered on it for a moment before he tugged his sleeve back down and popped a mint into his mouth. Being totally focused, Kurt is startled by a nearby voice.

Decker nodded, clipboard in hand. "Nice work, Sergeant. After the war, I see an artist's career for you." He returned to checking off logistics, eyes scanning the yard as he resumed reviewing pre-transport operations.

Kris sat perched atop the turret, his harmonica catching glints of sunlight as he played a slow, nostalgic tune. Ottmar lounged nearby in his usual relaxed manner, his gaze drifting across the train yard—but his thoughts, as always before a mission, seemed far away. Stefan leaned against the tank's side, a cigarette dangling from his lips, smoke curling lazily into the clear blue sky.

Kurt glanced at them. They weren't just comrades—out here, they were family. Decker gave an approving nod toward the freshly painted logo. Kurt felt a quiet flicker of pride.

The others gladly noticed too. Kris tipped his harmonica in acknowledgment, Ottmar gave a slow wave and a thumbs up, and Stefan smirked, flicking ash to the ground with a knowing grin.

Chapter 11—When Men Say No, Krakow

The tanks were secured now, lined up on the railway flatbeds like warhorses waiting for the charge. Behind them, boxcars held supplies, spare parts, and equipment—each car loaded with the essentials for battles yet to come. Behind the box cars were the rail tank cars which carried the precious fuel. At the very front of the convoy sat an empty flatbed, a standard precaution to absorb the blast of any partisan rail mines.

The shriek of a train whistle sliced through the yard.

Decker's voice rose over the noise. "Mount up!" he called, clipboard tucked under one arm. "Pack your pistols. Two tank train convoys were hit by partisans last week."

The words hung in the air for a beat. *Partisans.* The thought made Kurt's skin prickle. He patted the holster at his hip, reassured by the weight of the pistol and spare clip. Tanks were a juicy target for ambush.

Around him, the others reacted in their own ways. Stefan flicked away his cigarette, muttering something under his breath. Ottmar ran his hand over the breech of his gun, his expression darkening. Kris, usually carefree, stuffed his harmonica into his pocket with uncharacteristic urgency.

"Keep your gear tight and eyes sharp," Decker continued. "It's a long ride—let's not make it shorter." The crew climbed atop their tank with practiced ease. Kurt adjusted his gear and cast one last glance at the dragon painted on the turret of their long-barreled Panzer IV. He hoped it would keep bringing the luck they needed. The train jolted to life. Steam hissed. Pistons groaned. The whistle blew again, and the convoy began its slow crawl eastward. The tank's hull vibrated beneath Kurt as he settled into place beside the turret. He scanned the horizon—the tracks stretched endlessly into the distance.

From above, Kris's harmonica tune picked up again, brisker now but steady, like a heartbeat. Kurt reached for a mint and let its coolness settle in his mouth. Around him, each crewman found his own way to steel for what lay ahead. The sun bore down, the train rumbled forward, and war awaited.

Kurt leaned back slightly, running his hand along the turret. The cold, new steel felt good beneath his palm—reassuring. He, more than anyone, appreciated what their new high-velocity gun would mean in battle. He'd felt its power at the test range. He knew.

Below, Stefan exhaled a plume of smoke. "It's a long trip—almost five hundred klicks," Stefan said. "Good we're headed to the oil fields, but even with most of it by train, we'll need fuel—and probably a tune-up—by the time we get there." He chuckled at his own joke.

Kris, half-smiling, added, "That's near Rostov-on-the-Don River. Maybe we can all pitch in and rent a sailboat."

Ottmar looked uneasy. "But I can't swim."

Stefan snorted. "That's okay. You can just float."

With a heavy lurch, the engine strained against the weight of the armor-laden flatbeds. The steel wheels spun briefly, sparks flashing as they fought for traction on the rails before catching. The convoy shuddered forward, vibrations rippling through the tank's hull and up into Kurt's chest.

The Krakow Incident

At one of the many scheduled stops—Krakow Station in southern Poland—the train took on water and coal. Kurt and Stefan sat on the rear engine deck behind the turret, their eyes scanning the platform and nearby rail yard. Kurt's hair was longer now, and he sported a fuller, non-regulation goatee. Commander Decker stood in the turret cupola, absorbed in writing a letter.

Down in the yard, Kurt spotted an SS guard striking a prisoner in a striped uniform—one of the transport workers. The guard barked orders, each word punctuated by a brutal blow. The prisoner cried out in pain with every strike.

Kurt's fury surged. Without thinking, he leapt down from the tank and sprinted toward the scene. "Don't!" Decker shouted from behind.

Kurt didn't stop. "It's not right!" he yelled over his shoulder.

Now within a meter of the guard, Kurt barked, "Stop, you dog! You don't treat prisoners this way!" The SS man ignored him and kicked the prisoner again.

The guard turned, sneering. "What the fuck do you want? You love commie dogs? Maybe you want some of this yourself."

He raised his rifle and aimed it straight at Kurt. In one fluid motion, Kurt lunged, grabbed the rifle with his left hand, and wrenched it free. Without pause, he smashed it against the iron rail track, splintering it.

112

Still fuming, he shoved the guard hard, then kicked him square in the chest. The man stumbled and fell backward onto the tracks.

Kurt stood over him, chest heaving, hands on hips. The rage inside him had burned out—but the fire wasn't gone. He turned and walked over to the prisoner, handing him a single mint. The man stared at him, wide-eyed and silent. Back at the train, Commander Decker had watched the entire scene unfold. He muttered under his breath, "Jesus... thought I'd seen it all."

Kurt climbed back onto the tank. "Well," he said to Commander Decker, "it was about time somebody actually did something. I can't save the world—but today, I stood up for one man."

The train hissed to a stop at the next station. Steam rose from the wheels as workers moved quickly to refuel and load supplies. Tank crews sprawled across the engine decks and bow sections of their Panzers, stretching limbs and soaking in the brief reprieve.

Kurt leaned against the turret, his goatee catching the sunlight. He absentmindedly traced the edge of the dragon logo with his fingers. Commander Decker's voice snapped—sharp and urgent. "Kurt. Get inside the tank!"

The urgent tone left no room for argument. Kurt turned, confused. Without a word, he slid off the deck and dropped through the open hatch. As he settled inside, heart pounding, he knew something wasn't right.

At the far edge of the yard, five military police appeared—uniforms crisp, movements precise. Two carried MP40 submachine guns, the dull metal catching the late-day light. The other three had bolt-action rifles slung over their shoulders. Brass crescent plates hung at their necks, identifying them as the feared enforcers of the Wehrmacht. Their boots struck the gravel in synchronized rhythm as they advanced down the tank line with silent authority. Their faces were expressionless, the rigid calm of men trained not to react—but their eyes were sharp, scanning each tank like predators tracking movement in the grass. Stefan glanced up at Decker. "These chain dogs are on the hunt."

Their faces held the stiff calm of men used to power. Around the station, workers fell silent as the they passed. Their very presence was a reminder: here, the Reich didn't just control logistics. It controlled everything. Inside the tank, Kurt crouched low, listening. The muffled voices outside were growing louder. The military police were making their way down the line, stopping at each tank. Outside, the crew stayed seated, trying to appear relaxed, but their glances told another story—tight, tense, waiting.

Stefan took a long drag from his cigarette, exhaling slowly. Then boots—deliberate and hard—crunched toward them. The lead officer approached Decker's tank, each step punctuated by authority. His eyes narrowed as he drew close. When he spoke, his voice was clipped, precise, and cold. There was no respect in it—only disdain, as if Decker and his men were filth in his way. Tools. Livestock.

"We are looking for a short soldier with longish brown hair and a goatee," the officer announced. "At the last station, he violated strict rules and destroyed military property. We need to take him in for questioning."

Decker stepped down from the turret cupola to the tank deck, his clipboard tucked under one arm. His voice was calm but still carried his unmistakable disciplined Wehrmacht officer's edge. "We are a highly trained, cohesive veteran combat unit," he said. "With, as you well know, top priority to conquer all of Soviet Russia. I am in charge of this whole platoon. I will not tolerate any of my fighting team being broken up."

The military police chief's eyes narrowed, his lips curling in a sneer. "So, he is with your crew." The accusation hung in the air, thick with contempt, but before the officer could step forward, Decker's hand moved with swift precision to his chest holster.

In one fluid motion, he drew his Walther pistol and leveled it at the officer's forehead. His voice was low, steady, and deadly calm. "On this train, I am in command. Anyone who puts a single finger on any one of my men, or this whole platoon, will find himself with a 9-millimeter hole in his skull. Understood?"

The military police were used to being totally unchallenged—feared and obeyed without hesitation. Decker's defiance struck deep, a direct blow to the authoritarian core they represented. They stiffened, hands instinctively gripping their rifles, turning toward Decker with a volatile mix of confusion, disbelief, anger, and wounded pride.

But the tension cracked with the sound of boots scuffing against steel. The Dragon crew rose. Boots thudded to metal. One by one, Kurt's crew stood atop the tank—battle-grim and silent, their hands resting loosely, but deliberately, on their holstered pistols. They didn't move fast. They didn't have to. Presence was enough. Stefan flicked the ash from his cigarette and let it fall between them, slow and unhurried. The smoke curled in the space between the two groups, like a fuse waiting for fire.

Decker's gaze never left the chief's eyes—unflinching, unyielding. An iron fist in a velvet glove. The chief swallowed. A bead of sweat slid down his temple. He wasn't used to this. Not from front line soldiers. Not from men who also had stared down the enemy daily and lived by steel and fire. Then—from the two adjacent tanks—came two sharp metallic clacks.

Two turret-mounted machine guns cocked in unison. Commander Lilienthal and Commander Bergman joined the line.

The metallic gun cocking sounds reverberated through the silent yard like a warning bell.

Lilienthal leaned into his cupola. "Any problems, Commander Decker?" Across the track, Bergman patted the barrel of his machine gun with a wry grin. "Hey, if you two run out of ammo, I've got 250 rounds ready to go."

He stroked the weapon affectionately. "We don't want anything to trouble our platoon's Dragon Tank." The military police chief shifted awkwardly, clearly unsettling him by the escalating tension. His men exchanged uncertain glances, their eyes flicking to the tanks' machine guns now trained in their direction. The weight of the moment settled over him, and a cold realization struck. *This isn't just a couple of soldiers and a rogue officer. It's now three tanks and three crews on their way to the front.* He swallowed hard, his mind racing with the consequences. *If this whole damn train is delayed, I won't just be embarrassed—I'll be transferred to a prison camp guard. Worse, I'll have to answer to the higher-ups, and that means serious trouble I don't want to even imagine. Those higher-ups are insane and fanatical. I need to get out of this without drawing more attention.*

Even the other two tank crews, themselves, had begun to rise, their hands hovered near their holsters. Every one of them had the cold, steady stare of battle-hardened soldiers—men who didn't bluff. Men who stared death in the face for months. Men who had fought on the frigid and brutal Eastern Front. For a long moment, no one moved. The yard was now deathly silent. Finally, Stefan actually pulls out his pistol with deliberate slowness. One by one, the rest of the tank crews follow, the metallic clicks of holsters' snaps releasing filling the air.

The police chief raised his hands in a placating gesture. "Hey, no need for that," he said, his voice tight. He took a step back, and his men follow, shuffled into a huddle. After a brief, whispered discussion, the chief turned back to Decker.

"We understand and support your serious efforts," he said stiffly. "We don't want to compromise your mission. If you happen to see that man, let us know." He salutes.

Decker paused, then returned the salute slowly, with almost mocking disdain. Decker: "Yeah, he is probably on the next train." The train whistle blew, and with a lurch, the engine began to move. The military police watched helplessly as the tanks rolled out of the station. From the shadowed interior of the Dragon Tank, Kurt exhaled a long breath he hadn't realized he'd been holding. When the station was finally out of sight, he climbed back up to the deck, his face pale but composed.

Decker was waiting for him. The commander's expression was unreadable, but his voice carried a rare warmth. "I can't save the world," Decker said, echoing Kurt's earlier words. "But today, I stood up for one man."

Kurt nodded, the weight of Decker's loyalty settling heavily on his shoulders. "Thank you, sir. I guess I owe you some licorice." Decker smiled.

They never heard, officially, a word about the Krakow incident again. But the quiet, long-term consequences kept showing up—subtle, recurring, but never discussed aloud. Everyone knew.

***

As the train rumbled on, Kris began to play a soft love song on his harmonica. Stefan lit another cigarette, the glow of the flame briefly illuminating his face. Kurt pulled out a mint and offered it to Ottmar who shook his head. Decker had a stick of licorice.

For the rest of 1942, the crew of the Dragon Tank fought their way south toward Rostov, near the Don River. The long-barreled, high-velocity gun of the Panzer IV proved more than its worth, making quick work of the previously invulnerable T-34s. Each battle tested their resolve and sharpened their cohesion as a unit. The Russians now grew more wary of these newly dangerous, long-barreled tanks.

By the year's end, Commander Decker was quietly pleased as the Dragon's victory tally now reached thirty confirmed kills.

"We did it together," Kurt said that evening as they bivouacked near a smoldering battlefield. He sat with the others around a small fire, the heat flickering off their tired faces.

Kurt: "Stefan gets us into position. Ottmar keeps the cannon loaded under fire. Kris keeps us laughing even when there's nothing to laugh about. And Decker—well, he somehow keeps us alive and out of trouble. Me in particular."

After the Leningrad front had stabilized and after the Krakow incident, they were ordered to sweep 2,100 kilometers to the far southern end of the continent as part of Operation Edelweiss—the German drive to seize Soviet oil fields in the Caucasus. It was an astonishing logistical movement across half a continent. In August 1942, Kurt's unit had advanced far south of Kursk and reached Maykop—a key oil city nestled at the foothills of the Caucasus Mountains, just inland from the Black Sea. Just months earlier, they had been fighting through the dense, snow-choked forests of Tikhvin, over 2,000 kilometers to the north—near the opposite end of the western Soviet Union. Now, in Maykop, the mountains loomed ahead, the air heavy with heat and the scent of oil. From the frozen forests near Leningrad to the near-tropical south, the contrast was staggering. But by December, the cold returned with a vengeance, and the advance ground to a halt due to supply logistics and the winter cold at Maykop, Russia.

Then bad news arrived one day in February, 1943. Commander Decker called the men together, his voice carrying the weight of the news he had just received. "Word has come down," he began, pausing as the men gathered around. "Army Group South had been surrounded at Stalingrad. All ground and air relief efforts have failed, and they've surrendered."

A silence fell over the group as the enormity of the loss hit. The surrender of over 550,000 soldiers was a devastating blow. This was the biggest single loss in German military history. The realization settled heavily on their shoulders—this was no longer just a battle; this was the beginning of a new, grim reality for the German Army.

117

Now the Russians had seized the offensive all across whole the Eastern Front. The Russian campaign to recapture territory in the Caucasus was code-named Operation Little Saturn. In February 1943, they retook Maykop and Rostov. Under the very real threat of encirclement, all German units were ordered to withdraw from the southern Caucasus front. Kurt's unit retreated to Fastiv, Ukraine, where they were ordered to turn in their Panzer IV long-barreled tanks. Kurt then received orders to report to Pulsnitz, Germany, for his second "equipment upgrade and training."

Chapter 12—Tiger One–A Legend Is Born

1943

Due to his exceptional shooting record, Kurt and his crew had earned spots to train on the most advanced and revolutionary tank of the day: the Tiger I (Panzer VI Version E). He reported to the Pultos Armor Training Center in Germany in March 1943.

Sergeant Jannis Bergman stood before a class of 40 hand-picked elite Panzer soldiers. His voice cut through the air, firm and commanding. "Men, you're here because your combat records prove you are the best of the best in the German Armored Divisions. Today, you will witness the latest armored fighting vehicle the Fatherland has delivered to help us achieve our goals. Enough chatter. Let's see the real thing." The soldiers filed out of the classroom and into a large warehouse. There, sitting in the center, was the massive tank. They felt small standing beside it, its sheer size dwarfing them. They were given a full 360-degree tour of the beast—each soldier murmuring their approval. Sergeant Bergman, "Not only are you protected from a fiery death, but just look at this gun. You are now in the most powerfully gunned tank in the world. This is the 88-millimeter gun, capable of dealing decisively not only with the T-34s but also easily handling the heavier KV-1s and the new more heavily armored T-34-85s."

Kurt stood among the crew, his eyes fixed on the gun. His fingers twitched, eager for the moment he'd command its power. The sound of that 88mm firing, cutting through the air, would be something he'd never forget. He had faced battles before, but with this new weapon, they could break through any resistance. It felt like a new chapter in the war was beginning—and Kurt was ready to write it.

Walking over to the side of the tank, Sergeant Bergman pulled a white sheet off two shells standing upright on the floor. "The shell on the left is the 75mm used, as you well know, in your former Panzer IV, the T-34, and the American Sherman. The shell on the right is the 88mm of our new gun. It makes the 75mm look like a toy," Bergman explained.

Kurt's gaze lingered on the shells. He had worked with the 75mm for a long time—watched it tear through armor *if* he placed it just right, and saw it bounce off the front armor far too many times. But this 88mm... it was a different beast entirely. The sheer power it could unleash made the 75mm seem like a distant memory. His shots would now penetrate armor that once shrugged off his best efforts. He could already picture it: the satisfaction of the shot, the silence after it hit its target—one shot instead of three.

Bergman continued, "The 88mm shell is 30% longer and 20% thicker, giving it a total firepower advantage—almost double the volume of the 75mm. And you loaders, as you might guess, the shells are 46% heavier, weighing in at 10.2 kilograms (22.5 pounds)." Kurt caught Ottmar's grin. He could always count on Ottmar to lighten the mood. Even in the face of such heavy responsibility, Ottmar found a way to crack a joke.

"Looks like I'll be getting bigger muscles now," Ottmar said with a smirk. Kurt chuckled softly, but inside, he felt the weight of what this tank represented. It wasn't just the power it carried—it was the responsibility. He and the crew would have to master it, and that would take time. They would have to learn to move in sync, every shot, every maneuver, with no room for error.

Sergeant Bergman continued, "And for those of you who like to swim, this Tiger has rubberized exterior hatches, gun ports, and vision slits. That makes it our first 'deep wading' tank. No more searching for bridges—you'll be able to cross rivers up to four meters deep (13 feet)."

Kurt raised an eyebrow. A swimming tank? It sounded absurd—almost laughable. But the practicality struck him. Nothing was going to stop this machine. Not the Russians, not the rivers, not even the terrain. It was more than a tank. It was a symbol of German resolve.

Bergman handed out the Tiger I crew packets. "These are your manuals and reference photos. We'll cover everything during training." Kurt accepted the booklet, thumbing it open. But his mind was already leaping ahead—imagining the weight of the gun, the clarity of a distant target, and the silence after the shot struck home. They studied the new tactics. The Tiger was now dubbed "the Hammer."

Thanks to what they'd learned, they could now engage enemy armor at twice the range—up to 2,000 meters (6,600 feet). The Tiger's 88mm gun could pierce a T-34's frontal armor at 1,200 meters—double the reach of the Panzer IV. And with nearly impenetrable frontal armor, the Tiger I could shrug off T-34 shells at 1,000 meters (3,300feet). At that distance, and beyond, it was virtually untouchable.

Only Stefan had a complaint. "It's a beast, no doubt. But it's slower than the old tank. Still, the Tiger tracks are almost 50% wider than the T-34 tracks. That will definitely help with mud and snow."

It was as if the universe had been preparing him all along. The moment didn't feel random—it felt fated, shaped not by luck but by two years of fire and grit. The Tiger wasn't just a new machine of war—it was the natural manifestation of everything he'd been through. Its long-range precision optics and thick frontal armor weren't luxuries—they were new lethal tools forged for a soldier like Kurt, whose sharp eyes and uncanny depth perception had been already tested, tempered, and proven in the worst conditions possible. What had once felt like punishment now revealed itself simply as preparation.

But now, during training, Decker's Tiger consistently ranked near the top in accuracy. Kurt's control of the Tiger's long-range gun was unmatched. His gunnery scores became the envy of every crew on the range. He soared to the top of the class—Decker couldn't have been more pleased.

Kurt put the final touches on the dragon logo painted on the Tiger's turret. Commander Decker glanced up from his paperwork, nodded approvingly. "Looking handsome enough for war. That dragon has been good luck so far."

The crew had assembled and had poured some champagne into their glasses. From his kit, Kurt reached down and pulled out an unopened bottle. Kurt: "I christen thee Dragon Tiger". He smashes it on the turret. He stepped back, admiring his work. The assembled crew all toasted with their crystal glassware. And then the party was over.

Their first stop was a Ukrainian town called Bogodukhov, near Kharkov. Here, they joined the newly formed 503rd Heavy Panzer Division—a breakthrough unit unlike anything Kurt had seen before. For the first time, all 45 Tiger I tanks were grouped into one concentrated, deadly formation—the kind that could punch through anything. Unlike the early-war French and Soviet strategies, which scattered their heavy tanks piecemeal among infantry units, this formational strategy was significantly different. This was focus. Intent. A fist instead of fingers.

At first, the 88mm cannon felt like a stranger—massive, unyielding, a weapon forged for giants. It didn't speak to Kurt, not yet. But day by day, shot by shot, the bond grew. The recoil no longer jarred—it spoke. The optics no longer challenged—they guided. The gun wasn't just powerful. It was ordained. As if the machine had been waiting for him all along. By the end of the week, it was no longer steel and rivets. It was a fang in the mouth of a dragon. A hunter's weapon, fused to the will of the one who'd been forged by fire to wield it.

Kurt sat in the roomy (comparatively) turret of Dragon Tiger, the vibrations of its powerful engine humming through his body. The training had been relentless, designed to prepare him and his crew for the monumental task ahead. As they moved through the training grounds, the sense of anticipation was palpable, the knowledge that the war's most significant battle was now coming upon them.

The men of the 503rd Heavy Panzer Division, armed with the formidable Tiger, would soon face the Soviet forces in what was sure to be a brutal, life-or-death confrontation. Without thinking, his fingers brush the dragon pendant resting against his chest. Kurt set Nikol's picture next to his gunsight, a quiet reminder of what he's fighting for. The significance of the coming battle weighed heavily on him.

***

This battle was forming around Kursk, Russia. A massive German offensive was taking shape—called Operation Citadel—the first major push since the disaster at Stalingrad, and rumored to involve more tanks than ever before.

Kurt knew that everything hinged on this. His division, with its 146 brand new Tigers, was now poised to make its battlefield debut, and it felt like both an opportunity and a terrifying responsibility.

The Tiger combined firepower, armor, and psychological impact, earning its place as one of the most respected and ultimately on, the most feared tank of World War II. As the days wore on, Kurt found himself thinking more and more about the enemy he would soon face.

One evening, as the crew went through their routine, Kris, the radio operator, relayed the latest intel over the intercom. "Reports are coming in," Kris said, his voice steady but laced with a hint of caution. "Luftwaffe photo reports estimate Soviets to have fielded over 5,000 tanks—T-34s, KV-1s, and other models. And that's just a rough guess as of this morning."

Kurt's brow furrowed at the number. Over 5,000 Soviet tanks? His mind quickly processed the figures, calculating the disparity. Just back from a command briefing, Decker had told him that we have mustered just under 2,900 tanks, including 146 Tigers. The math didn't add up in their favor. They were outnumbered—almost two to one, maybe more. The odds didn't sit well with him, but he knew better than to trust the numbers blindly. In war, the truth was often distorted by deception and the deliberate haze of intelligence reports.

Still, the fact remained—they were at a significant numerical disadvantage. Their units were assigned to Army Group South, Detachment Kempf, commanded by Field Marshal Erich van Manstein. Kurt forced the unease from his mind, knowing there was little he could do about the numbers. What mattered now was the Tiger. He trusted in its power. The machine was nearly indestructible, and with the right strategy, it could turn the tide. The early models had suffered teething problems, but those were supposed to be ironed out by now.

The Germans only had 146 Tigers for all of Kursk, but Kurt had faith that the tanks would perform as they were designed to, and he knew the Tiger could be the difference in the battle. Even with that confidence, he couldn't shake the feeling that the Soviets wouldn't be easily defeated. They had survived hell before, and now, they were preparing to fight to the death. They were determined to halt Germany's advance once and for all, no matter what the cost.

Kurt could almost feel the weight of history pressing down on him. The Eastern Front had become a brutal stalemate, and Kursk was the epicenter of it all. This battle would be decisive, a turning point for either Germany or the Soviet Union. For the Germans, it was a slim chance to recover from their previous losses. For Stalin, it was the opportunity to crush the German forces and launch a counteroffensive that would push them all the way to Berlin. Every man knew what was at stake.

The 503rd Heavy Panzer Division (attached to army Detachment Kempf on the southern Kursk salient), though relatively small in number, carried the fearsome reputation of the Tigers. It was a weapon that could alter the course of the battle, and Kurt's heart raced with both pride and apprehension as he prepared for the coming storm. The front stretched out before him, a vast expanse littered with deep dug trenches, minefields, and fortifications—each inch a death trap. He had trained for this, but nothing could fully prepare him for the reality of war. His mind drifted back to his training, the months spent honing his skills, the endless drills. But no amount of preparation could steel him completely for the chaos that awaited. As the days passed, the tension in Kurt's chest only grew heavier. The battle for Kursk was imminent, and with it, his fate—along with that of his comrades—was about to be sealed. He could feel the weight of it in every step, every moment. The time for talk was over. The time for action was almost here.

Through it all, Kurt vowed to do his duty, keep his head, stay sharp, and, most of all, hold onto his humanity. Because when the war was over, that was what mattered most to him. No matter how many battles he fought, or how much destruction and carnage surrounded him, it was the part of him that remained untouched by war—the part of him that still clung to kindness, compassion, and honor—that he was determined to protect.

***

On the Russian side, Captain Marat knelt beside a sapper laying the final stretch of barbed wire, the scent of damp earth and cordite heavy in the morning air. All across the steppe, the land had been transformed into a fortress—mines, trenches, and camouflaged gun nests stretching for kilometers. His sector alone held more than 40,000 anti-tank and anti-personnel mines, buried in patterns meant to funnel the Panzers into kill zones. Behind the forward trenches, two more defensive lines waited—each 10 to 15 kilometers back, thick with dugouts, anti-tank ditches, and fresh artillery. Further still, beyond the tree line, the third and final reserve line crouched in silence, stocked with tank corps and mobile infantry, ready to strike when the enemy was weakest. Marat had memorized every turn of the terrain, every fallback position. The Germans were coming with armor and arrogance, but this time, the Red Army was not scrambling in retreat. They had been given time—weeks of precious time—and Stalin's order was clear: hold the line, no matter the cost.

Marat looked westward, the early sun glinting off his binoculars, and whispered, "Let them come. The earth is waiting."

Chapter 13—The Steel Inferno–Kursk, 1943

The forest edge hummed with activity. Rows of German Tigers, Panthers, Panzer IVs, and StuG III assault tanks stood ready, their engines growling low in anticipation. Horses strained against their harnesses, hauling artillery, fuel, and ammunition to the launch positions. The air was thick with tension, the kind that always preceded a major offensive, and Kurt could feel the weight of it settling on his shoulders.

Commander Decker gathered the crew, his voice firm as he outlined the plan for the upcoming battle at Kursk. The weight of the moment hung heavy in the air, each word carrying the gravity of the serious mission ahead.

"We will be employing the Panzerkeil formation," Decker began, his eyes scanning each man, ensuring they understood the significance of the tactic.

"The 'tank wedge'—a formation designed for both offense and protection." Kurt listened closely, already envisioning the battlefield in his mind. The Panzerkeil was a familiar strategy, one that had proven effective in previous engagements, but Kursk would be different. The stakes were higher—far higher. They were outnumbered, and the Soviets had dug in deep. This wasn't just about breaking through enemy lines; this was about survival.

"The Tiger tanks," Decker continued, his voice steady but resolute, "will lead the charge at the front, with their formidable firepower and thick armor. Our job is simple: we take the brunt of the enemy's fire. We absorb it, we push forward, and we break through. The Panthers and Panzer IVs will follow behind, arranged in layers within the wedge. Their role is to provide support, both fire and protection, while we keep the enemy's focus on us."

Kurt nodded. It was a familiar tactic, one that demanded flawless timing and absolute trust in the men to do their job. As the lead tank in the formation, the Tiger was meant to spearhead the assault, the heavy armor absorbing the initial blows. It was a role Kurt had trained for—one that required not just skill, but a certain mindset: to keep pushing forward, no matter the cost, and to hold the line while the others followed. The enemy's attention would be focused on them, and it was their job to make sure the rest of the formation could move through the breach.

Commander Decker's gaze locked with Kurt's for a moment, as if to underscore the gravity of what lay ahead. "We break their line, we shatter their resolve, and we take Kursk. We do this, and we take the first step toward victory."

Kurt could feel the resolve of his commander in those words, and in that moment, he steeled himself for what was to come. The Tiger would lead. The crew would follow. And they would fight, not just for victory, but for each other—for survival.

Kurt nodded, understanding the logic. The Tigers were the heavy hitters, designed to withstand the heaviest of Soviet blows while giving the more vulnerable tanks room to maneuver. It was a sound plan, but he knew the old military axiom: no plan survives contact with the enemy. Decker's voice grew more resolute.

"Behind the tanks, we have the StuG IIIs. They aren't typically part of the Panzerkeil, but we'll need them for this battle. They'll provide close support to our infantry, engaging enemy positions with their guns, making sure we clear the way for our troops."

Kurt shifted in his seat, feeling the weight of responsibility. The formation relied on cohesion—every tank, every gun, every soldier would need to perform their role flawlessly. There was no room for mistakes.

"Our objective," Decker concluded, "is to break through the Soviet defenses, encircle them, and crush their resistance. We may be outnumbered, but our strength lies in the Tiger and in the formation. We move as one—together, we will break them."

Kurt held his ear steady on the commander, the plan settling into his mind. The battle ahead was formidable, but their plan offered a path through the storm. And as the weight of the operation settled on his shoulders, he knew one thing for certain: this battle would define them all. This combined-arms approach, with heavy tanks leading the charge and assault guns supporting infantry, was central to the German strategy during the battle. The Tigers took the lead ("The Hammer"), forming the tip.

Atop one of the lead Tigers, Commander Decker was positioned in the cupola, headset tilted over one ear. The whole crew felt the tension, each man locked in his role. Preparation was equally intense. Ottmar and Kurt loaded all 99 rounds. Stefan checked and re-checked all engine logistics and babied his two batteries. Kris checked the radio frequencies tanks were assigned and double-checked all electrical connections.

At 5:30 AM on July 5, 1943, Commander Decker ordered, "Go." Below, at the open driver's hatch, Stefan ground out his cigarette on the Tiger's front deck. He glanced up, catching Decker's glare. The commander's disapproval was palpable, his expression promising consequences. Having been idling for 20 minutes already, Stefan grinned, brushed the ashes off the deck.

"Understood, sir. That's my last for the day. But don't blame me if an Ivan bird lands one on us, sir." Decker growled but said nothing, his focus already on much bigger things. This was a massively important day for him. On command, the Tiger lurched into motion, tracks biting into the earth as the spear tip of German armor moved out into the theater of war.

Ottmar stroked and babied an armor-piercing shell, kissing it as if sealing it with a personal signature. The Dragon Tiger joined the advancing platoon. Stefan steered the Tiger, cresting a low hill. The massive machine loomed against the horizon, a shadow of destruction in the early morning light. The cupola was open, and Commander Decker stood, binoculars in hand, radio headset perched over one ear. His gaze swept over the distant terrain, searching for battle signs.

"At two o'clock, at least 1,500 meters (4,900 feet). Do you see him, Kurt?" Decker asked, his voice calm but sharp, a note of urgency buried in the steadiness. Kurt's eyes snapped to his scope, his fingers hovering over the turret controls. The world outside the turret fell away as his focus narrowed to a single point—the target ahead resting on a distant mountain top. Kurt traversed the turret, leaning into the gunsight, his sharp vision piercing the haze.

"Yes, sir. I see him," he called out. "Armor-piercing."

Ottmar, ever meticulous, grabbed the shell and slid it smoothly into the breach. "That's my baby," he said, patting the shell before snapping the breech shut. "Ready! Special super heavy-duty delivery, with love, just for Ivan. Up!"

Kurt's fingers brushed against the coolness of his necklace, the dragon pendant resting lightly against his skin. Sweat trickled down his forehead, and he wiped his eyes with a silk cloth, steadying himself. "Now that I look at him, sir, it looks more like 1,800 meters, maybe more," he added, to himself, his voice quiet, *about 16 soccer fields.*

Decker nodded without lowering his binoculars. "Adjust, and fire when ready." His thoughts raced, though his face betrayed no emotion. *No way at that distance, but if anyone can...*

Kurt double-checked the rangefinder, then adjusted the sighting reticle for the greater distance. His breathing slowed as focus settled over him. He paused, letting the stillness of the moment envelop him, the tension building in the tight space.

Just before taking the shot, his fingers brushed lightly against Nikol's picture beside the gunsight. Her face flashed in his mind—an image that briefly overtook his vision. Time seemed to stretch in that fleeting moment.

Kurt drew a deep breath, reaching for the quiet place that never failed him. Then, in a low whisper meant only for the steel beast beneath him, "Fly, Dragon... fly."

The Tiger's cannon erupted with a deafening roar, its recoil shaking the entire tank. The shell ripped through the air at over 1,000 meters per second—a flash of light streaking across the battlefield.

The hiss of its flight faded into the distance... and three seconds later the far hilltop shuddered.

The T-34 rocked violently as the 88mm shell slammed into its side, a burst of flames erupting as the tank's ammunition cooked off. The muffled explosion echoed across the valley, the death sound rolling softly through the hills before settling into silence.

For a moment, all was still. The battlefield waited. Commander Decker lowered his binoculars, rubbing his eyes as if doubting what he had just witnessed. He raised them again, scanning the smoking wreckage in the distance. "Damn, that's 2,000 meters (6,600 feet). Sergeant, can you hit China while you're at it?"

"This gun... I think it likes me... And nothing else matters." Kurt commented while grinning faintly, patting the cannon breech.

Decker ducked into the tank and turned toward Kurt, his expression shifting to one of calm authority. "Sergeant, from now on, fire on your own command." Kurt nodded, the weight of the new responsibility settling in. He shot a glance at Decker, his lips curling into a wry smile.

"Or maybe you're just *extra* eager, sir, to earn that Knight's Cross in Gold." Up top, Decker's attention shifted skyward as a low-flying hawk glided past, its wings slicing through the air. with effortless grace.

For a brief moment, the explosions on the battlefield seemed to halt as the sharp, commanding screech of the bird echoed across the scene.

Decker smiled faintly, his gaze following the hawk's soaring flight. The bird's wings sliced through the air with the same ease and deadly grace that Kurt's Tiger gun had just unleashed. For a moment, Decker couldn't help but see the parallel: the sharp-eyed hawk, an embodiment of nature's untamed force, and the dragon, which Kurt had come to symbolize in his own mind. Both were creatures of power—one of the sky, one of steel—each striking with unmatched fear and finality,

Decker tipped his cap toward the hawk, acknowledging a silent bond. The bird answered with a sharp, cutting screech that carried across the battlefield. For a moment, it felt as though the hawk itself had given its approval..

Decker had finally unleashed his unprecedentedly lethal gunner— a moment akin to the pulling of the legendary sword from its stone, a symbol of destiny fulfilled. In that act, the world had changed. Now, as Kurt had taken his first long shot, Decker knew this was their moment to shift the course of the battle.

Kurt leaned back from the gunsight, his fingers rubbing his eyes in a brief moment of respite. For the first time, it all felt clear—like it had always been meant to be. In that quiet instant, he realized this was more than just a mission; he felt like destiny was unfolding right before him. He touched his necklace, took a mint, and let out a long sigh, decompressing as the tension in his body began to ease. He shook his hands and arms, rotated his neck to stretch, letting go of the strain. His gaze drifted to Nikol's picture posted near the sight, and he smiled.

Then, Decker's voice sliced through the moment: "Twenty T-34s, two o'clock, 800 meters." Kurt snapped back to reality, instinctively gripping the controls as adrenaline flooded his veins. The calm was gone—war waited for no one. This was only the beginning of the day. His eyes remained locked on the battlefield, scanning the smoke for any signs of movement. His senses heightened, every nerve firing with adrenaline. He'd already taken down one enemy tank, but he knew this was just the start. The Soviets were relentless, and there was always another threat lurking in the haze. As he tracked a Soviet tank through the smoke, its outline appeared—a T-34, barely visible through the mist of burning wrecks. Kurt's fingers tightened on the turret controls. This one would be trickier.

"Ottmar," Kurt called sharply, his voice steady despite the chaos. "Armor-piercing. Now." Ottmar moved quickly, his hands steady as he grabbed the right round. The click of metal against metal echoed in the turret, and in seconds, the heavy armor-piercing shell was loaded into the breech. Kurt's eyes never left the target.

Ottmar: "Up!"

Kurt adjusted the turret, calculating the distance and angle. The T-34 was trying to maneuver, but it wasn't fast enough. Kurt lined up his shot, the crosshairs settling squarely on the Soviet tank's previously impenetrable frontal armor.

"Fire." Kurt commanded to himself, the words feeling heavier than usual. It was the first time he'd given the order on his own, since Decker had granted him that authority. The command rang in his ears, not just for the crew, but for himself as well. He wasn't just firing the gun—he was taking control of his destiny, and it felt good.

The gun recoiled with its familiar, deafening roar, and the armor-piercing shell ripped through the air. It struck the T-34 dead center, the round carved a tunnel through the thick armor as if the steel had already surrendered. The Soviet tank exploded in a violent fireball, sending debris flying in all directions. Kurt exhaled, the tension in his shoulders easing slightly, but he didn't let up. There was no time for relief.

"Load another, Ottmar," Kurt ordered, his voice calm despite the turmoil still raging around them. Ottmar was already at work, sliding the next shell into place with practiced speed.

"Baby is UP," Ottmar shouted, his focus unwavering.

Kurt's hands moved over the turret controls, scanning the smoke for the next threat. He wasn't done yet. Not by a long shot. The battle at Kursk was still unfolding, and he was determined to prove to himself that he could do his duty, no matter the cost.

His grip on the turret controls tightened as the smoke thickened, the air buzzing with the constant whine of distant artillery and the roar of Dragon Tiger's cannon. The sounds of destruction were deafening, but his focus was absolute. He'd racked up eight kills by now, and his team moved with deadly cadence. Still, his mind kept drifting back to the disabled Tiger—the one that had hit the mine. He'd seen it earlier, its tracks torn apart, its crew still firing as if nothing could stop them.

The radio crackled again, this time with the voice of Commander Decker, cutting through the mayhem. "Listen up, everyone," Decker said, his tone carrying a hard edge of command. "We've got a Tiger down. Hit a mine, track is blown. They're immobile. But the crew's still in the game, firing like they're at the practice range. We can't waste any more time here." Kurt's stomach tightened, but Decker's next words were clear.

"We press on. We'll recover the tank and crew later, once the area is secure. We can't afford to be bogged down. Our mission is Kursk and we've got a job to do. Stay sharp. Keep the pressure on and don't let up."

Kurt exhaled slowly, pushing aside the anger and frustration that threatened to rise. Decker was right, of course. They couldn't afford to get sidetracked by one tank, no matter how hard it was to leave it behind. The crew inside that tank had shown incredible grit—fighting on even though they were immobilized—but the war was still raging, and every second counted.

Kurt's hands moved automatically as he swung the turret toward the next target, his mind already back in the battle. His gunner's sight locked on a Soviet T-34, its flank exposed through the smoke.

"Fire," Kurt whispered to himself, his voice cold and focused. The shell ripped through the air, striking the T-34's side with a thunderous impact. It was gone in an instant, reduced to a burning wreck. Kurt didn't have time to feel relief. He was already looking for the next target.

"Ottmar, another," Kurt commanded, his tone firm. Ottmar worked quickly, sliding the next round into place.

The Soviets were regrouping, and their tanks were closing in but the German Tigers had the upper hand. Kurt's crew moved like clockwork—efficient, deadly, and focused on the task at hand. Despite the loss of one of their own, they pressed on.

Kursk Unfolds- Week Two

In the second week of the Battle of Kursk, the Germans pushed forward, advancing 32 kilometers (20 miles) toward their goal. Tasked with supporting the southwest pincer, their progress was slow and punishing—hindered by rain, deep mud, anti-tank trenches, ambushes, massive minefields, swarms of anti-tank guns, and the blistering heat.

Kurt's score for the first week was 15 victories including some of the heavier KV-2s. Despite these obstacles, the Tigers easily defeated the T-34s, suffering few combat losses themselves. However, their own mechanical issues were mounting: broken transmissions, fuel shortages, and blown tracks plagued the units. In this part of the sector, their sister armored forces—now reduced to only a couple hundred of the lighter Panzer units—fought on with grim determination.

As the day dragged on, many crews were fueled by "tank chocolate"—amphetamine-laced rations designed to keep them awake and sharp during the extended, relentless offensive.

A breakthrough and northern link-up would slam the jaws shut on the Kursk bulge—trapping Soviet forces and flattening the entire front. To prevent this, Stalin deployed his elite, veteran 5th Guards Tank Army—615 tanks—against the II SS-Panzer Corps, which fielded 294 tanks. This clash occurred on July 11, 1943, near the small town of Prokhorovka, 80 kilometers (50 miles) southeast of Kursk, where the two armored forces collided. What followed was the largest one-day tank battle in history—nearly 1,000 tanks engaged in a chaotic, close-range melee of fire and steel, transforming the battlefield into a swirling inferno. While Prokhorovka ended as a tactical stalemate, it was a strategic victory for the Soviets.

Well south of that conflict, Kurt wasn't at that legendary battle of but his mission was no less critical. Kurt's unit, with the 503rd Heavy Panzer Battalion, was on the southern pincer and tasked with clearing Soviet armored columns threatening the flank of the 4th Panzer Army's thrust. The hulks of burning German and T-34 tanks lined the horizon, a testament to the ferocity of the strong and aggressive Soviet defenses.

Kurt's focus sharpened as the battlefield swirled around him in a chaotic storm of fire and steel. The roar of enemy artillery and the constant surging of his Tiger's Maybach engine filled the air, but none of that mattered. He was locked in, his hands instinctively guiding the turret and lining up the next shot. Every second counted; every move had to count.

Stefan, unlit cigarette dangling from his lips, stayed calm in formation, his hands firm on the controls. Decker, up top, read the battlefield and ordered Stefan to optimal engagement points. Kris, the radio operator, kept the comms flowing, his voice cutting through the noise with updates, while also manning the bow machine gun when necessary. Ottmar treated each round with the care you'd give a prized possession, ensuring every shell was loaded with speed and meticulous precision. Together, they were a seamless force, each member of the crew moving with unspoken coordination, like the parts of a finely tuned engine, all driving toward the same brutal purpose.

The first hits on their Tiger came quickly—T-34s and anti-tank guns firing from all directions. The Tiger's thick armor absorbed the brunt of it, but Kurt could feel every hit reverberating through the tank. The pressure was mounting. He knew the danger, but in the moment all he could think about was the next target, the next shot. There was no room for thought. Only focus. Nothing else mattered

By late afternoon, the fighting had reached a fever pitch. A T-34 suddenly emerged from a gully at nine o'clock, and before Kurt even realized he had pulled the trigger, Decker's voice rang out: "Hit!" Without missing a beat, Decker barked, "New target at three o'clock! 125 meters. Fast mover—they're circling us, setting up for a side shot!"

Kurt's heart skipped a beat as the urgency in Decker's voice cut through the chaos. He immediately started the eleven-ton turret traverse, gritting his teeth as the seconds seemed to stretch into eternity. Fifteen seconds for the turret to rotate—it felt like a lifetime under fire. The dust and smoke from the battlefield swirled around them, partially obscuring his view, but Kurt's focus stayed locked on the target.

Then, through the haze, he saw it—a silhouette flickering, closing fast. The enemy tank was charging right at them, obviously intending to ram, just like others had done that day when the tanks were so close. Inside the turret, the heat and the stench of cordite thickened the air, smothering them. Kurt fired, hitting the charging Ivan tank squarely in the front armor next to the driver's hatch. The tank stopped and started burning. The four-man crew was gone.

Once across the Donets River, the Tigers were in motion the entire time, but they couldn't achieve their strategic objectives due to strong Soviet resistance and the operational challenges of mines and anti-tank obstacles.

Five days after the Kursk battle began, on July 10th, the Anglo-Americans landed on the beaches of Sicily. Two days later, on July 12th, Hitler, over General Manstein's strong objections, halted the Kursk offensive and ordered several of the larger Panzer Divisions to Italy.

That evening, Decker called the crew together. They stood in silence, their uniforms streaked with sweat, oil, and the grime of battle. The battlefield still smoldered in the distance, a graveyard of twisted steel and smoking wrecks. The sky, once filled with the roar of engines and the thunder of artillery, was eerily quiet now. Decker looked down at the sheet in his hand. He turned to Kurt, his voice measured.

"Your tally..." He paused, scanning the numbers. "...for these two weeks of combat is another 27 victories. That's almost two per day."

A sacred silence followed. The number spoke for itself. Twenty-seven enemy tanks reduced to charred hulks. Twenty-seven Russian crews—men just like them—gone. Decker exhaled, folding the paper before looking at each of them—Kurt, Ottmar, Stefan, Kris—his men, his brothers in this war.

"The whole crew excelled today. Every one of you. We pushed, we fought, and we survived. That alone is victory in itself." He let the words settle. "I know we wanted Kursk. We wanted to break through, to take what command demanded of us. But the battlefield decides what is won and lost—not the wishes of headquarters, fifteen hundred kilometers away. We did everything we could. And we did it damn well."

He paced slightly, rubbing the dirt from his brow before glancing at their battered Tiger—the machine that had carried them through hell and back. "That tank held because of you. It's just steel—until men like you bring it to life with skill and grit. Stefan, your driving kept us moving when others got bogged down. You steered us clear of Ivan's Tiger-killing tactic—swarming us from multiple sides at once: the *'Circle of Death'*. Ottmar, you fed that gun like a madman. We never had to wonder if a shell was ready. Kris, your ears kept our eyes open—tracking where our brothers were, calling out when they needed help, and reporting windows of opportunity. You didn't just save our hides—you helped us strike harder, smarter, and more lethal."

Commander Decker paused, scanning their faces. "And finally, I think we all agree—we've got the finest gunner in the army standing right here. Kurt, you made every shot count."

He glanced at Kurt, his expression softening—just a bit. "Twenty-seven kills, and we're still standing. That's not just skill. That's duty through discipline." Decker let the weight of his words settle, then cracked a rare smile—one of genuine approval, something almost unseen amidst the war's relentless grind. "Not every battle is about capturing ground. Sometimes, it's just about proving we can stand. And today, we made our statement, and we stood. Be proud of that."

Stefan smiled and pointed to the turret. "We all love our dragon tattoo. As I recall, that was your idea, sir I think our dragon has nine lives." The crew chuckled, trading backslaps with pride.

Lighting a cigarette, Stefan leaned in, his voice lowered. "I was near the interrogation tent yesterday. One of the Russian tanker prisoners— young kid, maybe nineteen—said something that stuck with me." The others turned toward him. "I heard him say Ivan tankers are calling us the *Dragon Tiger* now," Stefan continued. "Word is, their crews are told to steer clear. Said if the Dragon even sees you…"

He inhaled on his cigarette.

"…you're already dead." Stefan paused, then added quietly, "The kid said, 'We stay away from the Dragon.'"

Silence settled over the group for a moment. Then Ottmar muttered, "Damn right they do."

Commander Decker nodded. "Yes—the Dragon of War." He turned toward the horizon, where the fires of battle still flickered. "Tomorrow, they'll send us somewhere else. Another front. Another fight. But whatever comes—we face it together. Nothing else matters." He gave a small nod, then clapped Kurt on the shoulder before walking away, his rare moment of sentiment fading back into the heavy silence of war.

After the withdrawal from Kursk, the battle raged on, but Kurt's mind raced. In the quiet moments between engagements, the weight of what was happening beyond the immediate battlefield began pressing more heavily on him. It dawned on Kurt that Kursk wasn't just another battle—they had thrown everything they had at the Soviets, and it still hadn't been enough. The Russians weren't breaking; they were getting stronger. For the first time, Kurt began to wonder if the war itself was slipping beyond Germany's grasp—and what that meant for men like him, who had given everything to it.

As the Soviets pushed the retreating Germans back, Kurt could feel the shift in the air. The impact of Kursk was undeniable. The Russians had taken their losses, but they had endured—and now, they were fighting back harder than ever. The Russians had replacements for their losses; the Germans did not.

Kurt sensed that momentum had swung, more than ever, in Ivan's favor, the battlefield vibrating with the shift. What had once seemed like a potential victory for Germany now felt like a distant dream.

The Russians now launched aggressive, large counteroffensives with precision, carving through the German lines with a ferocity Kurt had never seen before. He was getting concerned. By August 23rd, Ivan had regained massive territory, a stretch of 2,000 kilometers falling back into their hands. There was no denying it now: the tide had turned. The Germans were no longer the aggressors; they were being pushed back.

Kurt's thoughts were sharper than ever amidst the battle. Even as his crew moved through the fight, he couldn't shake the feeling that this wasn't just a temporary setback. This was the beginning of something much bigger. He heard over the radio from Kris that the infantry—likely including his brother Conrad—was retreating all along the front. The writing was on the wall. By the time "Operation Citadel" (The Battle of Kursk) was officially abandoned in late August, it was clear to him: the Germans had lost the initiative, and the Soviets weren't just defending anymore—they were coming for them, and they weren't stopping.

Kurt was involved in hundreds of new tank engagements, and he and the Dragon Tiger added an additional 60 victories after Kursk. With the transfer of several Panzer armies to Italy, the Russians grew even more emboldened in their march to Berlin.

***

Inside a Soviet Earth bunker, a new B-10 Armored Car was parked outside, bristling with antennas like a porcupine. The atmosphere inside was dense with the aftermath of Russian victory, tempered by the fatigue that always follows battle. Commander Taranko and Captain Marat stood together, their conversation laden with the weight of their recent successes, though the tension of the war never fully dissipated.

Taranko raised his glass, his expression neutral but not unfeeling. "Captain, you did it. You stopped them at Prokhorovka. I don't like losing half of our tanks, but I'll acknowledge you stopped them for the motherland. You played your part well."

Marat stood at attention, accepting the praise with quiet humility, his eyes momentarily glancing toward the B-10 command car parked outside. Marat replied, "First Stalingrad, now Kursk and Prokhorovka. We've pushed those fascist Nazi bastards back." His gaze lingered on the B-10 for a moment longer before his faint smile turned wry, tinged with envy. "I see you've been rewarded, sir—a command car with a heater, no less. Will be nice to stay warm next winter, Commander."

Taranko's expression remained as cold as slate, but a frigid edge crept into his voice as his eyes locked with Marat's. "I'll be sure to think of you then, Captain."

For a brief moment, the air in the bunker thickened with unspoken tension. Taranko's demeanor softened just slightly, though his tone remained firm. "Victory does bring rewards. And as you're now an official war hero with the Order of the Patriotic War Medal, I've had your records purged, as promised."

He took a slow drag from his cigarette, the smoke swirling around him like an ill omen. "No one will remember your misadventures—not even Major Polykauf, who heroically perished at Kursk... with his scar."

The words landed with quiet finality, but something in Marat's chest tightened. He tried to mask the reaction, but his mind reeled at the mention of Polykauf. The past, it seemed, refused to stay buried.

Marat said nothing, but the silence stretched between them like a taut wire. Taranko, for all his authority and discipline, knew exactly how to push the buttons that made Marat squirm. Not moving on, relishing Marat's discomfort, Taranko continued, his voice low and smooth, almost savoring each word. "Polykauf..." he murmured. "He always had a certain... presence. Shame we lost him in such a manner. I'm sure that scar you awarded him was a fitting testament to his service." The word "scar" seemed to echo louder than it should. Marat's jaw tightened, and his fists clenched involuntarily at his sides. Without thinking, his fingers brushed over his own scar—the familiar ridge beneath his touch. Taranko had struck a deep nerve. Marat felt it—the weight of the scar on his soul as much as the one he had drunkenly carved into Polykauf's face.

"I suppose it's fitting, in some ways," Taranko added, studying Marat closely now. "We all carry our burdens, don't we, Captain? Some are worn on the outside for all to see..." He took a slow sip of his vodka, savoring the moment. "...others remain hidden within. As you wear your scar proudly, I suspect, for you, it may be more internal than external. But we all certainly understand the wish to leave some mark on this world." The words hung in the air, deliberate and cutting.

Marat's jaw tightened, his fingers flexing involuntarily at his sides. He knew Taranko was enjoying this—needling just enough to stir the embers of something buried deep inside.

Taranko set his glass down with a soft clink, watching Marat's reaction unfold. He wasn't looking for words—just the silent confirmation that his barb had struck true. The words hung in the air, thick and unforgiving. Marat met Taranko's gaze, but the bead of sweat tracing down his temple gave him away. He knew exactly what Taranko was doing—pressing, probing, testing the wound that would never fully close.

Taranko took another measured sip of his vodka, his eyes never leaving Marat. He wasn't just speaking—he was dissecting, peeling back layers, watching for the slightest crack. He wasn't looking for an answer. He was looking for a reaction. For a long moment, there was no sound—only the soft buzz of aircraft overhead. Marat couldn't tell if Taranko truly understood the demons that haunted him. Either way, the words served as a harsh reminder: for us humans, nothing was ever truly forgotten. Desperate to escape the heavy atmosphere, Marat gave a sharp, almost dismissive nod, his expression hardening. "Noted, sir. I'll keep it in mind."

Abruptly changing directions, "Berlin is next," Taranko suddenly announced, his gaze narrowing, as if already envisioning the coming struggle. "Stalin wants us to beat the Americans to it. The race to Berlin will decide more than just victory—it will determine who controls the heart of Europe after we crush the Nazis. We move out at dawn," his voice cold and resolute. "We *will* be the first to plant our flag in Berlin."

***

Miles away, Conrad and Jan sat in the cramped, rattling back of a packed Hanomag. Their faces were streaked with dirt and exhaustion, hands trembling—not from fear, but from the gnawing ache of amphetamine withdrawal. The stale air reeked of sweat and diesel, pressing heavily in the confined space.

Jan muttered hoarsely, his voice brittle, "Where we going?" Conrad, slouched against the cold steel wall, stared blankly ahead. His eyes were bloodshot, empty.

"Back to Korsun-Cherkassy... again," Conrad replied flatly, the bitterness in his tone cutting through the hum of the engine.

The weight of the Kursk defeat pressed down on him, relentless and suffocating. The retreat, the endless marches back—always back— gnawed at his soul, stripping away purpose and pride. What remained now was a hollow anger, simmering deep, ready to ignite, but with nowhere to burn.

Chapter 14—Korsun-Cherkassy Pocket

1944

Kurt rested against the side of the Dragon Tiger, the cold metal of the tank biting through his uniform. Kris's footsteps crunched on the frost as he approached, breathless.

"You told me to keep an ear on the radio for your brother's unit," Kris said, his voice urgent. "An hour ago, I learned his grenadier unit is trapped on the south side of Hill 239 in the Korsun-Cherkassy Pocket."

It was February 1944, deep in the dead of winter. The Soviets surround sixty thousand German soldiers. Trapped west of the Dnieper, snow piling over them like the dirt of a premature grave. The town of Korsun was the anchor, but it might as well have been a noose—strung between Kaniv and Cherkassy, tightening by the hour.

Kurt stared at the map Kris had just rolled open, but his eyes weren't on the lines. They were on Hill 239—and the tiny ink mark just past it. That was where Conrad's unit had last been reported. His brother. His stubborn, reckless, grinning brother. Trapped.

The Soviets had done this before—at Stalingrad. They were doing it again, grinding their way through the snow with artillery and hunger and cold as their allies. And this time, his brother, Conrad, was inside the vice.

Kurt's jaw tightened. He could still hear Kris's voice: "They're completely cut off. No supplies, no airlift. Manstein's trying to get Hitler to send help, but... " That *but* had hung in the air like smoke from a burning tank. *Goddamn it, Conrad. Why is it always you?* Kurt had lost count of the times he'd pulled his brother out of one mess or another—bar fights, motorbike crashes, drunken teenage stunts. But this wasn't some bruised ego or broken wrist. This was a death trap. And there was nothing Kurt could do—yet.

Not unless Manstein got his way. Not unless Hitler listened—*this time*. Field Marshal Erich von Manstein, Commander of Army Group South, had flown to Rastenburg, Hitler's headquarters, hoping to convince him to send reinforcements for a Cherkassy breakout. He warned of the looming disaster—another Stalingrad in the making—and begged for a relief force to be assembled. Reluctantly, Hitler agreed.

Manstein moved quickly, organizing the relief operation under the codename "Blake Regiment."

Kurt's heart sank as Kris's words processed in his mind. Conrad—his brother—was one of the trapped units. Right there, on the wrong side of Hill 239. Trouble always seemed to follow Conrad, most of it his own doing. Kurt couldn't shake the nagging thought—had his brother finally run out of luck?

Decker's voice cut through his thoughts, sharp and commanding. "Listen up, men!" He raised a crinkling piece of paper in his hand, eyes scanning the men before him. "We've been assigned, with 17 other Tigers, to be part of the Korsun-Cherkassy Pocket relief effort. We're attached to the newly formed 'Blake Regiment'—that's the main tank force assigned to break the trapped units out of the encirclement."

He paused for a moment, letting the weight of the news settle in. "We need the Hammer Power of the Tigers to crack through the Russian lines. We're going in hot, and we're going in hard. The Soviets aren't giving an inch, and we'll have to fight our way through every yard. But we've got the strength. We've got the firepower."

Kurt's mind raced, absorbing Decker's words, but they barely reached him. "Blake Regiment." It was their best chance at getting Conrad and the rest of the trapped men out alive. But the weight of the situation hit him hard—he wasn't just fighting for his country or comrades now. His brother was out there, and this mission would be the difference between life and death.

"Get your gear ready," Decker continued, his tone stern. "We leave in thirty minutes. We're not just going to rescue them—we're going to take that hill and make the Soviets regret ever crossing our path."

Kurt's hands clenched around the straps of his gear. For the first time in days, a surge of purpose coursed through him. He might not be able to control the chaos of war, but this—this was something he could truly fight for: his brother and the men trapped behind enemy lines. And now, with the "Blake Regiment," there was hope.

There was no hesitation. No question in his mind.

Kris, always perceptive, asked, "Maybe there's some way we can help your brother?"

"We'll be closer tomorrow night," Kurt said, his voice pragmatic, though his insides were anything but. "Once there, we'll see."

"I thought you and he didn't get along," said Kris, his eyes searching Kurt's face, sensing more than Kurt was willing to admit.

Kurt's jaw tightened, and for a moment, the words burned in his throat. His mind flashed back to the time after Conrad and Nikol had gotten engaged. At first, it seemed like everything Conrad and she had hoped for, but as the months passed, Conrad had grown distant, slipping away little by little.

For Conrad, it had taken him a couple of years, but he had finally "won" the beautiful fiancée. Nikol loved him dearly. Yet, being Conrad, commitments meant nothing when weighed against his own whims. He was always chasing something shinier, something just out of reach.

From Kurt's perspective, it wasn't just selfish—it was emotionally reckless, needlessly cruel. And in the end, Conrad shattered Nikol's heart, left her in pieces, and never once looked back with remorse. Later, after realities settled in, he did have regrets—but, by then, it was far too late.

Kurt couldn't deny that even thinking of rescuing Conrad on Hill 239 felt complicated. Why should he even consider helping the man, his own brother, who had hurt Nikol so deeply? Conrad might be family, but Nikol was someone Kurt felt fiercely protective of. Conrad hadn't wronged Kurt directly, but, to Kurt, helping him felt like a betrayal to Nikol. Why should Kurt help the man who had caused her so much undeserved pain?

Kurt turned toward the Dragon of War Tiger, seeing it, his hand instinctively brushed against the dragon necklace around his neck—a quiet reminder of the bond he shared with Nikol. The camp buzzed with tension, men moving like sparks before the fire. But Kurt's mind was elsewhere—on Conrad. Stupid, selfish, unforgivable. But still his brother. And he couldn't let him die out there. Not in Russia. Not when capture meant torture, starvation, or worse. He climbed back into the tank, the weight of his indecision settling like a stone in his gut. Tomorrow would be a reckoning—not just for Conrad, but for himself. He paused for a moment, then popped a mint. In the morning, distant artillery rumbled faintly, echoing across the horizon like distant thunder. Kurt and Kris grabbed some rations and coffee.

"This cold might kill us faster than the Russians," Kris said quietly, almost to himself. His hand rested lightly on the frost-coated flank of their Dragon Tiger. "Let's hope this beast still starts."

Kurt, his lips cracked and chapped, replied, "It better. We've got a lot of men counting on us." He popped another mint. Kurt climbed inside the Tiger, where Stefan was coddling the batteries. Crouching beside him, Kurt tapped his shoulder. "Stefan, hey—do you know if our support crew brought everything we'll need for the Tiger? Spare tracks, rubber gaskets, grousers, jacks, firing pins, Leitz lenses?"

Stefan looked up, startled. "Are you serious, Kurt? This is Captain Krauss we're talking about. The man's a legend when it comes to Tiger logistics. If we needed a single spare track, he'd probably send someone to Hitler's bunker to fetch it. He saves everything. No surprises."

Kurt leaned closer. "But do you know if he has the original gear that came with the Tiger?"

Stefan nodded. "You know how anal he is about Tiger parts? Last month, he was bragging about a dozen crates of factory-original snorkels he's hauled all over Russia."

"We actually got the snorkels, huh?" Kurt raised an eyebrow, intrigued.

Stefan grinned. "Yeah. If we ever have to cross a river, I guess we're covered. Though in this freezing hell, let's hope it doesn't ever come to that."

"Hmm. Maybe…" Kurt's mind was already turning.

"What are you thinking?" Stefan asked, tilted his head, curious.

Kurt: "Never mind." He murmured to himself, half lost in thought: *A few months ago, Krauss told me only the first 500 Tigers got them. Like it says on the turret, said we were Tiger #301.*

Stefan shrugged without looking up, his focus still on the batteries. "Lucky us, I guess. Just hope we don't need them." Kurt's thoughts shifted, and the idea began to take shape in his mind, but he kept it to himself.

"I just love this world." He nodded faintly, muttering under his breath.

The biting wind tore at Kurt's scarf as he straightened, scanning the frozen horizon. Behind him, Kris cursed the cold, unaware of the mental calculus raging behind Kurt's eyes. Engines rumbled in the distance—subtle, but growing—while the wind carried the brittle echo of artillery. The relief force was on the move. But if they didn't break through…

Kursk had left a scar. This—Korsun—could easily become a second Stalingrad. Kurt sank into his seat as the cold of the early morning seeped through the steel walls of the Tiger. His fingers tightened around the controls, checking the gun sight again and making sure everything was in place. The rumble of the engine vibrated through the tank, but it was the silence that seemed the loudest. His focus was absolute now, his senses heightened as they prepared for the assault. Across from him, Stefan adjusted his position, his eyes flicking between the controls and the darkness outside. The engine had been running for 15 minutes already, just like all Tigers did before they moved. Stefan was always calm before battle, a steady hand amidst the chaos. But even he wasn't immune to the weight of what was to come.

The quiet was broken by Decker's voice crackling through the comms. "Listen up," he began, his tone as firm as ever. "We attack at 4 AM, sharp. We move fast, hit hard, and keep your eyes open. The Soviets are dug in, but we'll break them. Let's go." Kurt's heart quickened at the sound of Decker's voice. The words hit him with a force he couldn't ignore. This wasn't just another mission—it was their chance to break through, to rescue the tens of thousands trapped behind enemy lines. It was everything they had been training for, and the stakes had never been higher.

He looked over at Stefan, who gave a small nod, adjusting his grip on the controls. The low hum of the engine filled the tank's interior, and for a moment, time seemed to stretch. There was nothing more to do now but wait for the command.

The seconds ticked away, each one heavier than the last. Kurt's eyes flicked over the controls one last time before locking onto the sights, his breath steady despite the tension. And then, as if on cue, Decker's voice came through the comms again: "Now! Forward!"

As the Blake Regiment advanced on command, Stefan slammed the Dragon Tiger's throttle forward. The massive engine roared to life, and the tank surged into the darkness. Kurt felt the lurch beneath him—and with it, a rush of adrenaline. The rescue assault on Korsun-Cherkasy had begun.

The roar of the Dragon Tiger's engine drowned out the rest of the world as they charged into the fray, the rest of the platoon following closely behind. Target: Hill 239. On an opposite hill, the Soviets saw them coming.

A distance away, Captain Marat stood atop a T-34, gripping a field radio. From his elevated position, he commanded his section of the Russian defensive line, using the vantage point to direct the tank column advancing below. The roar of engines and the sharp crack of distant cannon fire filled the air, but his focus remained on the chaotic battlefield spread out before him. Through his binoculars, Marat watched in mounting fury as the Tigers decimated, in rapid succession, one T-34 after another. They erupted into flames, their crews scrambling—or failing—to escape the infernos. The landscape was now littered with blackened Soviet wrecks, smoke billowing skyward in a grim testament to the slaughter.

"Damn it!" Marat roared, slamming his fists on the tank's turret in frustration. His knuckles scraped against the rough-hewn steel, but he didn't care. The battlefield was a disaster, and the German Tigers were tearing through his column with surgical violence and precision.

He spun toward the command tank's radio operator, his voice sharp and urgent. "Call up the reserve company! We're losing too many tanks out there. We can't even get close before ours turn into flaming coffins!"

The operator made the call. Marat continued seething. He saw the facts: *these fucking Tigers are a nightmare!* Below him, the T-34s continued their brave but futile advance, Russian shells bouncing off the Tigers' thick armor as the Tigers' return fire picked them off one by one. In the Dragon Tiger, Kurt could squeeze off one round every thirty seconds if needed. Marat's jaw tightened as he gripped the binoculars harder. He knew he was sending his men to certain death—knew it in his bones. But retreat wasn't an option. Not for him. Not in Stalin's army. The Russian line had to hold, even if he had to burn through every last crew to make it happen.

Thick clouds of black smoke from the now burning vehicles filled the valley at the northern sector of Hill 239. Tank crews struggled to free themselves from their burning German and Russian tanks. Many did not make it.

As the battle slowed, a German Famo Tiger-recovery half-track and a 20-man infantry unit advanced through wreckage and shell-chewed ditches. Their mission: retrieve a disabled Tiger—its transmission blown and stranded deep in the chaos.

Though immobile, the Tiger was far from defenseless. Its 88mm cannon hurled high-explosive shells with thunderous defiance, while twin screaming MG34s—coaxial beside the main gun and bow-mounted—raked the front. Ivan had already tried two furious assaults... both failed with many of its assaulting soldiers cut down. Now they stayed low, wary of the wounded beast that still bit—and of the Panzergrenadiers and rescue Famo closing in.

The Famo engine groaned under the strain of the uneven ground. Flanked by a Hanomag and its suppressive M34 machine gun, the Famo pressed on, shrugging off bursts of small-arms fire snapping through the air. Once the heavy chains were affixed, bit by bit, they dragged the great beast toward safety. At last, after what felt like an eternity, the Famo crawled meter by meter into the rear with the Tiger in tow. The rescue was more than just a mechanical feat—it was a testament to courage and coordination. The Tiger crew had kept radio contact alive, guiding the infantry in with precise directions under fire. This kind of communication, drilled endlessly in training, had paid off when it mattered most. As the battlefield's roar faded towards evening silence, the men knew: today, discipline and teamwork had saved a tank—and the lives inside it.

Now back at the staging area, Kurt had been thinking of how to get Conrad and his team out of the south side of Hill 239. He remembered his father's words: *"You'll know when it's the right time to take chances and push it."*

Korsun-Cherkassy Relief | Day One | Afternoon

By late afternoon of day one, the Tigers were refueled and re-armed, getting ready for another push on the north side of Hill 239 tomorrow. Both fuel and ammo were in very limited supply. Kurt decided he needed to take action to save his brother if he could. Family was important to him, even if it was Conrad.

Kurt: "Since they'll be soaked and cold, we've got blankets, extra jackets, dry pants, socks, and laundry bags for their wet clothes. Krauss helped out. We can set up temporary warming tents with propane heaters for them to change. We've also got rubber river rafts for the wounded, with ropes tied to each end to shuttle them back and forth." Decker scratched his head, visibly thinking.

Kurt: "If we cross by midnight, we might get 200-300 men out before Ivan notices and tries to crash the party. That way, we'll still be fully operational for tomorrow's fight. We've trained for this, so this will be a Tiger first—a surprise for Ivan. And the German Cross in Gold for you! Plus, an ocean of publicity for the innovative, successful application of advanced German technology: the Tiger One tank." Kurt took a breath. Kurt's voice was steady, but there was an edge to it.

"I won't lie to you. From Kris's radio chatter, I've learned my brother's grenadier unit is on the south hill with the trapped men. If he's alive, I'll do everything I can to get him back." The words hung in the air—a solemn promise to himself and his comrades. The weight of his brother's fate pressed heavily on him, but there was no turning back now. The mission was clear, and whatever the cost, Kurt was determined to see it through.

Decker stepped off to the side, pulled out a map, and did some mental calculations. After a moment, he approached the truck and examined the unopened snorkel equipment boxes, feeling the factory-fresh seals. Nearby, two transport half-track trucks stood ready.

He found and spoke with Captain Krauss, who eagerly reinforced Kurt's plan and volunteered two experienced engineers to help prep the Dragon Tiger for the water crossing. Krauss added that, once across, he'd see to it the crew had warmth and shelter.

Commander Decker ran the situation through his mind. Hard times called for unconventional ideas, and the Tiger's designers had built solutions for moments like this right into the tank. He paused, thinking a moment longer. Kurt's plan was risky—but it offered a real chance to rescue 200, maybe 300 grenadiers, including, if fate allowed, Kurt's brother. And all with minimal losses.

Decker also knew Kurt had already been passed over for the Knight's Cross three times. The last recommendation was met with a single-word reply: "Krakow"—a pointed reference to the rail yard incident, when Kurt stood up to an SS guard over the mistreating of Russian prisoner. of war. It wasn't a question of courage or combat record. It was about ideology. Kurt hadn't bought into the Nazi dogma—and Decker understood the system would never forgive that.

And yet, Decker mused, he, himself, might even earn the German Cross for pulling this off—innovative leadership with the Panzer corps' most powerful weapon. Maybe even a future at Henschel after the war. The worst-case? They lose a Tiger in the river—but Krauss had chains and engineers ready if recovery was needed.

In addition, the post-battle Blake Regiment notes would likely highlight this as a bold, unconventional maneuver by Commander Decker—a decisive action that rescued 300 soldiers who would never have made it out otherwise. The safe, conventional path tugged at him—but Decker knew what was right. He thought back to something from officer training, a Goethe quote that had stayed with him: "Magic is believing in yourself; if you can do that, you can make anything happen." This wasn't about orders or protocol anymore. It was about doing what needed to be done.

This plan was bold, unexpected—exactly the kind of maneuver the Russians won't see coming. Decker is thought that sometimes, risks had to be taken. And if anyone deserved this shot, it's Kurt. After a few minutes, he returns. Decker to Kurt: "I've got a problem."

Kurt: "What?"

Decker: "I can't swim." (Joking)

Kurt: "I can."

Decker: "Ok, you take the Dragon Tiger and I'll take the backup Tiger. I'll first get it approved upstairs as an evening recon in force".

Kurt, "Thanks sir. When this works, I promise you will get the Knight's Cross for thinking this up, Commander." He winked at Decker. He popped a mint and gave one to Decker.

Surprised at the mint, Commander Decker said, "So you stopped smoking?" Kurt, "Yah. Someone reminded me that there is, if you look close enough for it, still some sweetness in life. Believe it or not, even here at the Korsun-Cherkassy Pocket."

Kurt and Kris met up with Stefan and Ottmar to gather the equipment and begin the water-crossing preparations. There's a lot of work ahead. Meanwhile, Decker went to round up Grenadier volunteers and a Hanomag Flak unit. To seal the tank turret ring, they inflated large rubber industrial inner tubes from the Henschel boxes. The vision slits and gun ports already have rubberized seals built in. They used grease to freshen the rubber seals.

With the help of Hauptmann Krauss's two engineers, they assembled and secured the snorkel vertically on the back deck to handle air intake and exhaust gases. The snorkel, a tall, ungainly pipe, stood 3 meters (9 feet 10 inches) above the back deck like a smokestack on a train. Krauss was thrilled just see the gear finally being used as intended.

Kraus and the driver, Stefan, review everything mechanical to assure a safe river crossing and return. Kurt joins them.

Stefan: "Remind me how deep we can go."

Kurt: "We have a solid safety margin. Kris and I checked it yesterday, and the deepest river spot here is currently only 2 meters (6 feet 7 inches), well below the turret top. We drown if the river's deeper than 4.5 meters (14 feet 10 inches). But that leaves me, as the commander, with a clear view for close-in fire suppression with the cupola MG34. For you, it'll be a piece of cake—you just drive straight as a ruler *but* you must keep us moving while in the water. It will be super slow. You can do that, can't you? Just like they taught us."

Stefan: "I'll do it, but I don't like driving with my eyes closed."

Kurt: "I'll be your eyes. You just have to trust me on this one." Kurt checked his watch and tattoo—it's 10 PM.

At that moment, Decker orders "Move out." The sounds of artillery fire masked their movements as the "recon force" headed toward the river crossing area Kurt and Kris scouted yesterday. They took cover behind bushes on a slight rise, waiting for the attack to begin. Kurt's in the Dragon Tiger, snorkel in place. Beside him is Decker in Tiger #2, with two transport trucks loaded with supplies and a Hanomag Quad 20 mm Flak unit. Troops were unloading blankets, food, extra clothing, water, and set up a tent with portable heaters.

Kurt told Ottmar: "We won't need a loader with the tank all buttoned up."

Ottmar is sad, "I wouldn't miss this for the world." Kurt smiled. Ottmar was clearly motivated.

Kurt: "Alright, big guy. Just this once. You get the loader's hatch next to mine. Pack a beach towel and lunch and get back here." Ottmar rushed off to grab machine pistols, grenades, and ammo. Kurt checked his extra ammo on the turret deck.

Kris radioed in, confirming the trapped troops are ready. There was still distant artillery fire, and machine guns chatter in the distance. The Russians love fighting at night.

Kris to Kurt: "The grenadiers are set— about 175 men, including the wounded. They report a picket line of Ivan light machine guns between us and them. When we start the crossing, the grenadiers will wait 10 minutes while we lay down suppression fire. After that, they'll advance to break out. They're low on ammo, but motivated. They'll clean up what we miss."

Kurt: "Excellent." Kurt checked his watch—midnight.

Kris, via the radio, reported: "Commander Decker says go!" "Excellent," replied Kurt. He checked his watch—midnight. The Dragon tattoo on his wrist caught his eye, and for a brief second, his

150

thoughts flickered to Nikol—her voice, her fire, the way she used to trace that ink with her fingers. Then he refocused. The crossing was on.

Kris snapped his head around. "Decker says go—move!"

Kurt to Stefan: "Drive straight ahead until we reach the river's edge. I'll let you know when we are there."

Suddenly, the air erupted in organized chaos. White flares lit up the far side of the river. The Russian picket machine guns opened fire. The Flak unit and Decker's Tiger #2 charged over the crest, stopped, and laid down suppression fire on the Russian positions. The Flak wagon unleashed an ungodly barrage of 20 mm tracer rounds. Kurt points to Ottmar: "Look". He pointed out the tracers from the Quad Flak Hanomag, "the fingers of death." In two minutes, silence fell, except for the distant artillery. Kurt's Dragon Tiger advanced, reaching the river's edge. Infantry check the fastenings of the four tied ropes off the back deck of the Dragon Tiger. Kurt: "Halt, Stefan. We're at the water's edge."

They froze. Gunfire erupted from the right, but —Kurt silenced it with a three-second burst from his MG34, and the threat went silent. He ordered Stefan, "Drive". The Tiger started its crossing. In a minute, the water rose over the front deck like a barge. Four knotted ropes spooled from the shore to the back of the tank. Four rafts, with armed infantry, shove off to join them in the crossing.

In the dim moonlight, Ottmar grinned: "This is fun. Hope we get submarine hazard pay for today." Halfway across, the tank submerged further, the water reached the base of the turret. Kurt and Ottmar get sprayed by the water, and a subtle sucking sound emanated from the snorkel. Kurt smiled. Kurt: "I'll have to send a personal note to the Henschel snorkel designers after the war."

Ottmar beamed, chewing gum with a wide grin. Kurt talked to Kris, "Get on the radio, let Decker know we're officially the first U-Boat in Russia." The engine was muffled by the water as they moved forward. The Tiger, moving slowly, finally reached the shore and had pulled fully out of the water onto the beach, dripping like a beached whale.

Kurt ordered Stefan, "Halt." With the pre-arranged 10-minute window over, the trapped Grenadiers stormed through the silenced picket line, rushed to the waiting Tiger and the attached life lines. They were starved, ragged, and freezing— but free— they were free. They lined up at the ropes, hand-over-hand through the frigid moving water. The wounded are were helped onto rafts.

The river, once a barrier, had become the gateway to their escape.

A wounded German soldier spotted the Dragon logo and called out from a stretcher passing near the Tiger. A bloodied figure shouted, "Kurt! Kurt Knispel! It's me, Conrad, your brother! What the hell are you doing here? This is crazy!" Kurt jumped down from the tank, and Conrad struggled to sit up from the stretcher, using a makeshift crutch. The brothers embraced.

Kurt: "Brother Conrad, I twisted some arms." He points toward Decker perched on Tiger #2, across the river. Decker, ever vigilant, noticed the brothers' embrace through his binoculars and tipped his cap.

Conrad, smiled through the pain: "Well, you little short shit sure showed your big brother you've grown up. Not only did you save my ass, but my whole unit—what's left of it."

Kurt scanned his brother's injuries, concern in his eyes. "Your leg looks like you ran into a wild pig. Get in the raft. I'll catch up with you. You need proper treatment. Don't die before I get there." Conrad struggled into the raft, and Kurt checked with the medic about where they'll take him. He gave Conrad a mint, who looked up with a painful grin. "Thanks."

The next morning at the indicated German aid station, doctors and nurses tended to a flood of wounded soldiers. Conrad laid on a stretcher on the ground, surrounded by moans and screams. A blood-stained nurse worked on his massive leg wound.

Nurse: "Stay with us, big boy. The doctor will get to you when he finishes with the others." She nodded toward the long line of waiting men.

Kurt entered the tent, looking a wreck—his face covered in soot, dark circles under his eyes. He checked with a nurse, who shrugged. The tent lights flicker as artillery shells land nearby. He approached another who can't help him. Kurt then approached a nurse with a clipboard, who, checking her clipboard, pointed him to his brother. Conrad looked up.

Conrad, "Kurt, you look awful." Conrad suddenly winced, pain shot through his leg. He clenched his teeth, his face contorting.

Kurt: "I brought this for you. It's been lucky for me, and it'll bring you luck too." He took the dragon pendant off his neck and placed it around Conrad's neck.

Conrad, through gritted teeth asked, "Isn't that Nikol's?"

Pain seized Conrad again, and he groaned. The head nurse arrived from the operating table.

Nurse: "Alright, soldier, you're next."

Kurt and the nurse helped Conrad up. He moaned in agony as they place him on a gurney. The nurse looked at Kurt.

Nurse: "We need your help. We're short-handed today."

They moved Conrad to the field operating table, and the nurse inserted a leather bit into his mouth. Dr. Schramm, the battalion surgeon, approached. Dr. Schramm: "This leg has to go." He turned to Kurt: "I want you to hold his leg. No matter what. He'll scream, but don't let go. I've given him some painkillers, but this will still hurt like hell." Kurt took Conrad's leg firmly in both hands.

The nurse handed Dr. Schramm a bone saw, and he began. Conrad writhed in agony, screaming. Blood spurted onto Kurt's face. Kurt flinched and wiped it away. Kurt gripped Conrad's leg tighter, his fingers sunk into the flesh, a desperate attempt to steady both his brother and himself. Kurt's eyes squeezed shut. Whatever they were doing, he couldn't watch—not this time. Darkness was the only mercy he could offer himself.

The sawing continued, each stroke a harsh, rhythmic sound that stretched time itself, dragging it out in a cruel, endless rhythm. The pain-filled screams tear through the air, echoing in Kurt's ears, searing into his mind. With every stroke, the weight of his brother's leg grew heavier in his hands, becoming an increasingly unbearable burden, until it feels like he can't do it anymore."

Dr. Schramm, his voice harsh: "Open your eyes, soldier. We've got more patients." Kurt blinked and opened his eyes. The tent lights flickered, casting an eerie glow. Then it hit him—Conrad had already been taken away to recovery. His mind raced, trying to understand why the weight in his hands felt so wrong. And then he realized: he was holding his brother's severed leg. The image wouldn't leave him.

Hours later, as Kurt trudged through churned snow and scattered wreckage, the weight of that moment clung to him like frostbite. Around him, the battered break-out survivors of the German force pushed west—silent, hollow-eyed, broken. The retreat from Korsun-Cherkassy was no orderly withdrawal. The Soviets were relentless. It was a German collapse. To Kurt, it felt like Kursk all over again—a second great unraveling. Another bitter taste of defeat.

Stefan and Ottmar joined him at the front of the Dragon Tiger. Stefan looked up and pointed at the scorched dragon painted on the turret side.

"Still got heart…" he muttered.

"And a gun," quipped Ottmar. He affectionally patted the barrel.

Ten days later, as Blake Regiment rumbled westward through thawing earth and patches of dirty snow, the chaos of Korsun still lived in their bones. Inside the turret, Decker's voice cut through the static on the platoon radio. "The Korson battle reports are in," he said flatly. "Of the sixty thousand men trapped, over forty thousand made it out." He didn't need to say the rest. The silence carried the weight of twenty thousand lost. Decker exhaled, then added, "We left behind virtually all the heavy equipment. But forty thousand lived. That's something. That's something the Blake Regiment can be proud of."

Kurt didn't answer. He stared ahead, jaw tight, the engine's vibration humming beneath his boots. This wasn't a victory—it was a blood-soaked retreat. And whatever had once felt unbreakable in the Wehrmacht had cracked. They had broken out, yes—but not through strength. Through desperation. Hill 239 still burned in his mind. The Russians had let nothing go unpunished. And as the retreat dragged on, one truth loomed larger than the road ahead: the Red Army wasn't slowing down. Kurt felt a bitter pang. The numbers Decker rattled off confirmed what he'd feared all along. This wasn't victory—it was survival by inches. Just like Kursk. The Tigers had led the Blake Regiment's push, and yes, they'd pulled off something resembling an orderly retreat. But it wasn't enough. The tools of war that were meant to protect those 60,000 men now lay abandoned—broken and burning on Hill 239, scattered like bones across the snow.

In the battle's grim aftermath, one truth stood out: the Red Army's push was far from over. Whatever plans the Germans still clung to in the East had become little more than illusion—flickering shadows retreating west, surviving on borrowed time, and unable to outrun what was coming. Kurt could feel the weight of the retreat in his bones, the loss of ground pressing on him. The Soviet advance wouldn't be stopped. How much longer could they hold out?

Even as they tried to regroup, the Luftwaffe's ability to support them from the air had been irreparably diminished, a final blow to their already fragile hopes. In spite of the success of the partial German breakout, the Soviets again seized the strategic initiative, their pressure unrelenting. For three grueling months, Soviet forces capitalized on the disarray within German ranks, launching continuous offensives that turned retreat into a test of endurance. What began as a tactical withdrawal for the Wehrmacht evolved into a desperate and increasingly chaotic semi-organized retreat westward.

By May 1944, Kurt's official combat tally had reached 113 confirmed tank kills—101 of them achieved in the Dragon Tiger. On May 20th, he was promoted to Feldwebel (Staff Sergeant) and became the third member of the 503rd Heavy Panzer Battalion to receive the German Cross in Gold. He was also awarded the long-overdue Panzer Assault Badge.

Kurt's kill count had far exceeded that of many tank commanders who had already received the Knight's Cross, the highest battlefield honor. Despite this, he remained without it. At least three formal recommendations had been submitted on his behalf—including one by Oberstleutnant Franz Bake, who led the stunning Korsun-Cherkassy relief rescue. But each time, the request was quietly denied—not due to lack of merit, but because of politics. It was well-known, and remembered, that Kurt was not "in the club". The shadow of the Krakow incident, where Kurt had openly defied an SS Guard, still followed him.

Things were way different on the real battlefield; Kurt Knispel was a legend. Across the Eastern Front, experienced Russian tankers whispered warnings: "Beware the Dragon Tiger." Unlike the Western Front, the Eastern Front had no rules—it wasn't about tactics. It was about raw survival. No prisoners. No food. No justice. No safety anywhere. And humanity was the exception to the rule.

But conversely in the comfy distant inner circles of the Nazi regime, Kurt Knispel was an embarrassment—a political complication they didn't know how to reward or erase. Had he been SS instead of Wehrmacht, things might have gone very differently. But he hadn't. He had a personal code he wouldn't violate. He wouldn't swear loyalty to Hitler. He swore it to Germany. And that made all the difference. Unlike the SS, he fought in the regular Wehrmacht—Germany's army, not the Party's.

But one legend alone couldn't stop the tide. He and his unit did their best to hold back the flood of never-ending Russian soldiers, artillery, and tanks. For every one they took down, three more would pop up in their place.

By the spring of '44, Kurt received orders for leave to return home. Even before he left, the orders came in: Kurt and the crew were selected as one of the few chosen for intensive training in the second generation of the Tiger tank. He was to return after his leave to central Germany, where he would report to Paderborn for a strategic briefing, training, and preparations for the new generation of armored warfare.

Chapter 15—The Dragon Returns

Kurt rode in the back of an open truck, shoulder to shoulder with a full load of soldiers. Clouds of dust swirled around the convoy as it rumbled down a rutted road. Just outside a small village, the column rolled to a stop to refuel and resupply. The men climbed down stiffly, grateful for a chance to stretch their legs.

Then, from just over a nearby ridge—short, sharp bursts of machine-gun fire. Without thinking, every front-line soldier dropped flat to the ground—Kurt included. Years of combat had drilled the instinct into their bones. But none of the local troops even flinched.

Kurt slowly got up, brushing dirt and dust from his uniform. He looked around, puzzled, then approached a nearby military policeman standing at ease near the trucks. Kurt stepped forward, looking over to the area of gunfire. "I'm just in from the front. I can guess what's going on?" The Military Policeman gestured toward the chaos. "Yeah, just more SS partisan actions. This particular unit purged more communists, Jews, gypsies, and partisans than three SS units put together."

The guard nodded in the direction of the nearby armored command car. Kurt's attention shifted, and he spotted the figure leaning against the vehicle, taking pictures. He recognized Major Berndt. Changing film, the Major looks up. Their eyes meet briefly, a silent recognition passing between them. The Major opened his mouth to speak, but before he could say anything, a crackling radio call demanded his attention. He turned abruptly, his focus shifting, as he answered the call.

Two days later, Kurt walked into his home in his Panzer uniform and cap. His uniform was more faded than before but still black and crisp.

Dad came in. Big hug. "I am so proud of you, son. They called you a 'Tank Ace.' They even mentioned you last week in an official Wehrmacht radio broadcast. It's the only time they ever mentioned a non-commissioned officer ".

Kurt smiled big with his father's praise. They hug again. Mom came in and they hugged. She had tears during her hug. Conrad hobbled into the room, in civilian clothes, on crutches, on his one leg. He's emotional.

"Hey lil brother! I told everyone what you did." Kurt and Conrad had a brotherly hug. "Welcome home. Thanks for what you did at Hill 239."

Kurt: "That means a lot to me. Thanks. So, what did you learn on your adventures?"

Conrad, "That's an easy one to answer. I learned I can't win every time." Points at his missing leg. He wipes his wet eyes. Conrad reaches around his neck and takes the dragon necklace off.

He hobbled over to Kurt. "You going to need this more than me. Hope I didn't use up all the magic." Conrad put it around Kurt's neck.

Sister, Katrina, and Nikol bounded through the front door. Kurt hugged Nikol and then Katrina. Then hugged them both again together. Nikol's parents, Dr and Mrs. Rezek also came to the door.

Dr Rezek: "Hope it's OK for Nikol's parents to join in? Nikol told us of your expected return today. We wanted to welcome you home also."

Kurt: "Of course, it's fortuitous you stopped by." Kurt motioned Dr. Rezek to join him privately in the other room. After a few minutes they return. All form a semi-circle. Kurt gets on one knee in front of Nikol.

Kurt: "Nikol, I want you to know—I've already spoken with your father. No matter what happens, I want you in my life, in my family."

Kurt paused, his hand slipping into his pocket. In his usual awkwardness, he accidentally pulls out a mint, eyes widening in surprise. He hesitates for a moment, then quickly shoves it back into his pocket, fumbled slightly before pulling out a small, velvet box.

He opened it carefully, revealing a shimmering ring. The world seemed to pause, the tension building for a brief moment. Kurt: "Will you marry me? What do you say?"

There's a beat of silence before Nikol, her eyes twinkling with mischief, leans forward with a teasing smile. Nikol: "Only if I get my mint first. And only if you say 'please'."

Kurt chuckled, letting out a breath of relief, as if this was the last response he expected. With a grin, he fished the mint back out of his pocket, as if it's the most precious thing in the world. He leans in closer.

Nikol takes the mint, her smile widening, before she gives him a quick wink.

Kurt: *"Please."*

Nikol: "Well, since you *finally* asked the right way... yes."

She grinned, and he slid the ring onto her finger. They kissed, holding each other tightly, their laughter mingling with the quiet joy of the moment.

A couple days later, they were married. He wore the only thing he had that passed for formal—his black Panzer uniform. It wasn't the black of the SS. It was the grease-stained black of a Wehrmacht Panzer crewman—cleaned up for the day, but still unmistakable.

The Iron Cross sat sharp beneath the ribbon bar. The Panzer Assault Badge clung to his chest like a symbol of everything he'd survived. The Eastern Front Medal gleamed beside it, earned the hard way, across four brutal years in the East. There was no Knight's Cross—not for men like him. Not without the party pin. But the steel in his eyes had earned him something rarer: the respect of every man who'd seen him fight.

They exited the chapel with rice and confetti everywhere. They got into the wedding car and leave for an all-too-brief honeymoon in the mountains.

Chapter 16—The Crowned Beast–King Tiger

The wedding was over. The mountain air still clung to his skin, but the quiet was already fading. War had a way of calling him back before he was ready. And when it called this time, it came on treads a meter wide and armor too thick and slanted to believe. Kurt had seen plenty of tanks—but nothing like this. He'd heard the whispers even before training began: each one cost over 350,000 Reichsmarks—nearly triple the cost of a Panzer IV and far more than the Tiger I. It was the most expensive machine the Wehrmacht had ever rolled onto the battlefield, and it demanded the best.

Kurt knew the expectations, especially now that he was a commander. These weren't just tanks—they were weapon platforms that required elite crews to unlock their full potential. Only 146 crews had made the cut from the hundreds evaluated. Kurt's entire crew had been selected—proof of their skill, and a sign that command was watching. But it was clear who had tipped the balance.

Kurt Knispel, with his unmatched kill count and unshakable calm under fire, had become more than just a gunner; his Dragon Tank was already a legend among the troops. With a record like his, it was inevitable that he would be entrusted with the command of the new Tiger II.

To the upper echelons, though, he was still a problem they didn't know how to market. He never joined the Party, refused to parrot propaganda, and saved his admiration for fellow soldiers—not dogma. While others with half his record posed for newsreels and dined in Berlin with the brass, Kurt stayed in the field. His four recommendations for the Knight's Cross were denied.

Upon receiving his new orders, this time as the commander, Knispel arrived in Paderborn, Germany, for four weeks of intensive training on the Tiger II. From the moment he saw the massive beast in profile, he knew this was no incremental upgrade—it was a leap. The King Tiger was a fortress on tracks.

The crew gathered for briefings, wide-eyed and half skeptical. But as they walked around it, as the engineers spoke, the reality began to settle in.

The Armor

Kurt ran his gloved hand along the sloped front glacis. *Fifty degrees, 150 mm thick.* It was like facing a moving bunker. Unlike the flat armor of earlier German tanks, the angled plates meant shells that once punched through would now ricochet uselessly. He'd seen the damage Soviet could take thanks to their T-34 sloped armor. Now, the Germans were returning the favor—with better steel and thicker plating. From the front, this thing was damn near invincible.

The Gun

But it was the gun that made Kurt's pulse quicken. "Oh my", said Kurt, when he was introduced to the 88 mm KwK 43 L/71. It was a monster—longer, heavier, and more precise than anything he'd ever fired. During live drills, he watched in awe as targets shattered at 3,000 meters (9,800 feet). The enemy wouldn't even see them coming. Kurt realized this was 1,000 meters *beyond* his own record 2,000-meter kill at Kursk.

He leaned over to their new gunner, Sgt. Gregor Dotzer. "They'll never get close enough to shoot back." Gregor nodded in agreement.

It wasn't just power. It was dominance. And behind that long, menacing barrel, Kurt felt it. The battlefield had shifted. He didn't have to wait for trouble anymore—he now had the potential to erase it before it ever arrived.

Ottmar's eyes bulged when he learned each Tiger II shell weighed nearly 50 pounds—about 20% heavier than before in the Tiger I.

The extra weight wasn't a flaw—it was deliberate. More propellant, more reach, more impact. A larger cartridge case and extra propellant boosted muzzle velocity by 30%, that allowed the incredible unmatched lethal reach of the gun.

At Paderborn Kurt met with Commander Decker. He shook Kurt's hand firmly. Decker: "Congratulations on your wedding. And, of course, congrats on your command which is long overdue. Your 126 victories tell that story better than I ever could. That well-earned 'Cross in Gold' suits your uniform perfectly.

Bad news and good news. Bad news is we tried again, for the fourth time. to get you the 'Knight's Cross,' but... well, the Krakow incident hasn't been forgotten by some very high-level types. Good news is I was able to wrestle with personnel to make sure you got all our old crew again and we got you Gregor one of the best gunners, after yourself of course." Kurt nodded; his gratitude evident.

Kurt: "Thank you, sir. I owe you everything."

Later, Kurt stood beside the new Dragon Tiger II, its imposing mass cast a long shadow in the fading light. The Dragon logo now adorned the turret, freshly painted and gleaming with purpose. One by one, the crew members approached the Dragon King Tiger, each pausing to touch the logo—a ritual of unity born from shared trials.

Kurt, the new commander, was the first to approach the tank. At his chest, Nikol's pendant caught the light, a quiet reminder of the world beyond the battlefield. Kurt paused before the turret, his gloved hand rested on the Dragon logo for a brief, almost reverent moment. There was no need for words; the symbol represents everything they've fought for—each of them, stood together in the gates of hell. His fingers tracing the contours of the logo, grounding himself. In this quiet moment, the weight of the past and uncertainty of the future press in. For Kurt, the logo had come to symbolize much more than just an emblem— it was a reminder of his love for Nikol, now his wife, and the promise a future family they shared. Her image and their shared future life together stayed with him, a constant source of hope and strength. While the other crew members may have seen it as their good-luck charm, for Kurt, it was a constant reminder of the bond and future they share.

Stefan, the driver, followed. He approached the tank with his usual quiet focus, the honor of his duties heavy, as a driver, on his shoulders. His touch on the logo was firm and steady, a promise to keep them moving forward, no matter the obstacles ahead. The tank may be a machine, Stefan may be the at the wheel, but the crew's unity is what drives it.

Ottmar, the loader, approached the side of the tank. He touched the Dragon logo with an easy confidence, as if the symbol had become a part of him. His rough hands lingered on it for a moment longer than the others, a quiet recognition of the sacrifices they've made to get this far. Ottmar takes the new gunner, Sergeant Dotzer, into the turret.

"This is yours." He stroked the whole breach and targeting gear of the enhanced 88mm cannon. "You take care of these and they will take of you." Ottmar gave a slight nod. "Welcome to the Dragon."

Finally, Kris, the radioman, steps up. He reached for the Dragon logo, his fingers tracing it lightly. His role may seem peripheral to the tank's firepower, but his connection to the crew is no less vital. The Dragon logo symbolizes his place in this family—quiet, but crucial.

With their ritual complete, the crew climbed into their positions, the sound of the hatches closed shut signal the beginning of the journey to another battle. Together, they were more than just a tank crew—they are bound by something greater than the battlefield, and with each touch of the dragon, they remind themselves that no matter what happens next, they will face it together.

As with Tiger One, the new Tiger II proved a formable weapon. Initially the King Tiger had considerable teething problems, as it had been rushed into production and Allied bombing had made things very difficult. There were many transmission failures due to the vehicle's 70-ton weight. Despite this, they had solid gunnery success even up 3,000 meters (2 miles).

Chapter 17—The Sky Fell First, Caen, July 1944

Kurt: "Let's show them what the best crew with the best tank can do. We are now truly the Dragon of War—every one of us forged by fire."

In July 1944, at Normandy, the 503rd Heavy Panzer Battalion, equipped with twelve King Tigers—including Kurt's—joined the fierce Battle for Caen, a critical road and communications hub just 14 km (9 miles) from the invasion coastline. Strategically straddling the Orne River and Caen Canal, the city was a key target for the Allies.

Kurt learned a harsh lesson about the stark difference between the Eastern and Western Fronts. On the morning of July 18, 1944, the Allies launched *Operation Goodwood*, a massive campaign designed to destroy and disrupt German operations in the Caen area. The geographic location of Caen was critical to the Allied breakout from Normandy, making it a key and vital target for the bombing.

That morning, the sky thundered with more than 1,500 bombers— British Lancasters and American B-17s—darkening the horizon like a plague of steel locusts. They came in waves, each releasing its deadly load before vanishing, but to Kurt it felt endless, as if the sky itself had turned malevolent and was birthing the bombs. The howl of engines merged with the shriek of falling steel, ripping the air apart in one long, punishing scream. The ground shook beneath him. German tanks, even the mighty King Tigers, were swallowed by the earth or shattered in place. What had been a staging ground was now a graveyard. And in that moment, war no longer felt like a contest between men—it felt like judgment from the gods.

Kurt's Tiger was fortunately positioned, with four other King Tigers, more remotely under the tree cover of the forest. The sound of the bombs was more than deafening—it was a force, a primal roar that swallowed everything. Inside the Tiger II, Kurt and his crew could feel the earth tremble beneath them, the shockwaves rattling the steel walls of the tank as if the very ground were alive. The noise was overwhelming—like the world itself was being torn apart. The crew braced themselves, their ears ringing as the roar of falling bombs seemed to echo forever. The vibrations shook the turret, the hull, the very air inside, leaving them struggling to breathe against the pressure. The once solid, invincible tank felt small and fragile, a tin can in the midst of an apocalypse. The thought of what was happening outside—

of the German positions being obliterated by wave after wave of bombers—was almost too much to comprehend. The fear wasn't just in the air; it was in the very ground beneath them.

Inside the Tiger, Kurt clenched his teeth, gripping the edges of his seat as the turret shuddered violently. The air thickened with dust and smoke, turning the dim interior into a stifling haze of heat and suffocation. Blast wave after blast wave hammered against the hull, each impact like a giant's fist pounding their tank that shook them to their bones.

Outside, four King Tigers—symbols of invincibility—were obliterated like smashed pumpkins. Men and machines alike had been vaporized by the explosions—some vanishing in clouds of dirt and fire, others buried beneath the turned earth. Only eight Tiger IIs remained functional… and even they were barely recognizable as war machines— half-buried in rubble, their crews, like Kurt's, dazed, deafened, and barely breathing. Several lucky ones were unscathed.

When Kurt finally forced open the hatch, dragging himself out, the area no longer looked like earth. It was something else— twisted, blackened, ruined beyond recognition. The smoke hung thick, refusing to lift, and the air was heavy with the stench of scorched metal, burning oil, and something worse— flesh. Kurt and the crew stepped through the craters and wreckage to the remains of the adjacent tanks. They saw that the once-impenetrable armor was peeled open like tin cans, their crew simply erased in the fury.

Kurt kissed his Dragon pendant. *Thank you.* He had survived. Of the twelve King Tigers in the Caen area, now only eight remained. But not because of skill or strategy— just pure, dumb luck and the fact that many had been dispersed beneath the forest canopy.

All around them, once-mighty Panzers lay broken, their barrels pointing uselessly toward the sky. Some crews would never climb out. Others would be dug out by hand—if they could be found at all.

Kurt choked on the acrid, ozone-laced smoke, the stench clawing at his lungs. This wasn't Russia. There, at least, the fight had felt human— steel against steel. The Soviets had the T-34, and they'd learned to respect it. But this—this was annihilation from the sky. Nothing in Russia could erase a Panzer division in minutes.

He clutched his necklace, feeling its warmth against his palm. Kurt: *Maybe we were never meant to win this war.* In the end, only two of those original twelve King Tigers would make finally it back to Germany for refurbishing and reassignment.

The survivors— including Kurt's crew— eventually withdrew to Paderborn, where the remnants of their once-feared battalion would be refitted, reinforced, and given a new mission. They would not return to full strength—45 King Tiger tanks—until October 1944.

Chapter 18—The Last 166 Days, 1944

Operation Panzerfaust (Budapest, October 15-16,1944)

3rd Company, s.Pz.Abt. 503 — Vienna Gate

After refitting at Paderborn with the new Tiger IIs (King Tiger), the 3rd Company of the 503rd Heavy Panzer Battalion was deployed to Hungary on a special operation. It was October 1944. Word had come that Regent Miklós Horthy, on his own, had declared an armistice with the Soviets and planned to pull Hungary from the Axis alliance. Having anticipated this, Hitler's response was immediate.

Hitler activated Operation Panzerfaust, unleashing 200 to 300 Waffen-SS commandos under Otto Skorzeny to seize the capital. And behind them came six Tiger IIs—the King Tigers—making sure no one misunderstood Berlin's intent.

Kurt commanded the second tank of the six.

As the Regent Horthy lived and worked at the Buda Castle. The column advanced there on narrow, ancient streets. Six Tiger IIs appeared, rolling like iron deities. Infantry accompanied them. Broad, angular hulls swallowed the road. The second tank bore a dragon insignia on its turret—Kurt's command tank. Their engines rumbled low and steady, echoing off the stone buildings. Cobblestones vibrated under their treads and the 70 ton weight of each Tiger.

Skorzeny's SS commandos had already spread through the city— shutting down radio stations, storming key municipal buildings.

Knispel watched from his cupola as a Hungarian officer at the gate scrambled to reach a field phone. Futile. German agents had already cut communications. The line was dead. The government was already finished. Only the formalities remained.

The tanks halted at the gate. Treads ground to stillness. Engines idled low, growling like leashed wolves.

Up top, Kurt watched without speaking. He didn't need to. The message was parked under him in seventy tons of steel.

Kurt ordered gunner Dotzer to traverse the turret towards the gate. The turret turned slowly, sweeping the gate area in one controlled motion. The long barrel of his 88 came to rest, for just a moment, on the archway itself—a silent question mark for anyone still considering defiance.

The Hungarian Royal Guards and regular troops at the Viena Gate were caught totally by surprise. Most hadn't even raised their rifles. Some stepped away from their sandbags, stunned by the sheer mass of armor and the approaching German Special Forces troops.

No shots were fired.

The Hungarian guards stared at the tanks, at the SS troops now emerging from alleys and stairwells, rifles ready. Slowly, silently, one soldier laid down his weapon. Then another.

Budapest fell—not through siege, but submission.

Kris turned from the radio set, his voice tight with urgency. "They've surrendered. The Regent's in custody."

The German weapons stayed silent. But the will to resist by the Hungarian guards had been crushed by six very unique machines, by hundreds of gray-clad ghosts, and by the unyielding weight of inevitability.

The Tigers didn't stay in Budapest long. Two days after the castle standoff, Kurt's company was already rolling east. The Soviets had broken through and were grabbing ground fast—whole towns were falling overnight. Orders were simple: get there, hit back, don't let them close the trap. Nobody said it out loud, but everyone knew the truth—if they didn't stop the Red Army out there, it would be Budapest's turn next.

Siege of Budapest (December 1944 – February 1945)

Kurt came back to Budapest—but not like before. This time, there was no ceremonial entry, no show of strength. Now it was snow and smoke. Soviet artillery had encircled the city, cutting off every road in or out. The King Tigers of the 503rd, including Kurt's, were ordered to make a breakthrough—to punch a hole in the Soviet ring from the outside. They called it Operation Konrad III. To Kurt and his crew, it just felt like just another frozen suicide rescue attempt in the middle of another Russian winter. "We're not relieving the city," Dotzer said, tightening the elevation wheel as they bounced over frozen ruts west of the capital. "We're trying to claw through a noose."

Stefan didn't respond. He just drove. The roads into Budapest were white with ash and snow. Stefan had to weave around blown-out tram cars and the frozen corpses of horses still hitched to shattered wagons. Trees stood like skeletons, stripped bare not by winter, but by shellfire. Each block closer brought the kind of silence only found in ruined places.

They reached the edge of the Soviet encirclement near Bicske— and that's where the real fighting began. Anti-tank teams moved like phantoms through the rubble: one shot, then a second, then nothing. The Tigers fired back, their 88s lighting the dusk, but it wasn't the kind of war they were built for.

"We're too big for these streets," Ottmar muttered one night, resting a hand on the icy breech. "And too few." Kurt didn't disagree. Supplies were thinning. The crew was worn raw. Even Stefan was getting jittery and he was up to two packs of smokes a day now. No warmth. No replacements. Each time Kris keyed the radio, the answer was the same: *Hold position. Hold pressure.*

One night, after a long silent stretch and a failed third relief attempt, morale cracked. Stefan slammed a wrench down in the mud. "They've left us here to die."

Kurt didn't yell. He didn't give a speech. He simply stepped out of the turret, looked around at his crew by the faint glow of a burning building, and said, "We've got one advantage they don't."

They stared back, hollow-eyed.

"We know how to fight when it's hopeless."

171

Then he climbed back in, his breath clouding the frozen glass of the gunsight. By mid-January, the city was a carcass. But the tank kept moving. And so did they.

Their final push had stalled on the shattered outskirts of the city. The Tigers that weren't knocked out were simply stuck—bogged down in cratered roads, buried in rubble, or wedged between buildings on medieval streets too narrow (3.75 meter wide (12 feet)) never built for the wide Tiger II.

Then came the word, just after dawn on February 11th: roughly 28,000 of the 70,000 men trapped inside Budapest had tried to break out. They'd gone in waves—desperate, cold, under fire from every direction. Almost none made it. Fewer than 10,000 got through. Some estimates said 5,000. Either way, the message was the same: the siege was over. Budapest had fallen.

Kurt didn't speak that day.

Operation Southwind (February 1945)

The orders came fast—redeploy 72 km (45 miles) north. The Soviets had crossed the Hron River and dug in. If the Germans didn't destroy the bridgehead now, they'd be fighting them on Hungarian soil again within weeks.

This time, the 503rd brought numbers—25 to 30 Tiger IIs, stretched across icy fields and rolling hills near Levice. The terrain was open, unforgiving, and exactly what the King Tiger was built for.

Kurt's tank moved with surgical purpose.

Dotzer calls: "On target."

Kurt: "Fire"

Dotzer was in his element, calling targets with the calm of a man at a shooting range. "T-34, left ridge, low profile."

Boom.

Smoke.

Silence.

Kris snapped through the radio headset. "Scratch one. Good job."

Stefan drove without comment, weaving through half-buried fences and the mauled outlines of burned-out trucks and carts.

Ottmar, as always, kept the gun fed like it was a living thing.

It was a tactical victory—one of the last. The Soviets were pushed back across the Hron river. The Ivan bridgehead was gone. But the cost still came.

They kept moving—north of Budapest, through villages with names no one could pronounce, into Slovakia under fire, and finally back west near Brünn.

By then, Kurt's kill tally had reached 165 confirmed tanks. But numbers didn't mean much anymore What stayed with them were the burned-out tanks—turrets split open, the crews still inside, frozen from the winter cold. Now they could be the ones who survived a dozen battles, only to die on the city's doorstep.

In the end, it wasn't medals or orders that kept them going.

It was each other.

Chapter 19—From Innocence to Iron, 1945

The Last Line– April 27-28, 1945

German Farmhouse Command Post → Vlasatice, Czech Republic

The barn creaked with wind and memory. It had once held horses. Now it held ghosts. In the early morning darkness, a cracked lantern swayed above a field map, tacked to the rough wooden wall with rusted nails. Area commander, Captain Seidel briefs, the two Tiger II tank commanders, Knispel and Skoda. Seidel stood in the dim light, his face hollow from too many sleepless nights, a half-burnt cigarette in one hand and a pencil in the other. He tapped the map once.

"Our one currently secure escape artery is Reichsstraße 22 that goes through Znojmo," he said. "Its the last one we have. It's not just a road—it's a lifeline. If the Russians take Vlasatice, they cut it. And we start bleeding out—men, materiel, the last of the wounded."

Kurt stood opposite the table, arms folded. His face was blank but not unreadable. Shadows from the lantern moved across his uniform, the black Panzer wrap now gray with road dust and age. Next to him, Sergeant Carl Skoda leaned in, eyes narrowed. The light caught a two inch scar under his cheekbone.

"You two will deploy here," Seidel continued, tracing a line east of the village. "Orchard rise near the ridge road. You'll dig in before sunrise. Make your presence known—but don't engage until they crest the hill. Then you fight. Hard."

"What's covering the rear?" Skoda asked flatly.

Seidel shook his head. "Nothing. Everyone else is moving west—artillery, supply, most of the medics. Infantry's already thinning out along the corridor."

Kurt tilted his head. "Air cover?"

"You know better. We're on our own." Seidel looked away, jaw tight.

Ottmar, Dotzer, and Stefan stood by the door, their boots muddy, jackets slung over shoulders. They said nothing.

"This isn't a stand-and-shoot," Seidel said. "This is a plug. Due to critical fuel shorages, you are the last two teeth in the jaw. Hold the line until the last retreating transports clears Znojmo. If you give us two, maybe three hours, we get several thousand men and civilians away from the vengeful Russians and across the border to Austria." He looked between the two of them. "After that... you're on your own." No one flinched. No one asked for orders beyond that.

"You're not expected to survive," Seidel added. "But you are expected to make them bleed for every meter." A long silence followed. The kind that fell not from fear, but recognition.

Kurt nodded once. "We'll hold."

Seidel extinguished his cigarette against the wall. "If any of them—any child, any soldier—makes it to Austria alive, it'll be because of you."

Dawn – *April 28, 1945*
Orchard Ridge, East of Vlasatice

The fog hung low over the orchard like smoke that hadn't finished its business. Pale light filtered through the tree line as the two *Tiger IIs* rolled down a narrow farm track—Kurt's tank front and Skoda's staggered some 80 meters (262 feet) behind. The engines growled in rhythm, each machine nearly seventy tons of steel and defiance, crawling toward a ridgeline they were unlikely to come back from. Outside up his commanders cupola, Kurt scanned the terrain ahead with his binoculars. The mist softened the world, but not enough to hide the threat. Somewhere beyond the rise, the Red Army waited.

"Cover my right flank. I'll take the left." he said into the intercom, speaking not to his crew but to Skoda's tank.

"Copy. I've got your shadow." Skoda gave a short reply through the shared field frequency.

Inside the turret, Dotzer sat hunched over the gunner's scope, making range adjustments.

"Visibility is under 1,000 meters," he observed out loud.

"Good," Kurt said. "Let them come close. Fewer shots wasted."

Ottmar, seated to gunner Dotzer's right, checked the ready rack. Three anti-tank shells on the left. Two HE on the right. More in storage, but not enough for the day that was coming.

"First round's hot," Ottmar said. "Anti-tank in the pipe."

"Stefan," Kurt called down, "take us to the tree line. Slow advance. Angle five left."

"Jawohl." Stefan's hands gripped the half-wheel, coaxing the Dragon Tiger forward. The tank crawled like a predator on a leash, tracks grinding toward the cover of the trees. Mud clung to the track guards. The trees began to thin. Ahead lay open ground and rising

176

slope—the Vlasatice approach. Kurt looked left. Skoda's Tiger had also halted, half-shielded behind a collapsed hay wagon. Its cannon was already trained east, hull slightly angled—a perfect fighting stance. Skoda's crew knew what they were doing. The orchard went still. Kurt took one long look through his binoculars, then lowered them. "We hold here," he said. "This is where it happens." Stefan stopped the tank.

The orchard remained deathly still, but the birds had stopped singing. Kurt adjusted his headset, straining to hear past the tank's idle. Then—movement. He caught it first: faint silhouettes cresting the rise through the morning haze. Five, maybe more *T-34s*, their boxy turrets cutting black shapes against the horizon.

"Targets spotted," he said. "Five T-34s, bearing ten o'clock, range seven hundred meters."

Inside the turret, Dotzer already had the cannon slewed left to meet the threat. "On target—lead tank just cleared the ridge. Holding fire."

Kurt gave it two more heartbeats.

"Fire."

Dotzer pulled the firing trigger and the 88mm cannon thundered. The turret filled with a bone-jarring concussion, steel groaning as the breech slammed back on its recoil rails. The air stank of cordite and oil. Even with seventy tons beneath them, the Tiger rocked gently with weight and suspension absorbing most of the recoil. A white flash lit the fog—then a bloom of flame from the far slope. The lead *T-34* erupted into fire, turret blown askew.

"Scratch one," Dotzer said flatly.

Kurt didn't reply. His eyes were already on the next.

"Traverse right five. Next one's cutting downhill."

"Up!" Ottmar barked.

"On target," Dotzer confirmed.

"Fire!"

The second shell streaked through the haze, slicing through the front plate next to the driver's hatch. It jerked to a stop, burning. Return fire came. The orchard lit up with the thunder of Soviet shells punching blind through the mist. Dirt geysers bloomed ahead of the Tigers, tearing craters in the orchard floor.

A shell screamed glancing off the back end of their turret—too close.

"Stefan, reverse—ten meters, then stop!" Kurt shouted.

The big machine groaned backward, crushing tree roots and orchard fencing as it crawled in reverse. Another Soviet round exploded behind them where they had just been.

"Thank you, Ivan," Dotzer muttered. "You missed."

Kurt checked Skoda's tank. It was still firing, holding flank position. Skoda lit up two more T-34's. Smoke drifted from its cannon, and now a total of three enemy tanks were now burning on the far hill.

"Two down for Dragon," Kurt confirmed.

"Up" shouted Ottmar.

"On target" reported Dotzer.

"Fire" ordered Kurt. A hit and another T-34 is stopped in its tracks and burned fiercely. It was followed directly with another tank clearing the ridge—and then another. The odds weren't looking good. But then, they never had been.

"Steady," Kurt said, quiet now. "We fight until we're out of shells... or time." The seventh T-34 crested the ridge, its gun already trained on them. Kurt was halfway out of the cupola, shouting to Dotzer, "Traverse ten left—wait for my—" The enemy round struck hard—slamming the turret's side with a metallic crack that echoed like thunder. It didn't penetrate. But it didn't need to. The shell ricocheted upward at an angle—just wrong enough. A jagged shard of steel peeled off and hit Kurt in the head. He collapsed instantly, falling inside with a sickening thud.

"Commander's hit!" Dotzer roared, scrambling over. Blood was already pooling near Kurt's collar. His eyes were open, but unfocused.

Ottmar froze for a second, then shoved the med kit open with shaking hands. Knowing full well of the impossibility he yells "We need a medic—now!"

Kris was already on the radio to Skoda.

"Dragon Tiger! Commander down! "

Stefan reversed the tank, track by track, grinding backward toward cover. Explosions lit up the orchard. Another shell slammed into the ground where they'd just been. Another ricocheted off the front plate.

Kurt blinked once. The head wound bleeding profusely. His mouth twitched.

Dotzer leaned in close. "You're okay, Commander. Stay with us."

Kurt's lips barely moved. "Hold the line."

They carried him back to the little aid station they'd passed on the way in. Stefan remembered his eyes—open, struggling to focus—and the faint half-smile he gave when they laid him down. But the bleeding wouldn't stop. Orders pulled them back to the line, leaving Kurt in the hands of the medics. For a while he drifted in and out, calling out commands none of them could catch. Two hours later, Kurt Knispel—Germany's greatest tank ace—was gone.

He was almost home.

Kurt Knispel died 153 miles from where he was born, ten days before the war ended.

The Dragon Tiger crew had already rolled back into the smoke to fulfill Kurt's last order: "Hold the line."

There was no priest. No farewell. No comrades at his side. Just another body in the churned soil behind Vrbovec—hurriedly laid to rest beside fourteen infantrymen he had never met. Fifteen men in a rushed grave. No headstone. No markings. Not even a name.

The European war officially ended ten days later, on May 8, 1945.

Epilogue

Kurt

Sixty-eight years later, in 2013, a Czech-German recovery team searching the old battlefield near Znojmo uncovered a long-forgotten grave. Fifteen sets of remains. Fifteen dog tags. One with Kurt's name.

Nikol

Nikol, whose life remained forever intertwined with the war, ultimately married Kurt's reconciled brother, Conrad, fulfilling Kurts's promise, when he married her, to have her part of the family forever. Their union stood as a testament to forgiveness, redemption, personal growth, and hope amidst tragedy. They welcomed a baby boy into their lives and named him Kurt, honoring the man who served as their shared connection and beacon of integrity. Baby Kurt was given the Dragon pendant, same as the one mom had worn for four years.

Stefan

Stefan, after enduring four years in a Russian labor camp, returned home to rebuild his life. He married Katrina, Kurt's sister, finding solace and love in her unwavering spirit. Together, they created a life filled with quiet joys. Stefan still smoked. He had a pet box turtle.

Ottmar

Ottmar, ever resourceful, returned to his family's farm after the war—its fences splintered, its fields choked with weeds. But he rebuilt it, acre by acre. In time, he began making sweets from old family recipes—selling them at the market. His honey drops and licorice twists became local favorites, especially among children who never knew the war. Quiet and kind, Ottmar never spoke much about what he'd seen. But his farm and his confections told the story: survival, patience, and the long art of healing. He still talks with the horses and the tractor.

Kris

Kris opened a small radio repair shop, his steady hands and sharp mind finding purpose in the delicate work. In his spare time, he nurtured a creative streak—playing harmonica at local events and delighting audiences with his music. He also dabbled in acting and writing, transforming wartime reflections into stories that explored duty, courage, and the quiet strength it takes to live by one's own code.

Decker

At a modest desk piled with papers and books, Marcus Decker began writing about his combat experiences. His work found an audience across the globe, serving both as a historical record and a form of personal catharsis.

Marat

In the quiet months that followed, the rage Marat once carried—hard as iron, sharp as glass—began to loosen its grip. Not all at once, and not cleanly. But slowly, as if the war had stripped away the parts of him that belonged to another man: the cold inheritance of his father, the shadow he had worn like armor. His wife saw the change before he did. She would touch the scar along his cheek—the one he had once cursed—and smile as though it were a mark of courage instead of disfigurement. "It makes you look kinder," she'd say, tracing it lightly with her fingertips. "Like a man who lived." Marat never understood what she meant until one evening when he caught his reflection in the window. The man staring back at him was not his father. The old fury was gone. The scar had softened the angles of his face, but something deeper had softened the angles of his spirit. He felt, for the first time, that the wound had not merely marked him—it had opened him. That night, he allowed himself to believe he was no longer bound to the past. He took his wife's hand and let her hold the part of him he had spent so long hiding—the vulnerable center he had buried beneath anger. And as she held it, he felt something settle inside him. A quiet acceptance. A reconciliation with the man he had been, and the man he was becoming. Outside the window, a dragonfly settled on the glass, wings shimmering in the last light. Marat watched it rest there—fragile, unafraid—and felt something inside him mirror it. A small peace, delicate but real. A reminder that some things emerge transformed. That some things survive, even after the world breaks.

The End

Appendix

Kurt Knispel
(Source: Wikimedia Commons, for historical purposes only)

Birth

Kurt Knispel was born on September 20, 1921, in the small town of Salisov (Zlaté Hory), located in what is now the Czech Republic but was then part of the Sudetenland region in Czechoslovakia.

Family Background

Raised in a modest German-speaking family, Kurt grew up in the Sudetenland, a contested border region deeply influenced by cultural and political tensions. The rise of German nationalism under Adolf Hitler shaped the environment, but Knispel often displayed disdain for Nazi dogma and authority. It is likely that he did not fully embrace or participate in organizations like the Hitler Youth. This resistance to blind adherence to Nazi ideology became a defining trait throughout his military career.

Education

Details of his formal education are limited, but Kurt likely attended local schools in his rural hometown. From a young age, he showed a strong mechanical aptitude, a skill that later became invaluable in his role as a tank gunner and commander.

Pre-War Occupation

Before the outbreak of World War II, Kurt worked as an apprentice machinist in an automotive industrial facility where his father was a manager.

Historical Context
<u>Sudetenland Annexation</u>

In 1938, the Sudetenland was annexed by Germany following the Munich Agreement. This event profoundly impacted the region's German-speaking communities, who were suddenly integrated into the Reich.

Transition to the Military
<u>Military Conscription</u>

With the Sudetenland under German annexation since 1938, Kurt (19 years old), like many young men from the region, joined the Wehrmacht, the regular German army, in 1940.

<u>Enlistment and Training</u> (1940–1941)

His background as a machinist and processed with a natural mechanical aptitude apparently quickly set him apart while training with a Panzer (tank) unit.

Kurt began his Panzer career as a loader, then progressed to the role of gunner on the Panzer IV. He later transitioned to heavier tanks, such as the Tiger I and eventually the Tiger II (King Tiger). In his books Alfred Rubbel reported Kurt had incredible 3-D vision that made him especially lethal in the long-range Tiger tanks.

Completed tank training at the Panzer Replacement Training Battalion in Pultos, Germany.

Kurt Knispel Military Career

Operation Barbarossa (1941):
Assigned to the 12th Panzer Division during Germany's invasion of the Soviet Union. Gained first combat experience in armored battles across the Baltic States and Russia.

Eastern Front (1942):
Continued to serve on the Eastern Front, refining his skills as a gunner and occasionally as a temporary tank commander in the Panzer IV. Demonstrated exceptional marksmanship and leadership under intense combat conditions.

Battle of Kursk (July 1943):
Transferred to the 503rd Heavy Panzer Battalion, operating the formidable Tiger I tanks. Participated in the southern thrust of the Battle of Kursk, achieving numerous (27) tank kills and countering Soviet forces in this pivotal engagement.

Defensive Actions (1944):
After Kursk, Kurt's next major action came during the Fourth Battle of Kharkov, where he and the 503rd fought desperate rearguard actions as the Red Army surged westward across Ukraine. He then engaged in additional critical defensive battles across Eastern Europe as the tide of war turned against Germany to counter Soviet advances.

Battle of Korsun–Cherkassy Pocket (January–February 1944):
Fought in the defensive battles near the Dnieper River in Ukraine, where Soviet forces had encircled much of the German line. Fighting with the Blake Rescue Regiment, he helped carve an escape path through the Soviet ring.

Hungary and the Defense of Budapest (1944–1945):

Deployed to Hungary in October 1944 to resist the advancing Red Army. Engaged in fierce winter combat, including the doomed attempt to break the Soviet encirclement during the Siege of Budapest. Of the 44,000 German soldiers who attempted a breakout, fewer than 2% survived. Those who surrendered to the Soviets fared slightly better— one in three returned home... years later. The rest vanished into the ice and ash of Siberia.

Final Battles (1945):

Fought during the German retreat into Austria/Vienna to protect the few remaining Axis oil resources.

*Note: **Note:** *Panzer Aces II* by Franz Kurowski (p. 190) places Kurt Knispel at Caen (Normandy) in 1944 in a King Tiger. While this account exists, it is not supported by official unit records. Most reliable sources place Knispel exclusively on the Eastern Front during that period as above.

Mortally wounded in April 1945 near Vrbovec, Czechia, during a battle with Soviet forces. He died on April 28, 1945, in the last week of the war. He died 246 Km (153 miles) from his hometown in Salisov, Czechia.

Military Achievements

Tank Victories: 168 confirmed (*up to 190 with shared victories*)

Kurt Knispel fought on the Eastern Front with teamwork, resilience, and exceptional skill. Credited with 168 confirmed tank kills, he remains history's most successful tank ace. His total includes victories earned both as a gunner and, later, as a commander. It was never just about the tally—it was about trust, survival, and precision under pressure.

Through four brutal years on the deadliest front of the WW2, Knispel's bond with his team kept him alive. Together, they battled not only the Red Army, but the merciless Russian winters and boiling summers, proving their grit on one of history's harshest battlegrounds.

He stood in the fire of war—and somehow, kept his humanity intact.

Top Russian tank ace:
Dmitry Lavrinenko – 52 confirmed kills.

Top U.S. tank ace:
Lafayette G. Pool – 12 confirmed kills.

(For Historical and Educational Purposes Only)

Legacy

Recognition and Honors

Despite being one of the most successful tank gunners/commanders of World War II, Kurt, while he was alive, never received the Knight's Cross of the Iron Cross, the highest military recognition in Germany. It did not bother him, as he knew that to receive such an honor, one had to not only demonstrate exceptional military success but also had to be deeply aligned with the Nazi ideology, which he did not. He wasn't "in the club."

Kurt cared little for such accolades, as his values and sense of duty were guided by far higher ideals.

While others stood by, Kurt stood up, driven by his own sense of honor and integrity.

Rediscovery

After they found his grave in 2013, Kurt's remains were moved to the German Military Cemetery in Brno. He was reburied with military honors, highlighting the enduring fascination with his legacy.

Top World War II Tank Aces

Name	Tank Victories	Notes/Assessment
Kurt Knispel	168 confirmed	Most reliable*
Martin Schroif	161	SS Generally Accepted**
M. Wittman	138	SS Public Icon**
Otto Carius	150+	Self-Reported***

Highest Rank and Award

Name	Highest Rank	Highest Award
Kurt Knispel	Feldwebel (Sgt)	Cross in Gold ****
Martin Schroif	SS-2nd Lieutenant	Cross in Gold**
M. Wittman	SS-Captain	Knight's Cross**
Otto Carius	2nd Lieutenant	Knight's Cross

*Official Wehrmacht Unit Logs of the 503rd and 501st Panzer Battalions, witness confirmation, postwar research, shared victories Knispel routinely gave to other tankers making his own total victory number up to 190 if shared kills included. Only tank kills are in his number.   **As an SS officer, his records were handled differently than those of regular Wehrmacht tankers, with less transparency and known Nazi propaganda influence.   ***By Otto Carius himself in his post war memoir "Tigers in the Mud".

Kursk– Behind the Scenes, Map

The Battle of Kursk

German Forces:

Tank Assault Gun Type	Quantity
Parther	483
Partzer Id	941
Sture I	244
Tiger I	146
Marder (Tank Destroyer)	163
Nudoon (Tank Destroyer)	89
Othe Types	862
Total	2.728

Note: The "Other" category include models such as Roroos a captified ram, and older

Soviet Forces:

Tank Assault Gun Type	Quantity
T-84	8.400
T-20	800
SId-12 (Assault Gun)	300
SId-22 (Assault Gun)	150
SId-30 (Assault Gun)	800
IS-1	10
Other Types	5.324
Total	5.322

Note: The "Other types" Includes older models like the T-60 and light tanks

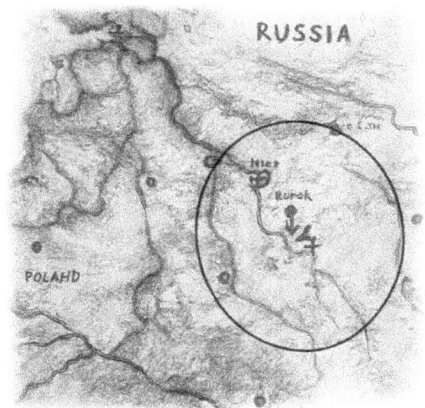

The Battle of Kursk, fought between July 5 and August 23, 1943, was one of the largest armored engagements in history. Both German and Soviet forces deploo-ed substantial numbers of tanks and assault guns. Here's a comparative overview of their armored strength:

Category	German Forces	Soviet Forces
Tanks and Assault Guns	Approximately 2,700	Approximately 5000

These figures highlight the significant numerical advantage held by the Soviet forces in armored vehicles during the battle.

193

Kursk by the Numbers

This was the single largest tank battle in history.

1. The battle was fought between 5 July to 23 August 1943, during good summer weather conditions.

2. The battle occurred 285 miles south of Moscow and around 55 miles from the Ukrainian border.

3. The Kursk Bulge straddled 150 miles across and 100 miles deep into German-held territory.

4. 300,000 civilians were used to construct eight lines of defense, including 9,000 km (5,600 miles) of trenches, with Soviet defenses reaching depths of almost 320 km (200 miles) in places.

5. All other civilians within 25 miles of the front were evacuated.

6. The German advance was halted at 10 miles in the north and 30 miles in the south.

7. The Tigers were adapted to carry 120 shells instead of the standard 90.

8. Soviets troops outnumbered Germans over 3:1, with 1,900,000 vs 780,000 troops.

9. Approximately 5,000 Soviet tanks were deployed against around 3,000 German panzers.

10. The Battle of Kursk saw overall Soviet tank losses of around 60% (approximately 3,000 tanks), while German losses were approximately 25% (around 750 tanks), reflecting the intense and uneven attrition of the conflict. Within this larger battle, the clash at Prokhorovka became a defining moment, where Soviet losses mirrored the broader trend at 60% (around 500 tanks) compared to 25% (around 75 tanks) for the Germans, yet succeeded in stalling the German advance.

11. Despite their limited deployment, around 4% to 6% of the Tiger I tanks (6–9 tanks of the 146) at Kursk were destroyed, highlighting their strategic importance and cautious use in the battle.

12. The battle showcased extraordinary defensive planning and resource mobilization by the Soviets, alongside devastating losses for both sides.

13. The battle marked the final strategic offensive the Germans were able to mount in the East. After Kursk, the Wehrmacht was largely on the defensive.

Sources:

Battle of Kursk – Wikipedia
The Battle of Kursk: Clash of the Tanks – HistoryNet
The Combat History of the German Tiger Tank Battalion 503 in WWII,
Lochmann, Von Rosen, Alfred Rubbel
The Battle of Kursk, Glantz & House
Hell's Gate (Cherkassy Pocket) by Douglas Nash
The Korsun Pocket by Niklas Zetterling & Anders Frankson
Atlas of the Eastern Front 1941-1945 by Robert Kirchubel

"The Dragon of War" Theme Song

This story was written to remember the men who fought not for glory, but for each other. To honor human courage and integrity under extreme pressure. Resistance in quiet forms. To remind us that even in the darkest hours, that, with courage, decency can still rise. The music that follows is not just a song. It's a heartbeat. A coda. A flame carried forward.

Written and Performed by
Celaine Andrus
Austin, Texas
"The Dragon of War"
is a bonus and song listening access is included with your book
for a limited time only.

For Print Readers:
Link: https://tigeronemovie.com/

Scan with your mobile phone to listen:

With Permission of Writer Singer/Songwriter, Celaine Andrus.